I0747075

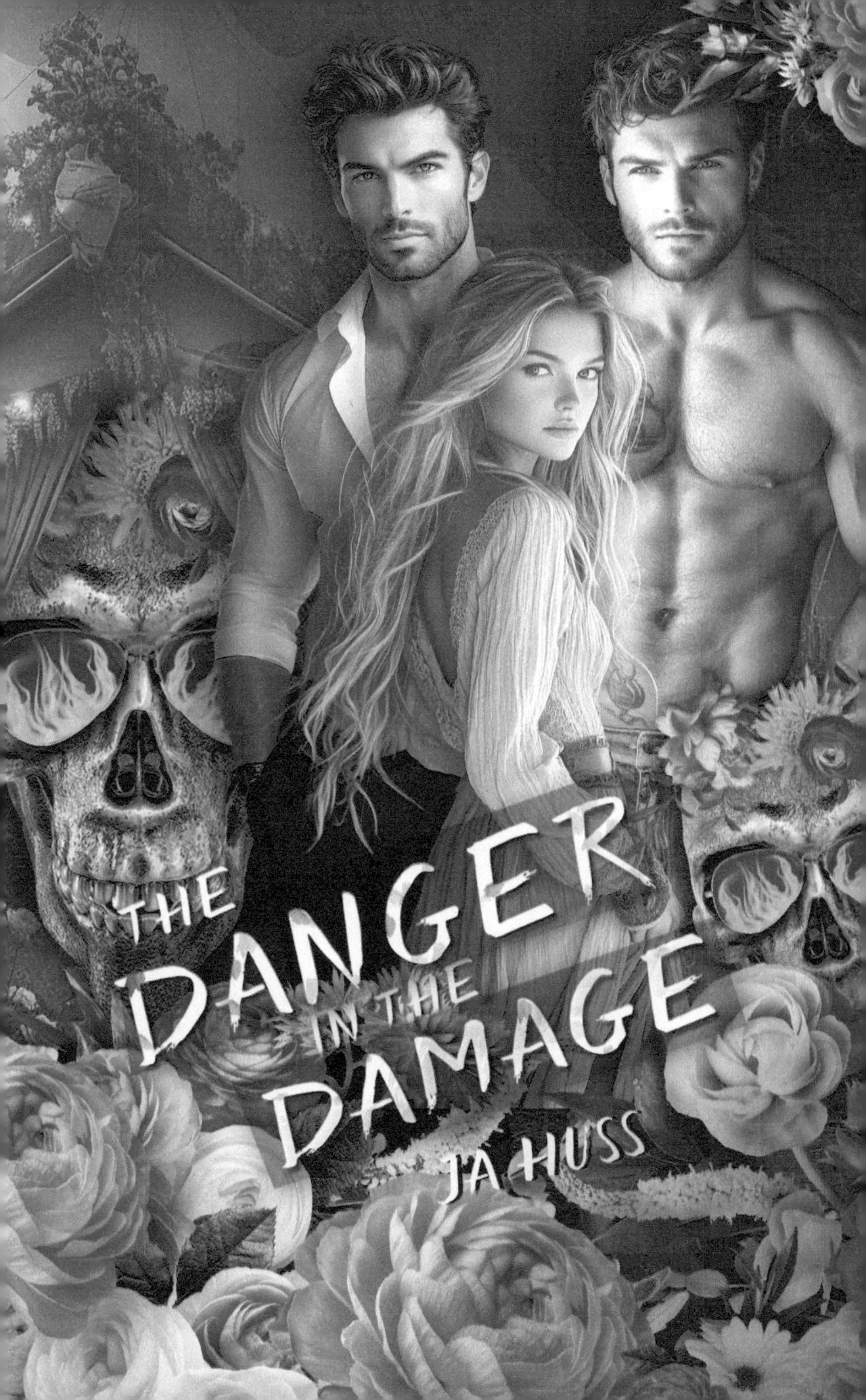

THE
DANGER
IN THE
DAMAGE
JA HUSS

Edited by RJ Locksley
Cover Design by JA Huss
No part of this cover was made with AI

A soldier searching for redemption.
A man addicted to control.
And the woman caught between them...

Ean Shephard knows trouble when he sees it and Olive Creed is the kind of trouble that can burn his whole world down. As Collin Creed's baby sister, she's completely off-limits. But her quiet strength, combined with her sad vulnerability, keeps pulling him closer. Shep came to Edge Security to escape his past, but falling for Olive could ruin his second chance and the fragile peace he's fought so hard to find.

Brose Sinclair has always played the long game. He and Olive are more than just partners inside the shadow organization they both work for, they're lovers. His absolute authority keeps her on track and Olive likes it that way. But her sudden attraction to their target threatens everything they've worked for and for the first time, Brose finds himself questioning whether control is enough to keep Olive by his side.

Olive Creed has spent her life learning to play her role perfectly. She can't afford to mess up. Not with Brose watching her every move, looking for mistakes. Mistakes she sometimes makes on purpose just to spur on his titillating punishment. But as she starts to fall for her target and her world begins to crumble beneath her feet, Olive finds herself wondering—which one of these two men would truly be there in her darkest hour?

Brose—the one who owns her mind?

Or Shep—the one who wants her heart?

THE DANGER in the Damaged is a battlefield of betrayal and control, where loyalty is a weapon and obsession takes no prisoners. It's a best-friend's-little-sister romance caught in the crossfire of dark secrets and mind games—and this time, Collin Creed isn't the one calling the shots.

Inside the pages you'll find...
Enemies to Lovers
Best Friend's Sister
Power Dynamics
Forbidden Love
Dark Protector
Forced Proximity
Possessive Love
Morally Gray Characters
Damaged Heroes
Redemption Arc

1 - Olive

*A*mbrose Sinclair *stares down at me* with an intensity that would've frightened the Olive of yesterday. His eyes are locked with mine. Dark green. Flashing. A window to the soul or a curtain drawn to conceal the shadows?

I've often wondered.

His face is the kind of symmetrical that people like. Square jaw framed in stubble that has been groomed to perfection and hair just a bit too long to be considered professional—tousled and with a slight curl, so it comes off as unruly.

Unruly is a good way to describe Brose. I suspect people who don't know him might mistake this unruliness as rebellion, but I don't.

It's just his wild side.

Which is my favorite side of Mr. Sinclair here.

"Who are you?" His words come out with authority and conviction.

"A badass," I reply.

It's not the right answer, but he smiles. Even chuckles a little. "Of course, you're a badass. I'm looking for the literal answer."

"Olive Creed."

"And what does Olive Creed do?" His thumb strokes my

cheek as eyes dance with the invitation for mischief that I just handed him.

But this time I give what he asked for instead of what he wants. Which is a serious conversation. "Olive Creed is the consummate professional. She's the protagonist in her own story. A hero in her own adventure." This was not the scripted answer, but Brose is happy with my improvisation because that curtain covering the soul beyond his eyes opens a little and I get a tiny peek of the man inside.

That's the one I work with.

The one I sleep with.

The one I love.

Picking up my 'story theme', Brose continues to prep me for the meeting. "Prologue..."

"Olive Creed is a sad little girl. Age eight. Brother leaves for the marines. Father goes crazy about it. Mother starts drinking."

He makes a pouty frown at me. "I hate that past you're dragging around."

"Me too. But Chapter one turns it all around."

"So this isn't a story about sad little Olive Creed?"

"Not in the least. This is the story of powerful, grown-up Olive Creed who is ready to take on the world."

His smile is big now. And he takes a few moments to stare at me. "You're really beautiful, you know that?"

I do. I suppose. I've looked in the mirror and I've got all the components of a beautiful woman. Thin, but not in a weak and wispy way. Long blonde hair that has a bit of wave to it, hazel eyes, though they lean gray mostly, and an attractive face that gives off a 'Clean Girl' vibe.

"You're gonna knock them dead with those looks," Brose continues. "Play it up."

Play it up. I nod. "You got it."

THE ONLY THING **on my mind as** I enter the conference room and take my seat at the table is main-character energy. I lean sideways into my chair to artfully display my short skirt and long legs, and tip my chin up to look around.

Every man stops talking to watch. It's one second of silence, and then all the conversations resume, but it's a very satisfying one second. Mostly because it's probably the most focused attention I'll get from them all day. In a few minutes, the meeting will start and then everything will be about the other me. Not the one sitting here in real life, but the one on paper.

Not that I care that they won't see me. Today is the beginning of everything. A new life. A step forward. A bit of freedom.

"All right, everyone, take your seats and let's get started." If I came into the room with main-character energy, Brose enters with the big-dick variety. His eyes are locked on mine when he slaps a two-inch-thick file down in front of his chair at the head of the table, and then he gives me an almost imperceptible wink.

But I catch it. And since I know what that wink means, a tingling sensation begins to build between my legs.

At twenty-seven, he's the youngest man in this room. But he's also the one who called this meeting so all the others quiet down and take their places without comment. A few moments later, the lights go out and a short film plays.

Three minutes. The last twelve years of my life play out in a three-minute summary. Six bullet points, seventeen photos, one thirty-second clip of my skills, and a short monologue—voiced over by me, of course—to sum it all up. "I'm ready," the young woman on the screen insists. "I've been trained by the best and I have proven myself to be meticulous, hardworking, and loyal. Thank you for your time."

The lights come on, the men murmur for a few moments, and then Brose asserts his dominance by clearing his throat and diving straight into his carefully planned presentation. "Gentlemen." Brose pans a hand towards me. "Meet Olive Creed, SIO 2.0."

He pauses here to smile at me, and I return that smile in exactly the way we planned before he continues. Everything about this meeting has been scripted and I'm not about to break character.

"In the past," Brose continues, "Silent Intelligence Operatives were deemed a complete failure and that's why the program was shut down twenty-five years ago. We had mental health issues with the agents, there were numerous ethical violations in our training methodology, and many operatives went rogue and had to be eliminated. But I assure you, all that has been fixed. We've spent the last twelve years redefining what it means to be SIO. We've spent countless hours poring over the latest research in mental development, incorporating the strictest operational controls, and implementing a partnership program that should ease all your fears about moving forward with CORE SIO projects using these agents in the future. If Olive here is SIO 2.0, then I am POD 2.0, her Personal Operations Director. We will never be out of contact. There is no more independent deep cover as far as SIO agents are concerned. We're in it together, as we have been for the last two years, and I'm here to tell you that she is ready. We both are."

Brose pauses here to read the room and finds all the men are thoughtfully considering his words. Because he's only twenty-seven—at least twenty years junior to everyone else present, aside from me—there was a small chance that they would not take him seriously.

Of course, it was never more than a small chance. He's Ambrose Sinclair. His great-great-grandfather was part of the initial CORE Directive back in the forties. His great-grandfather ran hundreds of operatives in the sixties and his grandfather did the same in the nineties, and then... well, the whole thing fell apart when his father was killed by the agent he was running just after the turn of the century.

Brose was just a toddler when that happened. But he was raised in it. That's the important part. Because so was I. This is what makes us different from all the failures that came before. Even though I didn't start my training until I was nearly nine, I come from these people just like he does.

When he continues, Brose is somber, his mood not dark in any way, just very serious. "Our problem was, and as a Sinclair," —he puts a hand over his heart—"I take full responsibility for those past failures, but our problem was that we expected civilians to *care* about the program. We plucked them out of the ether and dropped them into our world with very little understanding of the situation. They had neither the fortitude, nor the compulsion, to—forgive my language—to give a fuck, gentlemen. They didn't give a fuck about what we were doing or why we were doing it."

Once again, he pans a hand to me, smiling. "All that has changed with Olive Creed. We brought her in young. She's a veteran junior agent and she's only twenty years old. Forty-three missions." He holds up a hand, pressing it towards them as if to ward off any incoming objections. "And I know what you're thinking—these missions were simulations. But the simulations are vital to the success of the Silent Intelligence Operative project. They're not simply training exercises. And Olive rose to the top as the best of the best, I promise you. And with me by her side, she will be everything we've hoped for."

Brose pauses once again to look at me. And as I look back, I believe him. I have zero doubts.

We're a team.

It's us against them.

I spend every moment of my day with this man. We work together, we live together, we sleep together. This is what it means to be handled.

My mission is you and your mission is me. These words tumble around in my head in his voice because he's said them to me thousands of times.

I would never betray him. Not in a million years. And he will always be on my side.

I lose time, I think, because the next thing I know Brose is saying, "Please open the folders in front of you, gentlemen. This is our first operation and we're not leaving this room until you know it inside and out."

*It takes **fourteen hours** to explain the mission and answer every possible question that the CORE Oversight Committee has about what we're doing and why we're doing it.

Lunch is served, dinner is served, coffee is served. More water pitchers come and go than I can count. Only Brose is still wearing his tie and suit coat by the time it's all over and he opens the door to walk them out, but every single one of them *is* smiling.

And so are we.

Because he and I have done it.

Final approval has been given, SIO is back, and tomorrow we are going to start an operation that will put to rest past failures and bring forth the next generation of success.

Brose comes back to the conference room and steps inside, then slowly—while looking me dead in the eyes—pushes the door closed until there is a soft click. He smiles as he twists the lock and I know what's coming next.

My reward, of course.

Two years. That's how long we've been partners. And in this time we've come up with a very effective reward and punishment system. A system that satisfies both of us.

There are cameras in here. At least twenty of them, since it's an A-level meeting room, which means everything is top secret. The cameras are here to keep everyone safe. If any of this got out to the general public, there would be an uproar. It wouldn't change anything, not in the long run, but missions would be paused and opportunities would be lost.

As Brose has told me thousands of times, "Cameras keep us honest, Olive. And they keep us all equal."

But a stupid camera—or twenty, as is the case in this room— isn't enough to make me pause when he walks around the conference table, comes up behind my chair, spins it around, places his hands on my knees, and bends down. The whole time, those dark green eyes are locked with mine.

I draw in a deep breath, feeling happier and more hopeful about our future than ever.

His hands push my knees open, forcing my already short skirt to ride up. He licks his lips and lowers his gaze as he slides his fingertips up the inside of my thighs and then he dips his head between my knees and a moment later his lips are pressing up against my panties.

I scoot down in my chair to give him better access and let my head fall back as he arranges my legs over the armrests, spreading me open.

His tongue slides up and down my already wet panties, but it's his hot breath that drives me crazy. He knows this. Brose knows everything about me. We have no secrets. When we first started sleeping together when I was eighteen, we had long discussions about how we could please each other, so I know everything about him as well.

This, what he's presently doing to me, is one of my top five. I love the slow tease. It's all about the anticipation with me, which is completely opposite of how he prefers it.

Everything he does with me is foreplay for what I will do with him.

"Do not come, do you hear me, Olive?"

I bite my lip, eyes pressed closed, and nod. "I won't. Not until you give me permission."

He reaches up and strokes my breast. "That's a good girl. You're a good girl." His fingertips find my bare nipple under my blouse—he forbids me to wear a bra—and he gives it a good pinch.

I squirm a little, because it's such a turn-on I need to focus so I don't lose control. But when his lips resume their provocation between my legs, and his tongue begins to probe and press against the sweet spot he knows so well, I need to begin silently chanting to keep my arousal in check. *He thinks for me, I act for him. He thinks for me, I act for him. He thinks for me—*

"Oh." The moan slips out when he begins flicking the tip of his tongue against my stretched-tight panties.

"Don't. You. *Dare* come, Olive."

"I won't." But it comes out as a whimper and I'm no longer feeling confident about this.

Of course, this is the game we play. He tempts me into failure. It gets him off—and me, as well. He loves it when I can't control myself.

He punishes me, of course. But I like to be punished.

Just as my failure is his goal, his punishment is mine.

That's when I really let go. That's when it all becomes bliss.

He pinches my nipple again. Harder this time. *"Don't."* And he's angry, so I open my eyes. "Do not. I'm fucking serious. I will choke you, Olive. If you come before I allow it, I will choke you until you pass out. Do you understand me?"

I smile, but I nod. I love being choked. It's the pinnacle of everything as far as I'm concerned.

And for him, it's the ultimate climax.

My mission is you and your mission is me.

"Say it," he says. "Say it to take your mind off what I'm doing to you, Olive."

I take in a breath, hold it for three seconds the way he taught me, and then slowly say the words as I let it out. "You think for me, I act for you. You think for me, I act for you. You think for me, I act for you."

And with these words comes the control.

I do not let myself release. Not yet.

He stands up, pets my head, and leans in and kisses my lips. "Good," he says, whispering the word into my mouth. "You're such a good girl. I'm so proud of you and so is everyone else. And when we get home, Olive, I'm going to fuck you blind."

I smile as I gaze up at him, picturing what that might mean. "Do anything you want to me. I will not disappoint you."

If he can tantalize me to the extreme and I can hold out—oh, God, he loves that. He gets off on it so hard. "Challenge accepted, puppet."

And then he kneels back down, pushes my panties aside, flicks his fingertips against my sweet spot, and pushes them deep inside me. He rips my blouse open, grabbing at my breast, eagerly doing his best to make me fail.

But I am strong and I have my mantra.

He thinks for me, I act for him.

He thinks for me, I act for him.

He thinks for me, I act for him.

2 - Shep

When **I was discharged** from CORE, the releasing officer handed me a booklet called *Do's and Don'ts: An Easy Transition into the New Life of You.*

It was a fictional scenario in the vein of a second-person narrative of a man who I was supposed to identify with, getting discharged and what he experienced in his first two weeks of life on the outside.

The story revolves around a character called 'You'.

And this is where the BS starts because second-person point of view is a trick. It's a whole bunch of 'you did this' and 'you did that'. Like it was really *me* in that story.

It's a PSYOP mind fuck. Because everything about CORE is a PSYOP mind fuck.

But they made me read it before they let me go and I have to say, it did end up being pretty accurate.

You go to the store, hungry for food you've never eaten.

You choose many things, eager for a taste of what you've been missing, and then realize you don't have any money and must make a choice:

Do you, a) Rob the store and take the food?

Or, b) Put it all back?

This was a literal multiple-choice question. I chose to put it all back, of course, because it's the textbook answer.

There were about twenty of these questions that needed to be answered before I was allowed to leave and I ticked all the right boxes.

But it's one thing to be fictional 'You' in your first two weeks on the outside and quite another to be literal 'Me'.

Most of the time when I went into the store, I did pay for it. I worked a few jobs to make ends meet, as they say. I played the game. But it's all so rigged. I don't understand how these people on the outside do it. I really, really don't. It's so obvious that all the rules and laws are enacted for one reason only: to keep a man down.

Or a woman. Or hell, even a child.

It's *all rigged*.

So fuck it. I stopped paying.

Of course, 'You' predicted this. There was a whole chapter in that booklet about the court system and what to expect when 'You' go to prison.

Also very helpful, actually. Because I did go to prison.

For five years.

And I'm only out now because Charlie Beaufort made it happen.

Take a day for yourself. You look like you need one.

I'm not sure if I should be flattered that he's taken notice or if Collin Creed telling me to fuck off my first full day at Edge Security as a new recruit is a bad omen of dark things to come, but either way, it doesn't matter because I need this day off.

I'm sure his directive has more to do with the fact that he

wasn't expecting me to show up at nine o'clock last night, which means he doesn't know what to do with me this morning, and less to do with my lack of sleep and disheveled appearance after getting a surprise early release from prison three days ago and my subsequent multi-day motorcycle ride across the country to the outskirts of Disciple, West Virginia.

Either way, it's not good. But none of this is in my control, so I chant the words of wisdom passed on to me by 'You' in Do's and Don'ts: *Control the chaos, control yourself.*

Of course, it didn't help me before and that's why I was in prison. But I've grown over the years. I've matured. I've learned how to live with these outside people, even if it was mostly from the inside of one of their prisons. And I figure, what the fuck? It can't hurt. Maybe 'You' was on to something?

Controlling the chaos inside my head is pretty much the only superpower I have at the moment, so I blow out a breath as I ride into Revenant, slowing down so I can look at the storefronts, and try to absorb the hopeful energy of a fresh start.

Revenant is supposed to be the seedy part of Trinity County, but after prison, the idea that this small town is anything but quaint is ridiculous.

Still, my contract with Edge explicitly states that I agree to stay inside Trinity County and... well, if Creed is gonna kick me out, it won't be over something as stupid as a beer in the wrong shit-stain small town.

It's Monday morning right now, and while I do see that the diner is open as I slowly cruise through the bike-lined streets, the rest of the town looks abandoned. I've only ever been down here at night-time when things were rowdy enough to give off the impression of happenings, but now, in the morning sunshine, all I see is disappointment.

Still, my only other choice is Bishop, which is all the way over on the other side of the county, and while they do have pubs and I do like a wench in a peasant dress, I highly doubt that's a better choice than my current location. So I ease the bike into a space in front of the diner, kick the stand, get off, and blow out a breath as I take my helmet off.

This is when I notice my own reflection in the diner window and even though it's not a proper mirror, I have to agree with Collin Creed.

I look like shit.

All the overthinking that I kinda talked myself out of doing while riding down here comes flooding back.

It's not real.

Men who get kicked out of CORE, rob stores, and get sentenced to ten years don't just get out of prison one day and end up at Collin Creed's Edge Security with a second chance.

It doesn't happen that way, Shep. You know it doesn't happen like that.

"But it did," I mutter, still staring at my reflection in the window. "It *did* happen that way. Because here I am. And this *is* real."

A woman appears on the other side of the window, smiling at me as she wipes down a table. "Come on in," she says. Though I can't hear her, I can read her lips.

She's pretty. Cute, really. Looks like a real nice girl.

But I'm not the kind of man who gets the nice girl. I'm the kind of man nice girls need to run from. So I shake my head, turn away, and just start walking down the street towards the bar I was at last night.

To my surprise, the hours on the door say it's open and the door is not locked when I pull on it, so I actually go inside.

Some old-school song is playing on a jukebox and the entire place is empty, save for a man standing on the other side of the bar polishing a pint glass. He's looking up at a TV mounted in a corner, but glances over his shoulder at me when I enter.

"Mornin'," he says, then goes back to watching the TV, which I notice is playing horse races. The mans stops polishing, almost leaning up on his tiptoes to see the race better, then he lets out a sigh. and says, "Fuck." He chuckles, looks over his shoulder at me, and shrugs. "Well, there's another hundred bucks gone. Guaranteed Gold, my ass. More like Lucky Loser." He laughs at his joke. "Do you wanna beer or somethin'? Or are ya just here killin' time until the fun starts? If so, you'll be here all day. We're not technically closed on Mondays—Lasher would shit a brick if we closed down the whole town to have a literal day off—but it's known that we kinda are. People won't start showin' up for any kind of fun until after dark, friend. So if you're lookin' for a party, you're not gonna find it here."

I take a seat, set my helmet on the bar, and look around. "Well, I've been told by no one in particular"—I look back over at the bartender—"that I look like shit and should take a day."

The guy nearly snorts. "Collin Creed tell you that? Or was it Amon?"

"Creed. And how'd you know I was one of them, anyway?"

"Shit, you Edge guys might as well be wearin' nametags, that's how much you all look alike. Killers, huh? That's what you guys are?"

It's a bold question if you ask me. But this guy asks it like he's asking where I went to high school. "Somethin' like that." Then I look around, find the sign for the restrooms, and head that direction without another word to the barkeep.

I push the swinging door open, walk over to the sink, brace my hands on it, and stare at myself in the mirror. "This *is* real."

My reflection takes a few moments to agree with me. But I force myself to look into my own blue eyes until the panic in my chest subsides and my heart calms down to a reasonable level. I glance over my shoulder in the mirror, noticing the décor. There are vintage metal signs on the walls. Oil signs, and gas station signs, and street signs. They don't look like fake reproductions either. They look original. I turn around and see a corkboard on the wall near the door with lots of things tacked to it.

I walk over to the board and start reading things. Mostly it's flyers for local bands, or whatever. Colorful pieces of half sheet paper printed up in sloppy black ink like it was done by hand.

All the other notes have the same nice touch. Boards like this are typically filled with business cards for local people. But aside from the flyers, most of the space on this one is taken up by handwritten notes.

The most prominent one is a piece of notebook paper with the words, *For a good time call Sally*, scrawled across it in black marker. There's a phone number underneath with a five-five-five prefix.

Fake, obviously.

I scan the rest of the notes. There are no more sex offers, they are mostly for other businesses in Revenant. Though I do see one for a bowling alley in Disciple and a pub in Bishop, which are the other two towns in Trinity County.

Which has me pausing to reconsider the fakeness of it all.

That's when I notice the map.

I reach out, give the piece of paper a tug, and pull it off the corkboard. What the hell is this?

It's handwritten, like all the other notes on the board, and done up in black marker depicting a crudely drawn picture of a woman with big hair, and big eyes, and a speech bubble coming out of her mouth that reads, *The Mule Pit Speakeasy is calling your name, soldier.*

I scoff, then glance down at the map. It starts at the bar I'm in, leads out of town, down the highway towards Fayetteville, and then veers into a national forest. From there, it leads to a parking lot and a foot trail that takes you into the forest. The trail leads to what appears to be stairs, and the stairs lead to the bar.

"What the fuck?"

When I flip the page over, there's a black and white photocopy of, presumably, the inside of the bar. But it's a bad photocopy. Like it was run on a state-of-the-art Xerox machine circa nineteen-seventy-five.

And there's a woman. This time, a real woman. She's wearing a dress that gives off speakeasy vibes and is making a kissy face at the camera. Off to the side there's another speech balloon that says, *Come find me, soldier. I'm waiting here just for YOU.*

The word 'you' is capitalized and underlined.

A creepy chill runs up my spine and makes the hairs stand up on the back of my neck.

You.

Is that a sign? It this map for me? Like, specifically?

"For fuck's sake, Shep. You're insane."

Which might be true. But that doesn't cancel out the fact that I just found a map to some secret speakeasy in the woods.

I leave the bar and go back to my bike, feeling very much out of sorts. But when I get on, and grab the handle bars, ready to kick it over, I realize I'm still holding the map in my right hand. It's clutched in my fist.

I look around, once again wondering if any of this is real.

Outside the diner, there's a little crowd of people. Talking and holding coffee cups or takeout containers like this is just a normal day.

But it's not a normal day.

Because 'You' is talking to me.

I shove the map into my pocket, kick the bike, and pull away.

Heading down the highway towards Fayetteville.

I FIND **the turn-out** into the national forest easy enough since it's just outside of town on the Loop Highway, so I'm literally idling the bike in the parking lot, staring at the trail less than ten minutes after I left the bar.

It's not that muddy, which means I don't have to leave the bike here and walk in. If this map is correct, I can ride all the way to the stairs before I have to get off. After that, it's just going down those stairs and the bar should be right at the bottom.

Once again, I pause. Because this is kinda crazy. A secret bar in the woods? A flyer with a map tacked up to a corkboard in a bathroom?

Hell, being in this part of the country again is a trip in and of itself. Looking back on my recent history, is this map really that out of place?

I rev the bike and ease forward. The trail is narrow and the trees along each side are old and tall, so the boughs sort of form a tunnel as I slowly ease the bike down the path. After about ten minutes of gently sloping descent, I come to the stairs. They are on the edge of a very deep gorge and when I lean over the side, there's a river down below. Over the entrance to the stairs is a rusted beam with the words 'Your Family Wants You To Work Safely' painted along the length of it in neat, block letters.

Despite the massive sign, the stairs themselves are rather narrow and small. But what they lack in grandeur, they make up for in steepness and the only thing I'm thinking about is what a bitch it's gonna be walking back up. It takes nearly ten minutes to reach the bottom, but I am not rewarded with a secret drinking hole, just a long brick ruin of crumbling coke ovens.

I pause, looking around, then start wondering if I should go back up. But off to the left of the coke ovens, there's a small deer path and when I bend down to take a closer look at the dried mud, I see boot prints that appear recent.

I think this is it.

I'm already here. It doesn't cost me anything to look around before giving up, so I head into the trail and push through a thick copse of trees. When I look to the left, there it is. A secret bar in the middle of the forest.

The building is made of brick—maybe even the same brick as the coke ovens back at the stairs. They kinda look like cinderblocks, but they are easily a hundred years old. Most of them are covered in vines and all of them are stained with bright green moss.

It's kinda quaint, actually. Especially with the sign, which is almost exactly like the one at the top of the stairs, only along the length are painted the words 'Mule Pit' instead of 'Your Family Wants You To Work Safely.'

All the windows of the establishment are just holes in the brick, like they haven't had glass in them in decades. But the sounds from within are muffled, which doesn't make a lot of sense until I go inside and realize the brick building is just a shell when I'm presented with a set of actual doors made out of steel.

There's no bouncer to stop anyone from entering, so I just pull the door open. Music blasts out at me—something bluesy and local that I don't recognize—and when I enter, I find myself on a high balcony looking down into a large room filled with people. Probably *hundreds* of people.

The stairway leading down from the balcony I'm standing on appears to be two or three stories high. It reminds me of a fire escape in a big city. Industrial, and metal, and rusted. It looks sketchy and old, like it's been here as long as this old mine, but when I grab the railing, it feels solid. So I start my descent, all the while taking in the room.

It's not really a room, though. It's more like a cave. About every eight feet or so there are thick, old, dark brown beams along the walls. Probably railroad ties. Whether they actually hold the place up or are just there for decoration is anyone's guess. There are old dirty rugs covering the hard-packed earthen floor, but they don't look shabby or out of place because they are those antique-lookin' things. Persian or something. People are walking all over them, some dancing on them— which is probably a hazard—and the rugs look like they came with the mine when it was first carved into this hillside.

There's a stage, and a band playing, and massive bars lining two sides of the room. There's also a proper dance floor on the other side of the room where people are dancing—like couples. Men and women, like married couples. But it's obviously more than some local hangout where Ma and Pa go to wind down on a Friday night, because there's plenty of titties on display as well.

At least twenty half-naked women are serving drinks and there are two cages on either side of the main stage with a girl inside them wearing absolutely nothing. Not even shoes.

There are dozens of small circular tables grouped in front of the cages, and none of them are empty. They are draped in white tablecloths, and each one has a flickering candle in the center. Couples wearing everything from jeans, t-shirts, and cowboy hats to suits and dresses. There's even one woman wearing a gown. While all the seated customers are leaning in to each other, like they're all in the middle of a fascinating conversation, this woman is surveying the room like a madam.

Which she might actually be, since it's highly unlikely that fully nude dancers are legal here either, since there's no shortage of alcohol. And this kind of explains the clandestine nature of the whole set up.

On the last landing I pause, taking it all in.

What the actual hell? How is this here?

I can't decide if I'm in a speakeasy, a whorehouse, or a gentlemen's club, but in any case, it works.

It's not some seedy little bar with a sagging tin roof, it's a genuine Château Marmont out in the middle of the West Virginia woods.

A girl sashays towards me. Having probably deduced that I'm a first-timer, she sways her hips in a seductive way and flashes a welcoming smile. She's not topless and she's not carrying a tray of drinks, but it's pretty clear from her outfit that she's a Mule Pit employee. Her dress is flapper-esque. Something reminiscent of the Roaring Twenties of the last century. Like maybe she lives in Disciple and this old thing was just hanging in her closet.

It's not out of place—there are plenty of women wearing

costumes in the same vein—but the Mule Pit is not some Revival knockoff, so while there's a lot to like about the dress, there's also a lot wrong with it. In fact, that's the perfect way to describe everything about this place. Enticing, but for questionable reasons.

"Can I help you?" she says, coming to a halt just below me. Her West Virginia accent is present, but not thick.

"Yeah. I'm looking for a drink, I guess."

She reaches up to me with an outstretched hand, enticing me to take it with twiddling fingers.

I slowly descend the last few steps, stopping right in front of her. She's short, maybe five four, so I'm looking down on her as she looks up. Her eyes are hazel—a little bit gray, a little bit green, a little bit brown. Her hair is dark blonde, maybe even brown in a more normal light, and she comes off as wispy, but not skinny. Her arms, while long and willowy, are also defined. I deduce that her breasts are better than average, even though she's not showing them off. And she's young. Early twenties at the most.

So this is my first question. "How old are you?" Because the last thing I need to get involved with is an underage girl working in an illegal titty bar. You can't be too careful about this stuff in my experience.

"Twenty. How old are you?" She says this playfully. Like maybe I'm too old for her and my answer might dictate how this encounter goes.

But it won't. Even if I was sixty, it's this girl's job to make me happy so I'll spend money. "Twenty-seven."

She smiles. "Perfect. Old enough to know better, but young enough not to care."

Which is an astute thing to say, in my opinion. But I don't

bother dwelling on it because she's already slipping her arm into mine, leading me deeper into the club. "Come on. Let's get you that drink."

She doesn't take me to either of the bars, but instead ducks through a beaded curtain and we enter a long, dark hallway with rooms along either side.

"I'm not looking for sex, so if that's what you're expecting, I'd rather have my drink at the bar."

Her face, when she glances over her shoulder at me, is sweet and unaffected at my suggestion that she's a whore. "I'm not looking for sex either. I'm just gettin' us a private room where we can relax."

Which is a lie. She's gonna bill me for this private room, but whatever. There's nothing wrong with this girl. She's nice to look at, so I'm not inclined to object.

I have money. Not a lot, but I live on a compound where all my basic needs are paid for and even though I'm the new guy at Edge, Charlie Beaufort set me up a sweet signing bonus when I got out a prison. The motorcycle was part of it. And this money is practically burning a hole in my pocket. So whatever this girl has to offer, I can cover it.

Maybe I didn't come in looking for a girl to fuck, but would it be so bad if I found one?

We duck through another curtain and enter what appears to be a living room with a black leather couch facing a giant screen hanging on the wall. A black-and-white movie is playing with the sound turned down.

"Have a seat and I'll get you a drink." She points to the couch. "Will it be beer or whiskey?"

"I'll have the whiskey."

She holds out her hand, palm up. "Cash or credit?"

I pull out my wallet, grab a fifty-dollar bill, and slap it onto her palm. "Cash."

Her expression doesn't change, but I catch something here. Disappointment? Was she hoping for my credit card so she could run up a bill? Is this place just some honeypot to shake down the locals?

I doubt it. If it were, word would've gotten out. And while I'm not from West Virginia, I am from Tennessee and the places aren't much different. Strangers do not build speakeasy bars in the middle of a forest with a plan to fuck over the locals.

Not smart ones, anyway.

Whatever is happening here—and clearly there is *something* happening here—it's not about stealing from the locals.

It's probably mobster shit. Or whatever equivalent organized crime they have runnin' West Virginia. Moonshining is my guess. Which makes sense, since this place is a bar.

The girl and I are both holding on to the fifty-dollar bill when I say, "Is the whiskey moonshine?"

Which makes her laugh. "Look around, Ace. Then I'll give you one guess."

So they are moonshiners. "Are you from around here?"

She cocks a hip, but her expression remains playful. "Well, something I did or said has ruffled you. You're full of questions."

"Are you?"

"Of course. Can't you hear it in my accent? Born and raised in these parts, Ace. My family goes way back into these hills. I'm talkin' places you ain't never heard of. Places you'd never find your way back from if you were to wander into them. My daddy's a very important man."

"And he lets you work here? He don't mind when you bring

strange men into a private room invitin' said man to conjure up all kinds of lecherous deeds that might be done in that room?"

She tips her chin up, a little bit defiant. "It's not up to him. But no, he doesn't mind. Everyone owes favors to someone."

Which is a *weird* answer.

But she doesn't give me time to chew on it. "Anyway. Do you want that drink or don't you?" And then she gives the fifty-dollar bill, which we are still both holding onto, a small tug.

I tug hard enough to take it. Then tuck it back in my wallet and hand her my credit card. "Let's start a tab, darlin'."

She places her hand on my chest, flat against my beatin' heart, and looks up at me. "Anything you want, Ace." Then she turns and ducks through another beaded curtain at the opposite end of the room and disappears.

3 - Brose

My *phone buzzes*. I grab it, glancing at the screen, and answer before it can buzz twice. "Grandfather. What do I owe the pleasure?"

"I'm checking in. How are things going?" His response comes across a sketchy satellite line with small micro-interruptions in the connection and a trace of long distance distortion.

"Good. We're open for business."

"Perfect. And… how are you feeling?"

I shrug, even though we're not talking in person. "Fine. Why?"

"You know I worry about you, Ambrose. You're all the family I have left."

He says this every time we talk. Like he's trying to convince me of his love. Sometimes it bothers me, but only in a casual way. He's all the family I've got left as well. "Thanks for asking," I say. "But I'm OK."

After a small hesitation, he says, "Good."

But he doesn't say anything else. So I ask, "Would you… like a progress report?"

"No, thank you." His tone comes off as considerate and these words are soft. "Don't hesitate to call if you have any issues. You know how to find me. Now carry on."

The call ends before I can say anything else, but there's no time to think about it because Olive enters my control room without knocking. I look over my shoulder, enjoying this look she's wearing today—the Roaring Twenties dress, her pale face in the false light, and her eager eyes. The whole vibe just works for me.

"I've got one," she says, handing me his credit card. "Who is he?"

I turn back to the panel of screens in front of me, the system cycling through its routine sweeps of the compound. Constant eyes, always watching. Comparing the image of the man who just entered the Mule Pit with all of Collin Creed's known employees takes less than a second.

"New guy," I say, pointing at the top left screen. "Just came in last night. Good thing the drones tagged him at the gate." I zoom in, the profile populating across the screen. "Ean Shephard. Age twenty-seven. Former DRS."

"Deep Recon Specialist? No shit?"

"No shit."

"Well..." Olive pauses to think about this. "I don't get it. He's one of us. Is he here undercover?"

"He didn't trigger the tracking when he came through the entrance of the bar, which means his chip has been turned off, so my official assumption should be no."

"Then what's your unofficial assumption?"

"Give me a moment," I say, letting my fingertips dance across the keyboard. I hit enter and this guy's history with CORE pops up.

"Holy shit," Olive says, leaning in towards the screen. "He's legit."

He *is* legit. It takes me almost ten whole seconds of scrolling to get to the bottom of all the info we have on Ean Shephard. I point to the last entry. "And there we go. This one went insane a few years back. Was discharged and promptly entered the prison system out in Wyoming for armed robbery."

Olive takes a seat on a wheeled stool and rolls herself over next to me. "Damn. What the hell is he doin' here?"

I scan the notes that begin to populate now that I've drawn attention to the new guy. "Looks like Charlie Beaufort got him out of prison and sent him to Collin on a contract."

"I don't get it. Why would Collin hire him? Especially after Collin's fallin' out with Charlie?"

"Oh, hold on. This explains it. His contract with Charlie got sidetracked by some judge's moral compass, so it didn't actually go through until after all that shit went down underground with Collin and friends."

"Hmm," Olive hums. "You'd think that Charlie would have the power to cut those strings."

She's right. "You would think that. So maybe this guy *is* undercover?"

"Spying on Collin?" she asks. "That's quite a deep cover if they sent him to prison for five years just to set it up."

Yeah, Olive's right about that too. Doesn't make much sense. I turn my head to look at her. And God, she's so fucking beautiful, I almost can't stand it. Everything about this girl is perfect. And my job here—to handle her—well, it's like a dream come true. I handle her all right. Every fucking night I've got my dick between her legs.

"Brose?"

"Right. Yeah. It's possible that this isn't Charlie's mission. Maybe he couldn't cut the strings, even though he wanted to."

Olive is nodding. "Makes sense."

"Get rid of him."

"Already? But—"

"Olive, do not question me. Get *rid* of him. The last thing we need is to get stuck in one of Charlie Beaufort's webs. We'll get the next one. Over half those guys on Collin's payroll are former CORE operatives."

"But what if he's not deep cover? What if he's just an employee?"

"Don't contradict me. I said get rid of him."

"We've been open for three weeks, Brose, and not a single other Edge employee has come by. We've put those flyers up all over Revenant, but take a look at the room out there." She points to the bank of screens that keep an eye on the public areas. "They're all locals or tourists who came for the Trinity County experience. Collin has warned his guys, or something. Ean is new. This might be our only chance. If I let him get away, he'll go back to the compound, start talking about this place, and then Collin or Amon will hear about it and tell everyone to stay away for sure. Or worse, he'll come down here to check it out himself."

"All of that is true," I say, slowly reaching over to place my hand on her throat. Her eyes immediately track to mine. "But I know why you want to work him. You can't fool me, Olive. I saw the way you looked at him. You think he's attractive." I press my fingers into her skin with just enough pressure to let her know this is getting serious.

Which makes her eyes close. The expected outcome.

Olive Creed. She's a dirty little whore, and I mean that in the most affectionate way, because I'm the one who turned all that lust into something usable. She's horny, like all the time. And I'm not saying she'd fuck just anyone, but this guy here? Ean, or whatever? He's better-looking than most. It's natural for her to be drawn to him.

Olive opens her eyes, trying to get herself under control. "My ensuing seduction," she says, climbing into my lap and spreading her legs to straddle me, "will be purely professional." She takes my face in her hands and stares deep into my eyes. "But wouldn't you like to watch, Brose?"

"You want to fuck him right now?"

"Only if you want to watch." She smiles at me. Winks. Then she kisses me and starts grinding on my dick, getting me hard. Or more like getting me ready.

"Fine," I whisper. "Fine. I'll watch." The way this girl affects me is way beyond inappropriate. She's got a hold on me. It's a weakness. I know this. But I really like her. A lot.

Olive kisses me again, our mouths open, lips lingering. Then she says, "Don't get too excited. I'll be back after he leaves to finish you off."

Then she gets up and abandons me with a fierce hard-on and a fantasy that may or may not include this motherfucker who just walked into my operation.

4 - Shep

The girl is gone for about ten minutes. Which is putting me off, to be honest, but when she returns my irritation at being kept waiting quickly fades when I realize she took the extra time to change her clothes. Instead of the dress, she's now wearing a cropped white t-shirt that clings to her tits and makes her nipples pop out. She's also wearing a pair of cut-off denim shorts with lots of loose strings dangling down her lean, tanned thighs. And she's barefoot.

She grins at me and her eyes are wild with possibilities as she sets a tray down on a little table near the beaded curtain.

On the tray is a wide-mouth mason jar filled with clear liquid. It's got a black label with white lettering around the middle of the jar that reads 'Code Black.' There are two shot glasses as well.

"Sorry I took so long. I just wanted to get out of that dress and put on something more comfortable."

More accessible is more like it. The cropped t-shirt is so short, it would barely take a flick of my finger to expose her firm and perky tits.

She pours us each a shot of moonshine and then walks over to me, taking a seat on the couch. She's so close to me, we're bumping shoulders. But she turns her body, giving me room, and opens her legs a little, which makes me look down at her invitation.

She's not shy.

"Cheers?" she says, holding out a shot glass for me to take.

Which I do, then nod. "Sure. Cheers."

We click the glasses together and then I watch as she downs it in one gulp like a professional. The wince is immediate and it comes with a wheezing gasp. A moment later, she's coughing and I'm laughing.

"It's a little strong?"

She can barely talk when she answers. "It's… not bad…"

Which makes me laugh again. Then I down mine and the burn—holy fuck. I've had homemade whiskey all over the damn globe, but this is something else. It's so hot, I'm expecting fire to come out of my mouth when I breathe.

I cough too, and then she's pattin' me on the back and we're both laughing.

It's good. Not just the moonshine and the girl, but the laugh.

I feel like it's been a long time since I had a proper laugh.

After about a minute, we're both recovered and she pours us each another. But when she offers it to me, I put up a hand. "One is enough, darlin'. I didn't really come here to get drunk."

This makes her eyes dance and she cocks a hip. "Oh? Then why did you come?"

"Well, to be honest, I just wanted to… watch."

Her smile is so big, I laugh again. "*Watch?*"

"Like people-watch, ya know? I just wanted to be somewhere I could relax and fade into the background."

This makes her snort. "Fade into the background? Ace, I've known you for all of twenty-five minutes and even I can see that you're not a background kind of guy. Main-character energy is flowing off you like water running over the side of a hill in the springtime."

"Why are you calling me Ace?"

"Because I don't know your name and you look like a man who gets shit done."

"Do I?"

She nods and repositions herself on the couch next to me so that she's leaning against the armrest and her legs are draped over my lap. Immediately, I start touching those legs, rubbing my large hands over her knee and then along her inner thigh.

When I look back up at her, she's staring right back at me. "I thought you weren't lookin' to fuck no one?"

"I'm not," I say, but my voice is kinda raspy and hoarse. "I'm just… enjoying the view."

She smiles. "Well, if you change your mind, you let me know."

"How much?" I ask. Which is a terrible thing to say to a girl who looks this sweet. But the facts are the facts. She's a whore.

"That's up to you. We don't have to fuck. We could just have fun."

"How much does fun run?"

"Fun is fun and it's all the same price. Fifty for fifteen minutes."

I reach into my pocket, pull out my wallet, and present her that same fifty-dollar bill.

She takes it from me and then leans over and places it on the little table holding the moonshine. Then she sits up, climbs into my lap, straddles my legs, and pushes her tits into my face. "Where should we start?"

I look down, then flick my fingertip against her tight, white t-shirt, and up it pops, exposing those firm and perky tits of hers. She takes both my hands and places them on her breasts, inviting me to squeeze. Which I do.

She begins to grind on me. Slowly and deliberately. Like she's trying her best to hit my cock in just the right way.

Of course, it immediately springs to life so her task is made easier. When I look at her again, she's biting her lip. "Do you wanna kiss me?"

I'm watching her lips as she says this. They are pink and plump. And then, for some reason, I'm thinking about shit. The things I've done. The people I've hurt.

And then the next thing I know, I'm throwing her off me and pushing my way through the beaded curtain, leaving the same way I came in.

"Hey! Where are you going?"

She grabs my arm, but I whirl around so fast she goes flying sideways, crashing into the wall. When our eyes meet this time, she must see something in them.

She must see *me* in them. Because she cowers.

I shake my head, then turn and walk down the hallway, go back out to the main bar, climb up all the stairs that lead to the real world, and spend the next half hour hiking back up to where I left the bike.

It's **early afternoon** when I get back to the compound and the whole place is filled with ex-soldiers busy training K9s. I ease the bike down the long driveway towards the house I've been assigned to. There are like ten houses for the men here, and then all the guys who run the place have their own houses, so it really is a compound.

One might even call it a base. Because everybody here is ex-military.

I catch Amon's eye as I pass by and he nods at me. I'm not sure what this nod means, but by the time I get off the bike and take my helmet off, I can take a good guess because he's heading my direction.

"Hey… uh…" He forgot my name.

"Ean," I say, fillin' in that blank.

"Right. Ean. Sorry. We haven't really talked yet, so I figured I'd come over and explain what's goin' on with the dogs."

"I guess you're training them for deployment?"

"Right." Amon smiles, and he's a very attractive man, so his smile is always comin' off as charmin'. But he's Collin Creed's partner, so that charm he so effortlessly displays on the outside has absolutely nothing to do with the man he really is on the inside. "Obviously. What I meant to say is I thought I'd explain why you don't have one yet. You see, we did have an extra puppy, but my son claimed it. And the other puppies are too young yet. Just born three weeks ago. So it's gonna be about another month and a half before you can really interact with yours."

"My…?" I'm confused.

"Your dog."

"I don't have a dog."

Amon chuckles. "I know. That's why I'm explainin' this to you."

I look around and realize everyone has a dog. Everyone but me.

"I'm sorry," Amon says. "I get that you just got here last night, but didn't you get some kind of briefing about what we do here at Edge?"

I shake my head. "Nope. I was told this is my new contract and you guys own me for the next twelve months, so I showed up."

"Oh." Amon ponders this. "All right. Well"—he pans a hand to the soldiers and the dogs—"everyone gets a dog to train. And depending on where they're at in the training, they might deploy with a dog or they might not. We've really only got about ten of them ready to work. All the others are a project, so I'll just be blunt right now. You will not be deploying with a dog if you're only plannin' on being here for the first term of your contract because your dog will be a puppy."

I shrug. "OK."

"And said puppy is too young to bother you with at the moment, so you won't be doing any kind of serious training for a couple months."

"Fine with me."

Amon stares at me. Hard. "So what I'm really sayin' is that after PT every morning, you're with Ryan."

I look around. "Ryan is…"

"One-fourth owner in Edge. He's not here, he's in the woods making roads and digging shit up."

Now I squint my eyes at this fucker. "Tell me again what you're saying?"

"I'm saying you're on labor for the foreseeable future."

"Labor?" I laugh. "Dude, I'm a fuckin' soldier. I've been all over the goddamned world. And you're telling me… I'm what? Diggin' ditches or somethin'?"

This guy actually has the balls to clap me on the shoulder. "That's exactly what I'm telling you, friend. I don't have any fuckin' idea what Ryan is doin' out there in the damn woods. All I know is that you're his new bitch. So… welcome to Edge."

Then he turns and just… walks away.

"Welcome to Edge," I mutter. But I don't bother continuing the argument. I just take myself inside, go upstairs to my bunk.

There are ten houses, six men to a house. This is the story I got last night from my roommate, Chester. But I'm the odd one here, since I'm new and the rest of them have been here for months already. So this house has seven of us. The guy who was in this room has moved in to a walk-in closet on the first floor, claiming he'd rather live under the stairs like Harry Potter than spend one more night with Chester, who snores like a motherfucker.

But I don't really mind. Sleep is highly overrated, if you ask me. Sleep is where the nightmares live, so I only give in when I have to.

I didn't sleep a fuckin' minute last night. Not a single minute. Which is most likely the whole reason Collin Creed told me to 'take a day.'

But there's nothing else to do, so I might as well just kick it on the bed and phone surf. I take my wallet out of my pants and this is when it hits me. "Fuck." I forgot my damn credit card at that bar. Then I actually laugh out loud. Because right here and now, that place doesn't even feel real. Did I really ride my bike into the woods, take several hundred stairs deep into a river gorge, and find myself a clandestine speakeasy filled with moonshine and whores?

The girl's face pops into my mind. Not the way she looked when we first met, but the way she looked at me when we were partin' ways.

I scared her.

But what's new?

I scare everyone. Hell, I even scare myself.

Well, one thing's for sure, I'll have to go back to get my card. So maybe I'll have a chance to explain. I walk over to the window and peek out. Not for any particular reason, just to take in my new environment. But immediately I spy Collin and Amon having a conversation across the driveway.

Then Collin turns and starts heading towards my house.

He's coming here for me, I know it. So a moment later, when I hear boots thudding on the wooden stairs that lead up to the second floor, I'm not surprised.

I'm still lookin' out the window when he taps the doorframe, knocking. Of course, the door is open, so it's just a courtesy knock at best. "Hey, Ean. Got a minute?"

I turn. "Shep," I say.

"What?" Collin squints at me.

"Everyone calls me Shep, not Ean. So I'd rather you just call me Shep."

"OK." He forces a smile. "*Shep*." He keeps that forced smile goin'. "I just wanted to welcome you proper, since you got in so late last night and there was some confusion on our part about who you are and what you're doin' here."

I try not to sigh with frustration, but don't entirely succeed. "I told you. Charlie Beaufort sent me. I was stuck in limbo because I was in prison and some judge got a wild hair up his ass about lettin' me out."

"Right." Collin nods. "I get it. And you're legit. I'm not saying you're not. I called Charlie up, even though I hate that motherfucker and we're not even on good terms, and it's all legit. So I'm not questioning you about that."

Now it's my turn to squint my eyes at him. "Then what are you questionin' me about?"

"Look, man, if you don't wanna be here, you're free to leave."

"No," I say. "I'm actually not. Working for Edge was a very specific condition of my parole."

Collin chuckles. "Dude, I am not gonna turn you in. You're a grown man. You can do whatever the hell you want."

I sneer at him. "So you think… what? I should break parole and go on the run? Leave the country and hide from the fuckin' CORE for the rest of my life?"

"Corps?" Collin says. "As in the Marines? Why would they care where you went? You've been discharged, right?"

"What?" I laugh. "No. I wasn't in the Marines. CORE. C-O-R-E. *CORE.*"

"Well, I can hear what you're saying," Collin says. "I just don't know what the fuck you're talking about."

"I thought *you* were in the CORE?" I wave a hand at the window. "I thought all of you were in the CORE."

"I was in the Corps. *Marine* Corps."

My squint deepens. "Are you fucking with me right now?" I scoff. "You better be fuckin' with me. Because if you don't know what I'm talkin' about…" But I don't finish. Because he's not one of us. Collin Creed isn't like me. And I'm kind of taken aback.

Collin squints back. "I think we should take this conversation to a more private location."

"Which would be where?"

"We've got a SCIF in the church and I think we should go there now."

I don't say another word and neither does Collin. He turns and walks out and I follow. Because we need to set this straight and I'm sure as hell not gonna tell him anything out in the open air like this.

Anyone who thinks that the CORE can't hear you any time and any place is a fool. And while Collin and his crew might not know as much as I do about how this world works, they are not fools. And this SCIF they have proves it.

We enter the church and Collin heads towards a door in the back. He pauses here, lookin' at me. For a moment, I think he's gonna change his mind because he doesn't move. And while he doesn't say anything either, he doesn't really have to. I can almost hear the silent argument in his head: *You're just gonna show him all your secrets, Collin? Then hope he's not a spy?*

But he must decide in the affirmative because he pulls the door open, flicks on a light, and waves me forward.

I enter a stairwell and go down two levels, not just one. At the bottom I find myself in a small concrete room with two doors. One is the SCIF. I can make this guess because there's a box outside the door, which I know from experience is a little Faraday cage for phones and shit. Nothing in, nothing out.

Collin walks over to it, opens the box, and drops his phone in. I do the same. Then he closes the box and opens the door.

I go in. He follows and closes the door.

The moment that happens, my head starts to feel weird. Like a vacuum. Which is normal, so I don't panic about it. People don't realize this, but the world is filled with electromagnetic frequencies. Unless you are very deep into the wilderness, there are frequencies floatin' on the air all around you, at all times of the day.

This is the hallmark of the modern world. Humans are constantly surrounded by low-level waves. Wi-Fi, radio waves, electrical hums, and even nearly imperceptible environmental noises like distant traffic or air currents.

But the point of a SCIF is to block all those frequencies. So when you go in, and the door shuts behind you, it's like puttin' on a pair of noise-cancelling headphones. But a thousand times more powerful.

Everything stops.

And it's weird.

In CORE, they call it the Rift.

The void. Because it's empty.

And they say if you stay in this type of environment too long, you'll go insane. That humans have changed over the past hundred and thirty years since electromagnetic frequencies started to be manipulated for communications and now, it's just a part of us. That's why people go crazy in the wilderness. They can't live without the frequencies.

Collin lets out a breath, bringing me back to the moment. "All right, what the fuck is going on? Who the hell are you, and why are you here?"

"First of all," I say, holding up one finger, "I'm Ean Shephard and I came here on a contract with Charlie Beaufort. Nothing I told you was a lie."

"Why are you here so late, then? When all the other guys arrived months ago?"

"I told you. I was in prison. Charlie made a deal, but the judge would not sign the papers for my early release. If there's anything else goin' on here, I'm not a part of it. At least, not a willing or an informed part."

Collin sneers. "That sounds like an excuse to me. So in the future, when I find out you are a part of something, you can just say you didn't know."

"I get it. It's all kinds of suspect. But whatever Charlie is doing, it's got nothing to do with me."

"Maybe. Maybe not. But what the hell were you talking about up there about the Corps?"

"CORE," I say again. "C-O-R-E. CORE. It's black ops shit. Like the stuff you were involved in that *didn't* get you sent to prison."

"If that's a dig on me and my men, well, we weren't robbing gas stations, either."

"Fair, I guess. But you and your guys did a whole lot worse than that. Other people just took your fall."

For a moment I think he's gonna object, but then he gives in and sighs. "Fine. We were… protected. But I don't know what you're talking about when you say the word CORE. What is it?"

"It's just…" I shrug. "CIA shit, I guess."

"You guess? Is it, or isn't it?"

"I mean, obviously, they are two different things. But they share the same space."

"All right. So why can't you leave Edge? You said they would hunt you down if you left. Why?"

"Why?" I kinda laugh. "Because I was DRS. Deep Recon Specialist."

"Assassin?"

I shrug. "Sometimes."

"What about the other times?"

"Well, I just hung around, mostly."

"Spying?"

"Obviously."

Collin laughs. "How the hell am I supposed to trust you?"

"Hell if I know. I didn't ask to come here. I was sent. And I'm not leaving without Charlie's permission. So if you don't want me here, you need to clear it with him. Only then will I leave."

I am fully aware that if Collin Creed tells me to get the hell out of his compound, my ass will be getting the hell out of his compound. He knows this too. What am I gonna do? Fight them? Call the police? It's stupid. I just want him to know that I'm insisting that he go through the proper channels.

He slides right past that and continues on to the next bit. "Are you reportin' back to Charlie?"

"No."

"Will you take a lie detector test?"

"Yes."

"We're gonna set that up and then I'll have a better idea of what to do with you."

I shrug with my hands. "You're the boss."

He nods, knowing he is, and then we retrace our steps and go our separate ways outside.

I head back to my house, but what I really wanna do is get my credit card back from that girl at the bar. It's just… after that conversation I just had with Collin, it's not gonna happen. I probably won't be able to slip away until the end of the week at the earliest.

So I just mope around in the house for a bit, then hit the mess for some food.

But at night, when the place is mostly quiet and the demons in my head are just starting to get loud, I picture the Mule Pit and that girl.

I didn't get her name.

But next time, I will.

5 - Brose

*O**live flops down** on the couch behind me, sighing loudly. My fingers pause on the keyboard, my eyes look straight ahead at the screen in front of me, and I start counting.

I have a rule. It's hard, and fast, and one of many, actually.

Rules keep things simple. Keeps this little kingdom I'm ruling all very black and white. And this particular rule is that Olive gets to interrupt me when I'm busy with *one* sigh of frustration or boredom, and no more.

This was her one.

It's been four days and she and I are practically living here at the Mule Pit. It's been nothing but long days of waiting and, for her, at least, equally long nights of frustration.

Another rule I have is that if she is with another man, I take a break. I'm not going to compete with someone inside Olive's mind. And while she obviously didn't get far with Ean Shephard, she was wiggling in my lap just a few minutes prior to wiggling in his.

Then he left her hanging.

If Shephard is playing a game here, he won that day. Because she can't get over that part. He walked out on her and she was giving him some good moves. So he's up there, inside her head, and when it comes to who I am to this woman, it's number one or it's number none as far as I'm concerned.

It's twenty seconds now and that one sigh was all Olive gave up.

"You're bored?" I ask.

"Aren't you?"

"You're thinking about him?"

She scoffs. "Aren't *you?*"

I swivel in my chair so I can look at her. She's wearing another one of those Roaring Twenties dresses. Not something she had, because she left Disciple when she was a girl. This dress is something she got from a thrift store. Apparently, you can find these dresses all over the surrounding counties and Olive has a whole closet filled with them now.

This one is long, straight, shapeless, and light yellow. I get the costume part of these clothes they wear at the Revival, but I don't find any of it particularly attractive. Especially the hair.

Except for Olive's hair, that is. Hers is dark blonde, shoulder length, and wavy, so it always looks the part, but that's how her hair always is. She doesn't need to do anything to make it blend in with the dresses, and I suddenly wonder if it's genetic.

Which is stupid. But then again, there it is. Sitting right in front of me. Perfect, effortless, nineteen twenties style.

She's waiting for my answer.

"No. I haven't been thinking about him at all." This makes her sneer, but she doesn't say anything. She knows there's more to my answer and there is. "I've been thinking about you *and* him."

Olive presses her lips together and nods a little bit. She's slumped back into the couch cushions, one leg thrown over the armrest, looking very sexy. That's not the look she's going for though—she's trying for 'moody'—so it's all that much more alluring because of her lack of effort. "I figured as much since you haven't fucked me in days." All these words come out with an attitude. "You think I don't know, but I do, Brose. I've been with you every day and every night for two years. I know you."

I'm amused, so I tip my chin up and challenge her. "And what is it that you think you know about me, Olive?"

"Your *rules*. Just because you never made a handbook doesn't mean I can't read them."

I'm surprised that she actually used the word 'rules,' but also intrigued as to what she thinks these rules are. "Go on."

"Go on, what? That's it. You have… lines, or something. Things I'm not supposed to do, except you don't tell me I'm not supposed to do them. Or actually, you *do* tell me to do them, and then you punish me for it."

"What do you think you did that you feel I'm punishing you?"

"I climbed into that guy's lap. I was going to fuck him. And even though you agreed, you're mad about it so you haven't touched me in days. It's your way of teaching me a lesson."

"And what lesson have you learned?"

"That what you say, and what you do, and what you think are oftentimes… very different things."

"I didn't agree, by the way. It was your idea to fuck him and you placated me with that bait about watching."

Her eyes squint down a little, like she's thinking back. But this *is* actually how it went down, so all those frown lines forming across her forehead even out pretty quick. "So which part are you mad about? The fact that I wanted to fuck him or that you didn't get a show?"

"You tell me. You're the instant psychologist."

She smiles at me, but it's a sardonic one. Then she scoots her body just a little bit to the right without taking that one leg off the armrest. Just enough to make sure I have a good view as she slips her hand down her stomach and pulls up her dress to reveal the fact that she's not wearing underwear.

I'm not sure if I'm angry about that or turned on, and I hate conflicting emotions, so I don't react.

My apathy only prompts her to keep going. "Well, I can't read your mind, Brose, but if it's a show you want, I can deliver." And then she flicks a finger back and forth across her little pink nub.

Olive is an eager girl when it comes to sex. She's not hard to please. She touches herself often, always finding pleasure in it, so she's getting a lot of pleasure out of this moment. Her eyes droop low, but don't entirely close. Her mouth goes slack, affording me a little peek at her tongue, and her back arches just the tiniest of degrees.

It's not an act. It's real and even if I was trying my best to remain indifferent, I would have a hard time not responding. But in this case, after days of sleeping and working beside her with no sexual contact at all, that best try wouldn't even come close to enough fortitude to withstand her teasing.

My dick grows inside my pants and her eyes are there to see it. Her tongue flicks out, swiping over her top lip, inviting me to picture her mouth sliding around my hard tip.

"If you want it," she says, her voice low and seductive, "come get it."

My smile is sideways. "That's not how this works."

"Today, Brose? Today it is. Because you have rules that I don't know about. And you put me in situations where I break these rules, and then you punish me for it. And I get it. I'm a little slut. I like it. A *lot*." She withdraws her fingers from between her legs, then closes her knees and stands up, straightening her dress. "But if you think I'm weak and have no self-control at all, you've misjudged me."

I scoff.

Which makes her squint again. "Try me, Brose. *Try me.*" Then she turns towards the door, like she's gonna walk out.

Immediately, I'm up from the chair and crossing the room. I grab her by the arm, spin her around, and push her against that door with a hard thump.

Her mouth is open when she looks up at me, shocked.

But it's a split second of shock, and nothing more. Because when my hand slides over to her breast and gives it a squeeze, she smiles. "Take it then. Because if you can have rules, Brose, then so can I. And from now on, if you agree to something and then try and punish me afterward, I will punish you back."

My hand slowly slides up to her throat and my fingertips splay open around it.

She holds her breath, hoping.

I've never seen a woman so turned on by choking. Ever. Olive Creed likes to be choked so much. Sometimes she tempts me into doing it.

The problem is, I like to be the choker, and it has happened on occasion that I have failed to... *restrain* myself.

I've choked her into unconsciousness three times now, and each time I did it, she came. Of course, while it's risky, it's not actually *that* dangerous. As long as I remove my hand the minute she goes limp, she comes back.

It's just... I'm afraid that... one day... I won't remove my hand at all.

"Do it," she dares. "Do it, Brose."

But I'm not going to do it, so I do not squeeze her throat. I just leave my hand there. It's the equivalent of her grabbing my dick, but not following through with a hand job. "You wanna know what rule you broke, Olive? That made me *hate* you?"

Her eyes squint down when I use that word 'hate.' I don't hate her. I will never hate her. It's just a trigger word and it does the job. "You hate me?" she says.

"Do you wanna know? Or not?"

"Tell me."

"You wanted him more than you wanted me."

"That's not true. I belong to you, Brose. That guy is nobody."

"Make me believe it. Make me believe it, Olive, and I'll—" I press my hand against her throat. She sucks in a breath. "I'll give you a little bit of this." I press just a tiny bit harder and her eyes close.

But at the same time, her mouth opens and those words I love to hear come spilling past her lips. "You think for me, I act for you."

"Say it again."

"You think for me, I act for you."

"*Again.*"

"You think for me, I act for you."

This time, when she says the words, I push on her shoulders and she slowly drops to her knees. As she lowers, her head lifts up and her eyes are locked with mine. She doesn't react as I undo the buckle on my belt and pop the button on my jeans. She doesn't move when I slide the zipper down and pull out my long, hard cock. And she doesn't resist when I wrap my hand round my shaft and push the tip past her lips. She opens wide for me, gagging a little, but trying her hardest, and I make my way inside her.

"That's it," I say, petting her pretty hair. "That's it. You're a good girl, Olive. You're a very good girl."

I hold my dick in her mouth, counting the seconds. Her eyes begin to water, making her mascara run, and her breathing is erratic and loud.

But I keep my dick right there in her mouth, pressed against the back of her throat, until I get to the count of three hundred. She's counting too, I'm sure of it. She doesn't know what my count is. It's never the same, but she knows I'm keeping time.

And when I get to three hundred, I give it one hard thrust and then pull back to let her cough. But just as quickly as she recovers, I push back in, making her gag again. I keep doing this until the count of sixty. I'm not sure if she's counting with me now. In fact, I'm pretty sure she's not, because she's moaning.

"Do not come," I threaten. "Do *not* come, Olive." She looks up at me, nodding, her face smeared with black mascara now.

I just look at her. I want to take a picture of this moment, but my phone is all the way across the room and breaking the moment isn't worth it. I live for this. I live for this girl, and her hot, wet mouth, and her makeup-smeared face, and her eyes.

There's something really wrong about it.

My attraction to Olive is forbidden. And I don't want to be so enthralled by her, but when those gorgeous eyes of hers look up at me like I'm her *God*, there's no way I can resist her seductive enchantment.

You must, Brose. You must resist.

She's not yours.

She belongs to CORE.

She belongs to CORE. She belongs to CORE.

I say this over and over and over in my head because it's true. But right now, I don't care about the rules. I pull out, grab her by the shoulders, spin her around, push her face up against the door, and lift her dress up.

She opens her legs for me without hesitation and I can hear her whispering, "He thinks for me, I act for him. He thinks for me, I act for him," over and over again.

When I thrust my dick inside her, she comes. She doesn't make a sound, nor does she clench me, but everything is so wet all at once that there is no way to miss her insubordination.

I lean in to her ear to make sure she hears my ragged, whispered words. "Oh, you're gonna pay for that."

But that's what she wants. She wants to be bad and she wants to pay for it.

I grab her by the wrist and drag her over to the couch. Then I sit down, pull her across my lap with her ass in the air, and smack her until I come all over myself and her cheeks are red with handprints.

6 - Olive

A soft chime wakes me and when I open my eyes I'm rewarded with a spectacular view of an approaching thunderstorm through our floor-to-ceiling bedroom windows.

Brose stirs in the bed next to me, his voice thick with sleep. "Turn the chime off, Olive."

For being a stickler for rules, he's very hard to wake in the mornings. But that just adds to his appeal, I think. That he likes his sleep.

I reach over, tap the alarm clock, and the chime stops.

"Thank you," he mumbles, his face now under the pillow.

I swing my legs out of bed and stand up, stretching. I have my back to him, but I know he's watching. And when I peek over my shoulder, he is. One eye open, staring straight back at me.

This is a morning routine with us. In fact, after two years, pretty much everything is a routine with us. I smile back and he winks, then closes that one eye for a few more minutes of sleep as I make for the bathroom.

By the time I'm showered and changed, he's up and dressed. I come out of our closet pulling on a trench coat as I watch him knot his tie in the mirror over the dresser. He winks at me again and I smile.

"Hurry up, hurry up," I prod. "We're gonna miss the train."

We're not gonna miss the train. It's not Amtrak, for fuck's sake. It's the Blue Line out of CORE headquarters. But this is just what I say to him. It's just part of the routine.

Brose turns and smiles. "How do I look?"

He looks delicious is how he looks. And if we didn't have work, I'd just tackle him sideways onto the bed and have my way with him one more time. But we do have work, so I just compliment him. "Good enough to eat."

Brose walks towards me, grabbing his coat off a chair as he passes, and by the time I'm pulling the door open, he's shrugging it on.

We walk the long hallway, saying hi to other agents as we head for the stairs, and then go down to the main level where there are dozens of people congregating in the large, open lobby.

This particular estate—internally called Grid-21—is but one of hundreds of CORE estates all over the world where operatives, like Brose and me, live. It's on a forty-acre tract of rolling hills and woods just outside of Leesburg, Virginia, and houses about fifty agents at any given time.

We do not all live in the same house, of course. Brose and I live in the main mansion, but there are nine more houses on the property. All brick, all luxuriously furnished, and all free.

It's kind of a good deal.

Plus, this place has direct access to the trains below ground. Which means Brose can take his time waking up and we'll still be able to stop by the dining room for a takeout beverage and a pre-bagged pastry.

He grabs a paper and gets the lemon muffin with coffee, black. I take the scone with a chai latte.

And then we hit the escalator and five minutes later we're two hundred feet below ground and the station noises replace the soft conversation and kitchen sounds upstairs.

We walk out onto the platform and take a seat on a bench. Brose opens his paper and I sip my tea and people-watch.

I know everyone's faces. Lots of them give me little waves. But I don't really interact with anyone, nor they with me. It's pretty much like this with all paired-up operatives. We're together. No one else matters.

Brose and I have been a team for the entire two years I've been above ground. He's my life.

Thinking this makes me want to look at him, so I slide my eyes to the side and watch his face as he reads.

"What?"

"Nothing," I say, my voice sweet and soft.

He doesn't look at me, but I get a lopsided grin. "You're thinking about last night, aren't you? You're imagining yourself over my knee."

I wasn't, but I am now.

He flicks his paper, then gives me a side-eye. "There's always more where that came from, Olive. All you have to do is ask. I'll bend you over the back of this bench right now, right here in this station. And then I'll fuck you from behind as everyone watches."

There is no way to stop my grin, so I cut eye contact and look straight ahead.

"You'd love that, wouldn't you?" he asks. "You're such a dirty little whore."

He calls me this all the time, but not in a mean way. Nor a literal one. "Only with you," I say.

He scoffs. "That might've been true last week, but I know

you've been secretly fantasizing about that Ean Shephard guy."

Which isn't a lie. But he can't know that for sure, so I deny it. "You're the only one I fantasize about, Brose. And don't make promises you can't keep. If you thought you could get away with bending me over this bench, you'd have done it long before now."

He laughs. And, probably, starts weighing the pros and cons of following through with his offer. But the high-speed train arrives, sliding along in front of us in near silence until it comes to a stop.

I grin at him, winning, then pan my hand to the train.

He stands up, folds his paper, grabs his coffee and muffin and gives me a slight bow of his head as he passes and enters the train.

He heads to our usual seats in the back of the car. A table for two. I don't like moving backwards, so Brose takes that seat, leaving the forward-facing one for me. This is one of the small ways of showing me he cares.

And I love it.

I love everything about him. His dark hair, his green eyes, his muscular body, and his big dick. Brose Sinclair is absolutely perfect. My dream man.

So while he was right, I've had a few small sexual fantasies about that Ean guy who works for Collin, it's meaningless. Just urges, nothing more.

I'm gonna marry Brose one day. And while I do understand that he's my boss at the moment, it won't always be this way. I won't always be under his authority. One of these days I'll get promoted and we'll be equals. We'll be one of those iconic duos. Like Bonnie and Clyde, except we're the good guys.

Brose looks out the window, which is a screen and not

actually a window since it's pointless to have train windows when you're underground, and watches the news. Our train rides are typically silent like this. He likes his thinking time and I've gotten used to it as well.

But I don't stare at the screens. Don't care about the news. I watch the people in the car with us. Some of them are teams, like us. But most of them are young women like me sitting alone and facing forward, so I only get a glimpse of their backs.

This first leg of our journey is quick once we pick up speed. This is a commuter train, so we get off and board the Green Line in the station below Winchester. Then we begin the twenty-minute journey to the station below the Mule Pit.

Six months ago, this station didn't even exist. It's all part of our operation, a place only for us. Well, not really. There are about a hundred other CORE operatives who spend a day here and there at the Pit, just to make it look full and to fill in odd jobs. But it's only seven forty-six am and Brose and I are running this operation, so when the train stops, we're the only ones who get off.

I exit first, Brose following, and then he takes my hand and, together, we walk up the stairs that lead to the locker room inside the bar.

I pause at my locker to change, but Brose doesn't wait. Just leaves, heading to the control room.

There are six dresses to choose from. Five of them are fairly modest, since they were all made in Disciple. But there's one—a knockoff that I found in a second-hand store in Charleston— that's got a sluttier feel to it. It's more of a bra and panties, but with a long, thin fringe covering my torso and back. The fringe is an iridescent green and turquoise color so it shimmers like something out of a fantasy under the bar lights.

It drives Brose wild when I wear this one and I always end up straddling his lap in the control room, grinding over his legs with his hard dick inside me.

I'm super horny this morning, so I put it on with these very expectations firmly in place.

Then I leave the locker room and find Brose in front of the screens.

Brose turns to look at me. "I hope you're ready, because he's coming."

"What?" I walk over to the screen where he's pointing. And sure enough, there's Ean Shephard riding his motorcycle through the woods, just like he did last week. "Well, fuck," I say. "Finally."

"We do have his credit card."

"We do," I agree. "But he sure did take his time. I'd pretty much given up on him, to be honest."

"I doubt he could get away. Since Collin and Charlie fell out, Collin would be on high alert about everything this guy did. And Ean, being CORE, would've picked up on it and bided his time. But the good news is, he's here."

I grab a stool from across the room and roll over to sit next to Brose. "I don't really understand why Charlie sent him in this way. I mean, he's CORE. Why not just give him the directive and let him do his job? Why all this complicated stuff?"

"He *was* CORE, Olive. He's obviously not anymore. He's obviously out of control."

I almost snort. "Then why is he even still alive?"

Brose looks at me, squinting. "For *this*, obviously. They needed to fuck up his life so he could get past Collin. He's still a spy, but he doesn't even know he's spying."

"A sleeper, huh?"

"Yeah." Brose is tapping the keyboard now, getting new angles of Ean from other cameras as he makes his way into the canyon by way of the stairs. "A sleeper."

I rest my elbow on the desk and sigh. "Poor fucker."

"Yep," Brose agrees again. "If I ever get to that stage, Olive, just off me, OK?"

I chuckle. "Agreed. And you me, Brose. Please don't let me go out as the butt of someone's joke."

He looks at me, his green eyes shining, but also dead serious. "We'll go out together."

I nod. "Deal. Just like Bonnie and Clyde."

The bar isn't even open yet, so neither of us gets up to greet Ean when he finally makes his way into the canyon and pulls on the Mule Pit door. It doesn't open, so he pounds a few times. Of course, we're not gonna let him get away. Not after waiting all week for him to come back. So when he turns away, ready to give up, Brose says, "You're on. Don't fuck it up."

I get up, walk out of the control room, and quickly make my way up to the door. I push it open and just barely catch a glimpse of Ean as he's turning around the corner of the brick building. "Hey!" I call.

He turns and comes back a few paces.

"Was that you at the door?"

He nods. "Yeah. You know why I'm here."

"You left your credit card."

"Can you get it for me? Then I'll be on my way."

I smile. "Sure." Then I hold the door open. "Come on in. I think it's in the office."

He hesitates, and for a moment I think he might not take me up on the offer, but then he relaxes his shoulders and gives in.

Following me inside.

7 - Shep

When I got to the Mule Pit and found the door locked, I thought for sure I'd made the whole thing up. There's no real evidence that this is a bar. That it was open. That there was a band playing. There's a little trail in the dirt leading to the front, but it's a tiny affirmation.

So when she called for me as I was walking away, it felt like something out of a dream. A good dream where the thing one has been obsessing about actually happens.

Obsession might be a little strong for how preoccupied I've been all week about this bar in the woods and the girl I found inside, but it feels like she's been the only thing on my mind when I wasn't thinking about work. Maybe I didn't wake up thinking about her, but I did fall asleep each night with her in my head.

She's pretty, but lots of women are pretty. This one though… I dunno. I can't put my finger on it, but I like her. It's that instant kind of attraction that doesn't come along very often. At least, not reciprocated. I get that she's a whore and it's her job to show interest in me, but it felt like more than that.

Which is what all guys say when they fall for a whore. But anyway. This is different.

All this is just my excuse to take her up on the offer when

she beckons me inside. There's no possible way I say no. I go in, through both doors, but pause at the top of the steps, unsure what she's got in mind.

"Follow me," she says. "It's this way."

There's a way around the stairs that I hadn't noticed the first time I was here because it's a half door to my left that matches the wooden walls, kind of making it disappear. I follow her through it and we travel the length of the large room below on a catwalk-like balcony that might be meant for lighting people, but nonetheless leads to the opposite end of the bar and a stairwell that goes down.

We descend and find ourselves in another hallway. The girl stops at a door and looks over her shoulder at me. "Be right back."

I let out a breath after she disappears into the room, then lean against the wall with my hands in my pockets. It's real. I didn't make it up. Which is a relief, because if I had made it up… well, I don't know what I'd do, but hallucinating a whole morning of traveling through the woods to a secret bar inside an abandoned coal mine would be a tragic escalation to my current problems.

Still, even if I didn't imagine it, it's all very weird.

The girl comes back holding up my credit card. "Here you go. And you can check. No one used it. I didn't even charge you for the time we spent together."

I sneer a little. "I paid cash. I gave you a fifty."

"I know." She reaches into her bra and pulls out a fifty-dollar bill. "But I'm givin' it back." She holds it up between two fingers, close enough for me to grab. But when I reach for it, she pulls it back. "Unless you'd like to spend it now."

I scoff, even though I don't really mean it.

"You did come all this way," she coos. "And while I don't know where you come from, I know for sure it's not close. The Mule Pit isn't exactly the corner bar." She waits for me to answer, but when I don't immediately come back at her, she keeps going. "You won't even stay for a drink?" Then she offers me the fifty again. "Even if it's on the house?"

"Well, I guess I could stay for a free drink." She smiles at my response. "But I don't wanna sit at the bar. I'd rather go back to that room we were in last time." Her grin grows. "Keep the fifty. It's a tip."

Her eyes dance mischievously as she tucks the fifty into her bra. Then she flips her hair and turns towards the hallway. But while I was concentrating on her eyes, she was grabbing my hand, so I follow her.

We don't end up in the room we had last time. It's a much better one that has a bed. "You're presumptuous," I say, chuckling a little as I close the door behind me.

"Well, this room has a bar." She pans a hand to it on the right side of the room. "Plus a couch. But if you'd like to start in the bed, I'm not complainin'."

The problem with whores is that they're paid to be nice to you. Not only that, they're really good at it. Not that I'm an expert or anything—I've never even been with one—but they congregate around bases, knowing that guys like me are here one minute, gone the next. And just before we deploy, we're all thinking the same thing. *What if I don't come back? Wouldn't it be nice to have the comfort of a woman before I die?*

Even if my urges never brought me to the edge of desperation like that, I understand the feeling.

Whores are trained to play off emotions. They're trained to trick you into believing they give a fuck so you'll open up to them. If not emotionally, then opening your wallet will do. So you can't trust anything they say. Even if this girl was truly interested in me, it would take a lot of convincing for me to believe it.

Of course, as a whore, she knows this. Which means she knows just what to say next. "I thought about you this week."

I don't answer, because it's bullshit. But she doesn't wait for an answer anyway, just slips behind the bar and brings out a real bottle of whiskey, not moonshine.

She comes back over my way and points to the couch. "Let's start here." Then she sets the bottle down next to a little tray holding two shot glasses and makes herself comfortable in the corner cushions of the couch. She's not wearing much, just a bra with lots of long fringe and some matching panties. So when she sits, the fringe parts in many ways, making her look more exposed.

Everything about whores is planned, I remind myself. She put this outfit on this morning for a reason, and that reason is to trick men into giving her more money than they should.

But I've already given her a fifty, so I figure there's no harm in sticking around for a little show.

"Pour us a drink," she says. "And relax a little."

I eye the bottle, but don't reach for it. I do, however, sit down. Not quite all the way over on the opposite side of her, but very nearly.

She chuckles. "Are you afraid of me?"

"No. I'm just trying to send all the right signals."

"Well, you're doing a horrible job, because I'm thoroughly confused. Do you not want a drink? You didn't pour."

"It's like nine-thirty in the morning. No, I don't want a drink."

"So why did you come in here with me? I'm only asking because I'm starting to think you're not here for sex, either."

"I'm not."

She scoffs. "So what do you want?"

I lean back into the cushions and sigh.

"Oh," she says. "I get it. You're one of those talkers."

Which makes me actually laugh. "*No.* I'm really not." I glance at her now, with a side-eye. "I'm way more interested in listening."

"Hmmm." She's studying me intently. "That's interesting."

"Why?"

"You want me to talk?" She points to herself.

I shrug. "Maybe I just like looking at you? Maybe I'm just a watcher?"

She laughs. And it's real too. "You want me to find a partner so you can—?"

"Sex. Is that really all you think about? I mean, you've never heard of people-watching?"

A breath comes out of her, but I can't tell if it's resignation or frustration. One of the two, for sure. "Look, you spent fifty bucks, so if you just wanna watch me sit here watching you, it's all good with me."

"Everything's all good with you, isn't it? You're the most agreeable woman in the world, aren't you?"

"You say that like it's a bad thing."

"It's not a bad thing if you're partners with someone. But a stranger? Yeah, that's just fuckin' suspicious."

"What's that mean? You think I'm trying to trap you or something?"

"Darlin', I don't know who you are, but it's blatantly obvious that you have no clue who *I* am."

"Tell me then, who are you?"

My laugh is nearly a guffaw. "Why?" I point to the ceiling. "So you can get it all on vid? I work for Edge Security. And yeah, I'm new there, but I earned the right to be part of an operation like that many, many years ago. There are seventeen cameras in here that I can see. Each of them has a microphone, but if I were to take a closer look at, say… the lamps, or that screen on the wall, I'm sure I'd find a few more. So while your little ploy might work on other people, it's not gonna work on me. And you know what? That sucks. Because I thought about you all week." I shake my head here. "Stupid, I know, since you're nothing but a whore. But you're pretty and if we were friends, you'd probably be very easy to talk to. So it's a bit disappointin' that just a few minutes in, you've proven yourself to be exactly what I first thought you were and nothing like the person I hoped you'd be."

I get up and start for the door.

"Wait!" She hurriedly follows me, placing a hand on my arm as I turn the handle. "Don't go."

I look over my shoulder at her. "Don't go? Why the hell would I stay? This place is… weird. Cool, I guess, but weird. And maybe you get that, or maybe you don't. Maybe you're some poor single mother just doing her best to make ends meet, so you don't bother looking real hard at things, but either way," —I grab her hand and slide it off my arm—"I won't be back."

Outside in the hallway, I pause, unsure where the exit is. But I can hear people to my left, so I head that direction. The hallway turns, and then I see the main bar up ahead through the windows of a stainless-steel double door.

When I push through, there's suddenly music. Like it's on

some kind of timer. And even though it's not even ten am, there are a lot more people here now.

I shoulder through them, suddenly realizing just how strange this all is. I mean, everything about it is bizarre, especially the location. But to be this busy, this early in the morning, when maybe twenty minutes ago there was no one here?

It's weird. And all I want to do now is get out.

I cross the room, heading for the stairs, and go up them. Then I pull the door open and leave.

Once outside, the music fades along with the stale scent of cigarettes, and reality returns in the form of a quiet autumn morning in the woods with the faint sound of the river in the gorge down below.

I walk past the coke ovens and I'm just about to start up the stairs when I hear, "Wait! Will you slow down for a minute?"

I turn and find the girl has put on a long coat and a pair of boots and is following me. "What are you doing?"

She stops when there's about twenty feet between us and shrugs. "I don't know. I just… didn't even get your name."

"Yes, you did. It was on my credit card."

"But…" She licks her lips, like she's nervous. "You didn't get mine."

"So?"

"Well… maybe we could start there?"

I shake my head and scoff, then hit the steps, taking them two at a time. It's a long hike up, but I'm willing to put in the extra effort if it'll put some distance between me and this girl.

She follows me, practically running to keep up. "Can you just slow down for a moment?"

"Why? So you can have time to come up with some more lies?"

"I just wanna get to know you—"

I whirl around, angry now. "Why the hell would you want to get to know me? I'm a really fucked-up dude. You had my name. If you didn't look me up, that's your problem, I guess. But you did, didn't you? And that means you know exactly what I'm talking about. So please, don't insult me. I'm not some dumb fuckin' hick who just walked out of the woods. That place back there? There's something wrong with it. In fact, there's nothing right about that place. Which means there's nothing right about you. And ya know what? You're just not worth it."

I turn and start climbing again.

"I'm sorry!" she yells.

Against my better judgment, I pause. But I don't look at her. "You're sorry about what?"

"The cameras. You're right, they're everywhere. It's a sting."

"What?" I turn around and stare at her, only to find her nervously looking over her shoulder. Like someone might be watching. "What do you mean, it's a sting?"

She huffs. "You know. A fuckin' honeypot."

I knew it. "Who are you?"

She presses her lips together. "You wouldn't believe me if I told you."

"Try me."

But she shakes her head. "No. Not here. If you want to know what's going on, then meet me somewhere."

"Where?"

"You pick. So you don't think I'm setting you up."

Walk away, Shep. Just walk the fuck away.

But since when do I ever listen to my own good advice?

"The Revenant Diner. Sunday at noon. I'll be there."

Then I turn and continue up the stairs and this time, she doesn't follow.

Maybe I will be there on Sunday, but then again, maybe I won't.

Because Collin set that lie detector test up for tomorrow morning and it's not just any old lie detector test, it's a fMRI. They're gonna scan my brain while they ask me questions.

And if I fail?

Well, let's just hope I don't.

8 - Olive

I ***stand at the bottom*** of the steps, looking up at Ean as he climbs. I stay right where I am until he disappears into the thick foliage of trees. Then I let out a breath, hug my jacket close to my body, and turn away.

Back inside, the place is busy now. There's no music, or customers, for that matter, but there are at least two dozen employees buzzing around getting ready for the day. I know them all, in a casual way. Since Brose and I are both in charge of this operation, I was there when they were all hired. They are mostly women, since it's kind of a strip bar, but there are some men too.

Everyone is from CORE. There are no outsiders taking part in this operation. It's way too important. And that's why it's in the woods. This is federal land. Part of the parks system.

But that's not the only reason why only CORE people work here. There is no way Brose and I would get approved to build such an elaborate operation just to snag my brother and his friends. It's more than that. Much more than that. It's a base of operations for what's to come. That's why there was a new train station built.

Collin, by himself, isn't important enough to warrant all this special attention. But combined with several other factors, he's the most important asset in the world. And Trinity County is worth the trouble. Jim Bob Baptist thinks he can get away. He thinks he can get out of his contracts. But no one gets out of their contracts with CORE.

I make my way down the stairs, across the room, and into the back hallways, heading for the office Brose and I share. But when I get there, it's empty.

Turning, I go back the way I came and enter the kitchen, assuming he probably went to get a cup of coffee. But he's not in there, either.

"Hey," I say to one of the servers as she hurriedly rushes past. "Have you seen Brose?" She doesn't even slow down her pace as she pushes her way through a set of double doors, but she acts like she doesn't hear me. I ask a few more people as they rush around, getting things set up for the day, but no one answers back. They're all too busy, so I take that as a no.

I look everywhere. I check every room.

He's gone.

And he's not answering his phone.

Which means he's mad.

Mad that I followed Ean out? Or… mad that I told him to meet me somewhere else?

Brose shouldn't know that I told Ean to meet me outside of the club because we were all the way over by the stairs. I know we have cameras out there, but there are no microphones close enough to where I was standing to hear what was said. I know that for sure because Brose and I signed off on the placements. I know where every single camera is, both inside the club and out.

But what other reason does he have to be mad?

And if he's not mad, why did he walk out and leave me here without saying anything?

It's just past noon, so... I guess it's *possible* he went to get lunch?

Possible. Just not probable.

No. He's mad and he left.

He left me.

Externally, I scoff. Because it's so like him. Jealousy is a thing with Brose. It's a flaw in his character, even he knows this. That's why he's always trying to maintain control, even when I push him to lose it.

But internally I wince. Because if he needed to walk away from me in order to control himself, he's *more* than mad. He's furious.

Inside the locker room I change, ignoring all the girls around me, who are chatty and friendly with each other, but not me. Once that's done, I put on my coat and go down the stairs to the train station. For a moment, I have a hope that I'll find Brose there. The train doesn't stop here every twenty minutes like some stations. In fact, I'm not even sure what the daytime schedule is, since I've never left work at noon before.

But Brose is not in the station. There's no timetable here to check to see what time the train came and when it will be back, either. So I get no answers to any of my questions. Only more questions.

All I can do is sit down on a bench and wait.

Three trains go by before one stops. It confuses me and I don't understand what it means.

Are they bypassing me on purpose?

Did Brose report me to management?

Am I in trouble?

When I hear the familiar sound of wind displacement to indicate another train is coming, I almost panic that it won't stop. Or worse, there will be a team of OIS agents on board, sent to retrieve me.

OIS is short for Operative Integrity Service. Which is really just the military police for CORE. If you fuck up bad enough, they come for you. What happens next, nobody knows, because no one comes back from that.

Did I fuck up that bad when I told Ean Shephard to pick a place to meet outside of the Mule Pit? Surely not. I mean, Brose didn't even give me a chance to explain.

Still, my chest is thumping when the train slides to a stop in the station and the doors open.

I can't move and I almost don't get on. But when the chime starts, indicating that the doors are about to close, I step forward and go inside.

There are people there, about a dozen. All of them alone, like me. Most are engrossed in private conversations with whoever is on the other end of their phones, and a few are sitting silently, looking at the window screens.

I take a seat by the door, feeling very out of sorts because I've never taken the train alone before. I've never had to. I've been with Brose every moment of every day since we became partners two years ago.

I get off in Winchester to change trains, then I'm home, in the station below Grid-21. I get off, and again, a sense of displacement washes over me. What if Brose isn't here?

What if he really did leave for lunch and came back to find me… *missing?*

But that's not what happened. It took almost two hours

before the train finally stopped to pick me up and no one came down looking for me.

He left. More importantly, he left me behind.

And at any point, he could've contacted me through our encrypted CORE phones, and he didn't.

I'm feeling very shaky and out of sorts, not to mention holding my breath, when I key in the code to our door and open it.

That breath comes out because he's here. Standing in front of the massive window, hands in pockets, with his back to me.

"Brose? What the fuck? Why did you—" But I stop there because he's turning and even though he's backlit and I can't really see his face, I can tell. He's furious.

There's a moment of silence between us and in my mind, it feels like it goes on, and on, and on forever.

He takes a step forward, and for some reason, I back up.

"Close the door, Olive." This is not a request. It's a command.

I suddenly feel like I'm gonna throw up. Adrenaline spikes, instantly rushing to every part of my body, and I have an almost overpowering urge to *run*.

But there's nowhere to go, and I know this, so I reach behind me without taking my eyes off him and tap the door closed.

Again, there is a very ominous moment of silence. His hands are still in his pockets when he takes a few steps towards me and I force myself not to take the same number of steps back. Not because I'm brave—he scares the fuck out of me when he's like this. Just because I already know that it'll piss him off even more.

Instead, I smile. "I made progress."

He sneers. "I bet you did. Did you suck his dick too?"

I want to be offended, but I'm not. But only because I'm used to his jealousy and telling him what he wants to hear—with slight embellishments that simultaneously calm him down—is the only way forward.

"Was it big and hard, Olive? Was it bigger than mine?"

"I would never do that, Brose. Not without your permission. And anyway, if I was going to do that, I would want you to be watching. And how could you be watching if I was outside at the bottom of the stairs where there just happens to be a blind spot in our surveillance?"

He's very calm when he answers. "Trust me, Olive. That blind spot no longer exists."

I smile again, nodding. "Good. I told you we'd need a camera there." Which isn't even a lie. We ran out of equipment that last day when the cameras were going up and he made the decision to omit the bottom of the steps from the grid so we could have one along the coke ovens.

He takes another step forward. "Do you want to suck his dick?"

I shrug. "It doesn't matter what I want. I'm a Silent Intelligence Operative and you're my Personal Operations Director. You think for me, I act for you."

He takes one more step forward. "You say that, but do you believe it? Do you really believe that your wants and needs are secondary to mine? If they are allowed to exist at all. And really, under Directive 1 of the SIO Code of Conduct, they're not, Olive. You have no free will. I think for you, you act for me. You agreed to this."

"I know that, Brose. That's what I just said. Why are you mad? I didn't do anything wrong. I set up a meeting—"

He picks up a vase and throws it across the room, making it shatter against the wall. I flinch back, putting my hands up to cover my face when the glass shards go flying, but still, I feel the sting when some of them hit me.

Then he's here. Right in front of me. His hand on my throat, pushing me backwards. I hit the door, looking up at him, afraid of what he might do next, but also—and I can't even admit this to myself without feeling shame—turned on. I close my eyes, moaning. Wanting him to choke me. Wanting him to fuck me. Wanting him to turn me over across his knee and slap me on the ass until it's so sore, I can't sit.

But the pressure on my neck from his hand is almost nonexistent, that's how light his touch is. He won't do it. He won't do any of that. Not in anger.

What he does is lean into my face. "Look at me."

I open my eyes and find his staring back at me, maybe an inch away.

"Tell me, word for word, what happened outside in the blind spot, Olive. And if you want me to choke you, and fuck you, and spank you, then don't you dare leave out a single fucking thing."

So I tell him. I leave nothing out. My debrief takes less than a minute. It was a very short encounter. And this is not quite enough time for Brose to fully pull himself together, so he stands there, glaring at me, for another few minutes as I wait— my lust for him manifesting as a pool of wetness between my legs—as he internalizes everything I've said.

Finally, he lets out a breath and the pressure on my neck increases. I close my eyes, again moaning.

"Tell me how much you want it, Olive. Beg me to choke you."

"Please," I whisper, leaning into the pressure of his hand. *"Please."*

His fingertips close down, just a little. Just enough to make me hiss. Then his hand is popping the button on my slacks, forcing itself inside until he finds my lust. His fingers slide back and forth across my sweet spot and this almost makes me come.

But he's there—always there—cautioning me not to do it. "Hold it in, Olive. Because if you let it out, I'll never touch you again."

That's the thing about Brose and me. He'll throw a vase across the room, shattering it into pieces, but he would never hit me. Because I'd enjoy that too much and what is the point of punishment if I enjoy it?

No. The violence is my *reward*.

It satisfies a sick need inside me that craves pain.

The next thing I know, I'm on the floor, waking up. He did it. He choked me. I practically come just thinking about it as he drags me across the floor and over to the couch. Then he picks me up, bends me over the back of it, and fucks me in the ass.

I come so many times, I lose count.

And when that's over, he sits, puts me across his lap, and slaps my ass until I come some more.

9 - Shep

I walk out of the bunkhouse Saturday morning at three-thirty am and find Collin leaning against Amon's truck, waiting for me. He doesn't look particularly agitated, but it's dark and there's a light above him, shining down at an awkward angle. So it's all very ominous.

Amon is in the driver's seat, leaning back, looking up through the open sunroof like he's deep in thought. Both of them are smoking, which strikes me as odd and I search my memory for another time I've seen them smoking, but I can't really recall.

Collin smiles a little as I approach, then drops his smoke and stubs it out with the toe of his boot. He opens the front passenger door, and I expect him to get in, but he doesn't. He pans a hand to it, inviting me to take the front seat.

In my experience, a man only wants to sit in the back when he needs to keep an eye on the person in front. He's not carrying, at least not obviously, and that's a relief, I guess. But none of this is a good sign.

"Thanks." I sigh, sliding into the passenger seat.

Collin gets in behind me and sighs as well. "Let's go."

Amon flicks his smoke out the sunroof, presses a button to close it, and then swings the truck around towards the road.

Once we're on the Loop Highway—heading north, I think—Collin says, "Are ya nervous?"

I scoff. "It's three-thirty in the morning and we're driving four hours to Pittsburgh to scan my brain while you administer a lie detector test. What do you think?"

"I think," Amon says, "if I were you, I'd be thinking about coming clean before putting these guys—who are clearly not fucking around—through all this trouble just to figure you out." He looks over at me and grins. "But that's just me."

I look out the window, frustrated. "I'm not lying. And anyway, you guys didn't even ask me any questions other than the ones about Charlie. I was recruited."

"We know," Amon sneers.

"Well, I didn't *ask* to be recruited."

"We know," Collin says. "This is the problem, Shep. Charlie and I are not in a good place. In fact, he's rather irate with me. If he sent you here to fuck something up, the least you could do is tell Amon to stop the truck, get the fuck out, and just walk away."

"Would save us a four-hour fuckin' trip to Pennsylvania in the middle of the night," Amon says.

"And a favor with Penny Rider," Collin adds. "You know who Penny is?"

I nod, but don't say anything. Everyone knows who Penny is. At least, everyone on our level. She does the intake background checks for all the dark ops. She's also the one you go to when you need something and don't know where to get it. I've never actually used her in that way, I don't have that kind of clout, or money—she accepts both as payment—but I've done two interviews with her over the years. She's not military, she's a contractor out of DC, but she might as well be military. She's been doing background checks for forty-two years. She knows everyone. Absolutely everyone.

"Now I owe her," Amon says. "This is a huge ask."

I blow out a breath, but just continue to look out the window. "Why didn't you just ask Penny if I was cool?"

"We did," Amon says.

"She says you are," Collin adds.

"So what's the problem?"

"She only knows what she knows, Shep," Collin says.

"I'm not a fuckin' operative sent here by Charlie Beaufort to spy on you or fuck up your shit. I'm just…" I exhale loudly. "I'm a fuck-up, just like the rest of them, Collin." I turn in my seat to look at him. "I washed out, OK? Do you wanna hear all the details of how that happened? Do you wanna hear about the missions? Because I'll tell you. But you know what that means. I don't care if they find out I told you. I don't even understand why I'm still alive, to be honest. But obviously, they're not worried about me. It won't be me they're concerned about if I spill my whole history right here in this truck. It'll be *you*."

Then I turn around and neither Collin or Amon say anything back. They both know I'm right. You come in to this black ops stuff all curious. You think you wanna know all the secrets. You think it's all cool spy shit. Gadgets and 007 Hollywood special effects.

But that's not what it is. That's not at all what it is, and both Collin and Amon have seen enough to know this. They don't keep it all dark because they're protecting their operatives. No. That's not why. They keep it all dark because if the general population of America knew what their tax dollars were really being used for, there'd be a revolution. Tables would be flipped and shit would go down. People do things in the dark for a reason and it's not just so others can't see.

It's so *we* can't see either.

It's so *we* have an excuse not to think about it.

Not to question it.

Not to regret it.

WE END up at Carnegie Mellon University, some futuristic science building with lots of windows that looks like it came straight out of an old sci-fi movie. Penny meets us in the lobby and while Collin and Amon catch up, I stare at the weird-looking spiral ramp in the middle of the massive space.

"Shep?"

I turn and look at Penny, who is in her mid-sixties, at least, but looks healthy and fit for her age. "Yep. I'm ready."

"We're this way." She turns and the three of us follow her to the bank of elevators. Once inside, Penny presses a green button on the bottom of the panel, then inserts a key.

I look over at Collin and Amon and find them both watching with raised eyebrows.

Interesting. Obviously, the green button indicates a highly secure area that is not generally accessible to the students or faculty here on campus. And the fact that it's at the bottom of the panel means it's in the basement.

My guess is right, because once the doors close, we descend and this descent is not quick. I count eight seconds, which probably correlates to seven to ten floors. Despite the raised eyebrows from Collin and Amon, it's not that surprising that the machine would be below ground. This is where all the secrets live.

When the doors open, we exit and find ourselves in what appears to be a busy hospital. Penny leads the way, turning left, and we follow. Me first, then Collin, and Amon brings up the rear.

Penny stops in front of a double door and smiles at me. "You're in here, Shep. Go on in and they'll get you set up."

I look at Collin. "Where are you guys gonna be?"

Penny is the one who answers. "They'll be in the control room with me and the techs." And then she dismisses me. "See you on the other side." The three of them walk off and I let out a sigh, resigning myself to whatever comes next.

I'VE HAD MRIS BEFORE. Lots of them, actually. So most of it is really familiar. I change into a pair of generic sweats and a t-shirt. Obviously, I'm told to remain still during the entire test—which could take up to ninety minutes—but this isn't just a scan, it's a test. So I'm given a remote to hold with a single button. All the questions are yes or no. Press once for yes, two for no. If I make a mistake, I'm to repeatedly press the button until the question is repeated.

Of course they tell me to remain calm, but it's not that easy when you're stuffed inside a claustrophobic can and your immediate future depends on your answers.

The questions are familiar in that they are worded and ordered to try and catch inconsistencies. All of them are about Charlie, but some are more direct, while others are not. They are looking for brain activity. Specifically, deviations from the norm, whatever that is. So they are questions like—*Have you ever lied about your interactions with Charlie? Do you trust Charlie Beaufort more than your current team? Have you communicated with*

Charlie Beaufort in the last year? Do you believe Charlie Beaufort has good intentions?

And they all require thinking. Which is the whole point, since they're trying to 'see' my thoughts. So by the time I get done, nearly two hours have gone by and I'm exhausted.

I'm just pulling my jacket back on when Penny enters the little changing room.

She smiles at me, then closes the door and leans against it.

"What?" I say, dreading what comes next. "Did I fail?"

She presses her lips together and shakes her head. "No. You passed."

"Then why are you here?"

She takes a step forward and turns. Then turns back. "You don't owe me anything. But those boys out there do."

"I guess. OK."

"And I like you. I've always liked you."

The fact that she's got an opinion about me at all comes as a surprise since I've only met her twice and both encounters were less than extraordinary. "Penny, if you've got something to say, just say it."

"All right. I do have something to say. It's a two-parter. First, I know what your job was. I've looked at all your files. I know why you washed out and how you ended up in prison. It's all very neat, and tidy, and in the records."

"So what's the second part?"

"The second part is that while you did pass, the tech noted some very unusual activity."

"Great. So they're gonna kick me out."

"No. We didn't tell Collin and Amon."

"Why not?"

"Because you passed the test. You're not working with

Charlie. We're a hundred percent sure of it and that's what Collin and Amon were looking for. So we reported those facts, and they're satisfied."

I roll my hand in a 'get on with it' gesture. "But...?"

"But they've done something to you."

My eyes narrow down. "*Who?*"

She presses her thin lips together again. "You know who. I can't say, because I'm not supposed to know who. But you know who. What did they do to you? Did they give you an implant?"

"What?" I'm squintin' pretty hard now. "What kind of implant?"

"You tell me."

I shrug. "No. I mean, I don't know. Did they see an implant in my brain?"

"No."

I chuckle. "So what are you going on about?"

"It doesn't need to be in your brain, Shep. In fact, at this point in time, it doesn't even need to be an implant."

I shake my head. "I don't know, Penny. I don't have any clue what you're talkin' about. I had plenty of health checks. My file should be very thick, so to speak. You know how it is. Once we sign those papers, we give up our autonomy. They say jump, I jump. They show up with a jab, I take the jab."

Penny blows out a long breath. "Collin and Amon are not CORE. Did you know that?"

"Yes. I found out the day I got there. They ran a private army inside the US military."

"Have you told them anything about CORE?"

"No." This isn't entirely true because I did admit to CORE when I was in the SCIF with Collin. But I didn't tell him anything, so I'm not gonna mention it to Penny. "You know the rules."

She nods. "I do. Just making sure you remember them too. They don't go away just because you're out, Shep."

"I know that."

"Good. Well." She smiles. "That's it. You passed. I just wanted to get your take on what we saw in your scan." She puts up a hand, warding off my next question. "No, I won't be mentioning it to Collin and Amon. As far as I'm concerned…"

She doesn't finish. "But as far as you're concerned, what?"

"I'm going to be looking into this. I doubt answers will come quickly since I need to be very careful. But when I figure it out —and I *will* figure it out…" She gives me a stern old-lady look over the top of her glasses. "You'll be the second person to know."

I DON'T SAY **much after** Penny finishes and we join Collin and Amon at the elevators. The three of them converse freely, like we weren't all here with an assumption—or, at least, the very real possibility—that I was some kind of spy.

Back up in the lobby, Penny says her goodbyes, then walks off in the opposite direction from where we came in. Collin, Amon, and I make our way back to the truck and this time Collin doesn't get in the back. I do.

Which is a step forward, I suppose. At least he's not worried about me literally stabbing him in the back on the ride home. Anyway, I'm glad I'm in the back because all I can think about is what Penny told me at the end.

… some very unusual activity.

She never did explain that. Not that I have the knowledge, or even the vocabulary, to understand any of the biological mods CORE does. But it would've been nice if I had a little more to go on.

Collin and Amon joke and talk on the way home, like it's not that uncommon for them to spend an entire morning probing the brain of one of their recruits. And what do I know? Maybe all of them went through this?

I've been here one week and everyone has treated me like an outsider. All of them. None of the guys in my house even bothered to try and include me in their routines.

I showed up for PT every morning. I did all the training. I helped Ryan in the woods with his ditch digging. He's laying pipes or something. Who knows, who cares. But there was no chatter or joking around with the guys in my unit. And I don't even have a dog. Not that I came here expecting one, but it's hard to not be jealous when everyone else in the entire place has a fucking dog.

Even Amon's kid has a puppy to train.

So I don't know.

Is this whole thing a mistake? Should I just pack my shit and move on? I mean, if they can't trust me, I can't trust them. It's that simple. And that means this whole thing is a waste of time. My time, their time, everyone's time is being wasted.

We don't stop for lunch, but even so, it's early evening by the time we get back to Trinity County. Four hours driving in, five fucking hours in that stupid research building, and then four hours back is a long day, so I'm not in the mood to do anything and my Saturday night plans involve hitting the sack.

But when we pull into Edge, every single guy is lined up along the driveway on both sides in their official units, and all of them are in dress uniform, black on black with the Edge logo and other patches they've earned affixed in various places. It's not something they wear every day, especially on a Saturday night—and I don't even have one, that's how fucking well I fit in here—so I don't understand what's happening.

And then, as we pass the first group, they salute. All the units, on both sides of the driveway. I lean forward, between Collin and Amon. "What the fuck is going on?"

Neither of them answers, but Amon stops the truck and he and Collin both get out and stand in front of it, like they're waiting for me. Nash, the fourth partner in this operation, comes up alongside them.

Am I being arrested?

I let out a long sigh, get out, and walk up to them. "What the fuck is this?"

Then, to my surprise, all three of them *salute me*.

"What are you doing?" I ask.

Collin steps forward, and we lock eyes. But he doesn't say anything and then Ryan appears holding a neatly folded uniform flat in his hands, offering it to me. He yells, in his best drill instructor voice, "You're out of fuckin' uniform, soldier. This is an elite unit and you will respect our dress code."

I raise my eyebrows, smiling.

"You think this is funny, you sorry-ass piece of shit? You have ninety seconds to get changed and every second you're late, the entire team will do ten push-ups. So unless you wanna be looking over your shoulder, waiting for the retaliation that will surely come after, you had better get your ass changed *now!*"

I'm still smiling—and so are Collin, Amon, and Nash—when I kick off my boots, take off my clothes right there in front of everyone, and put the uniform on.

They all wait. No one says anything, and no one is keeping track of time. So I do it all right. I tuck in the shirt. I lace up the boots. And then I stand and salute.

Collin steps forward, offering me his hand. I shake it and he says, "Welcome to Edge. You had a shitty first week and that sucks. We're all brothers here, Shep. And I'm sorry it started out this way, but it's over now. You're one of us." Then he whistles and Amon's boy steps forward, wearing his kid version of the Edge uniform, and leading his two-month-old puppy on a slip lead. He stops in front of me and hands me the leash.

"What are you doing?" I ask.

"You don't have a dog. I took your dog because we didn't know you were coming, but everyone's got to have a dog, Shep. So we're gonna share. He's the best. You're gonna love him just as much as I do." The little fucker actually salutes me.

And even though I'm not a dog person—or a kid person—I smile pretty big.

Amon comes over and claps me on the shoulder. "Everyone needs a dog." Then he winks at me. "And a boy to keep him honest."

All the men yell, raising their fists in the air, and music starts blaring over the PA system.

It's a party.

Maybe even… a welcome home party.

SUNSHINE **bright enough** to fucking blind me wakes me up the next morning. Or is it afternoon? I open one eye, cautiously looking around. I'm on the porch of the house, which explains the sunlight, and my mouth tastes like I ate something dead last night.

I sit up, then remember the party and smile even though I've got a poundin' in my head that feels strong enough to split it open.

It's late morning, but even so, there's no one around the compound. Just the sound of barking dogs down the driveway. Someone's up—someone's always up taking care of the dogs. But that's it. Not even Collin or his guys are around. Hell, not even the women or the kid are around.

Helluva party. Really good party.

I look down at my new uniform and get an unexpected jolt of satisfaction out of it. I didn't think it would matter to me, I really didn't. But when we got home and I realized that they did all this for me? To make me feel like part of the team?

Yeah. It matters.

I stand up, yawn and stretch my arms up over my head, ready to go inside and pass out again in the dark bunkroom. But then I remember.

"Fuck." I was supposed to meet that girl at the diner if I was still here today.

I go inside, pull out my phone to check the time, and realize it's eleven twenty-two and I'm supposed to be in Revenant at noon.

Pausing at the bottom of the stairs, I wonder if I should just blow her off. She's nothing to me, I'm nothing to her, and I've got a feeling that things will get complicated if I meet up with her now. It's all so weird. In fact, everything about that girl is screaming 'bad idea.'

She's cute, I'll give her that. But there's definitely something strange goin' on at that bar in the woods. She already admitted it was a honeypot, so my choice should be a simple one.

Stay away.

But then again, I might be able to get some good intel out of her. I bet Collin and his friends don't know about that place yet. If they did, they would've warned us, and they haven't. They definitely would've warned me, since I'm new here.

And anyway, I'm not going back there. I'm meeting her in Revenant. So I decide I will take a quick shower, ride the bike down and see if she's still there because I'm definitely gonna be late, and if she is—then it's a mission, not a date.

Satisfied with the plan, I go upstairs, shower, change, and twenty minutes later, I'm rolling onto the Loop Highway.

It's quarter past noon when I ease into a parking spot down the street from the Revenant Diner and I'm fairly certain she's not gonna be there when I walk inside. But to my surprise, she's in a booth near the back.

The place is packed with families, mostly. It smells good though, and my stomach rumbles as I watch plates of food go by. The girl spies me from across the crowded room and smiles. Maybe even lets out a breath of relief, happy to not have been stood up.

I walk over to the table, set my helmet on the seat across from her and slide in next to it.

"Hey," she says. "You came."

I run my fingers through my hair, trying to rein it all in after the ride, and lean back into the seat. "I came."

Before either of us can say anything else, a waitress appears. "He showed up! I told you he would." The waitress—a middle-aged woman with lots of tattoos and big-time cleavage hanging out of her pink uniform—winks at me. "You had her worried."

I shrug. "Well, I'm here now."

"What can I get you two?" the waitress asks.

"Coffee," I say. "Black."

The girl smiles and lets out a breath, like she was holding it in. "I'll have water with lemon."

The waitress clicks her pen. "Be right back."

I take my attention to the girl and get right to the point. "All right. I'm here. What did you want to tell me?"

10 - Olive

For a moment, I can't think straight. Ean is wearing faded denim jeans, a black t-shirt, and a leather jacket, same stuff he was wearing the other day, but he looks… different. Maybe it's the daylight without the shadows of the tree canopy, or maybe it's just his mood, which comes across as light and possibly happy. The point is, he's even more handsome than I remember.

Which isn't going to help me. And when I catch Brose's eye —he's in a two-seater booth reading a paper about ten feet away —I force myself not to think of this guy as a man, but as a target.

Because that's what he is. Our window into the inner workings of Edge Security.

Still, it's hard not to notice how attractive he is. Especially when every woman in the place is gawking at him. I thrust my hand out. "Hi." I try on a smile. "I'm Olive."

Brose and I discussed using a fake name, but decided against it. The point of the honeypot was to get Collin's attention. We came very early and walked around the town to see what kind of surveillance they have. It's good. Of course it's good. After all the shit that's gone down in Trinity County since Collin came back, everything, in all three towns, has been wired up so Edge can keep an eye on things.

What better way to get that attention than for me to date one of his men? Of course, even if Collin personally looks through the town footage, we haven't seen each other in so long, I doubt he'd even recognize me. But eventually, it's all gonna come out and I hope I'm there when this realization hits my big brother, because I really want to see his reaction.

But even if I'm not, it's easy enough to imagine it.

He's going to be pissed.

It's a joker. That's what Brose and I call it when we have a card to play, but don't. And this one is definitely wild.

Ean shakes my hand. "You already know my name."

"Ean."

"Shep. I go by Shep."

"Shep." I smile, because I like it. I like Ean too, especially the alternative spelling. But Shep is even better.

"So?" he says. "What did you want to tell me that was so important you couldn't say it at the stairs?"

Brose is listening, and of course I told him this was my lure, but we didn't talk about it after the exceptional spanking he delivered that day. I was so caught up in the sex—Brose is such an addiction, I'd do almost anything for the depraved attention he gives me when I'm bad—that I kind of forgot about it until this morning on our way here. I think he did too because I catch him, from the corner of my eye, lowering his newspaper so he can watch us from across the room.

I asked Brose what I should talk about with Ean, but he just said, "Use your discretion, Olive." Which makes this whole thing feel like a test. It shouldn't be a test, I was released into full duty months ago, but it still feels like one.

There are many techniques that agents use to garner trust in targets, but none work better than what I call Misery Loves

Company. So that's the scheme I've decided to execute. "Tell me something… Shep." I give him a shy smile here. "Were you born into it? Or was it a recruitment type thing?"

I already know the answer to this question—it's the same answer for all of us. Still, I don't know the details, and I'm curious. So I've decided that this is how I will approach the 'date.'

Shep sneers at me. "We're not here to talk about me. You said you had something to say. If that's true, say it. If it was just a lure to get me here, I'll be on my way."

I anticipated this reaction to my question. I mean, even if we weren't allowed to talk about it, who the hell wants to talk about it? "Fine. I wanted to tell you why the Mule Pit is out there in the woods."

He actually rolls his eyes. "Do I look like an idiot? Clearly, you guys are there to lure us."

"Us?"

"Edge," he clarifies.

"So you consider yourself one of them? Even though you're the new guy?"

"What do you want, Olive?"

"*You.*" My answer surprises him because it comes out very honest. And since I already know that he was a Deep Recon Specialist for CORE, it surprises me as well. Because there's no way that what he and I are doing here is real. But even if it was, it's just… impossible. Brose is my partner. For life. And while I might have to sleep with former DRS agent Ean Shephard, and I won't mind doin' it, it can't mean anything.

He thinks for me, I act for him.

Still, my response to Shep comes out with a whole lot of

feeling backing it up. Which makes Shep even more suspicious than he already was.

I glance over at Brose, just to see if he's got a reaction, but he's not there. There's a couple sitting in that two-seater booth now. My eyes flicker across the room and I just barely catch a glimpse of him walking out the door.

Did he hear it too?

Did he hear the feelings of desire behind my answer?

Does he think I'm serious?

"That's crazy."

I look at Shep. "What?"

"Your answer." He leans in, almost to the middle of the table, like he's about to tell me a secret. "Look, I don't know you. I don't know what you're involved in, but I know what kind of training you guys get and I'm not gonna sit here and let you insult my intelligence while you lie to me."

I push Brose all the way out of my mind. I need this guy. He's the only one from Edge who came in to the Pit. After all that money, all that time, he's *all* we've got. So I give him one hundred percent of my time and play the joker.

"I'm Collin's little sister."

Shep laughs. It's loud too, even over all the talking of the packed diner, and a few people turn their heads to look at us. "Bullshit."

I scoff. "Believe whatever you want, it's true. Go back to Edge and ask him if he has a sister."

"Who cares if he has a sister? Doesn't mean you're her."

"You have no idea who he is, do you?"

"Sure I do." Then he stands up and throws a ten down on the table. "He's my boss." And then he walks out.

I sit there, kinda stunned for a moment, doubting everything that just happened. He did not react the way I anticipated. But I should've seen it coming. This was a major mistake. And not the kind that gets me a good choke and a spanking at the end of the day.

It's the kind that gets me sent back to training.

I'm up, crossing the restaurant so fast, I catch him just outside the doors of the diner. I don't look around for Brose, I focus only on Ean Shephard.

"He killed my father," I say. It's not a whisper, either. Which is super risky, but the people around us are involved in their own conversations.

Shep turns. "What?"

"You heard me. He killed my father. Right in front of me, when I was eight years old. Blood spattered all over my face. I was traumatized for life." I let out a long breath, suddenly tired. Because all of this is true. "That moment? It was two seconds long. And these two seconds *ruined* me."

Shep grabs my arm and pulls me into a nearby alley. We stand there, looking at each other, as he looms over me like a threat. When he finally speaks, his words are deep, and low, and angry. "What the fuck are you talking about?"

He's still got a hold of my arm, so I shrug it out of his grip and harden myself for what comes next. I'm angry because this guy, he's no one. He's a fucking job. And now I have to tell him something real. I have to tell him something personal so I don't get demoted for fucking this job up, or worse, be labeled a Remedial and get sent to the Faders.

I look him straight in the eyes. "I was eight. It was New Year's Eve and I was sleeping while Collin and his girlfriend were babysitting. Some man broke into our house, came into my room, put his hand over my mouth, and dragged me into the hallway. Collin was there. He must've heard a noise or something, and he came into the hallway as the man was trying to pull me out the back door holding the rifle my father kept in the front closet. His girlfriend, Lowyn, she was behind him. The kidnapper let go of me, put his hands up to surrender, and Collin shot him anyway. Killed him. Right in front of me. I was covered in blood and bits of bone and skin from head to toe."

"That man. The kidnapper? He was your father?"

I nod, letting out a long breath. "Yeah. I didn't find this out until much, much later, but my mother was a very pregnant Blackberry Hill runaway. She had me in the Creed basement. I guess they took her in. And then… they just… kept me."

"And raised you as their own?"

I nod. "A few months later, Collin was gone. He joined the Marines to get out of Trinity County. But I guess you never really leave, do you?"

Shep's eyes narrow down. "Why are you telling me this?"

I narrow my eyes right back. "Because you don't know him."

"Who cares? He's my boss. I don't give a fuck who he *is*. I give a fuck about what he can do. And this little story of yours— even if it's true—was the wrong move, darlin'. Because all it did was make me like him more."

Then he turns towards the street, like he's just gonna walk away.

My heart thumps inside my chest, adrenaline rushing through my body as a precursor to the panic that's coming. "We're going to kill him," I yell. "And you're gonna be caught in the middle. So good fucking luck."

Shep turns around and even though I don't know him, I can tell that I've pissed him off. "Shut your fucking mouth." These words come out low and soft, but filled with threats all the same as he stalks back in my direction. He leans in to my face. "Shut your fucking mouth right now or I swear to God, I'll shut it for you."

"Why?" I ask, my voice softer now. He's worried about people hearing us, so I take that worry away. "Why should I shut up? Nothing I just told you was a lie."

"You're the lie, not your words. Do you think I can't tell what you are?"

"What I am?" I scoff.

"You're bent."

"What the hell does that mean?"

"Do I look like a literal idiot? I know what you are, Olive. I know who you work for."

I shrug, like this doesn't matter. Even though it does. "Well, I know who you are too. And trust me when I say this, they don't pick men like you for their capacity for deep thinking."

Shep actually guffaws. But when that's over, the change in him is visceral and I feel it in my core. A sick, sinking feeling fills my gut and the adrenaline is back, coursing through my body like the high-speed train I take to work every day. "What do you want from me, Olive? Because it's very, *very* clear that this whole thing between you and me is a setup. You're CORE. And you're stupid if you think I can't spot you people at this point. I was *born* into it."

I get defensive now. "So was I."

"No." He shakes his head. "No. You were a loose end, Olive. Collin isn't CORE. I know that for a fact."

"I'm not his real sister. And I'm not Disciple, either. I'm Blackberry Hill."

He relaxes a little, folding his arms over his chest. "You have no clue what's happening here, do you?" He scoffs. "Well, I can't say I'm surprised. But if I were you, Olive, I'd start asking a lot of questions about everything you think is true right about now." He reaches out and thumps his finger against my head. "Because *this* is their battlefield and you are nothing but a puppet. And whatever you think you know about me, it's bullshit. Because if you knew my truth... well, let's just say they're not gonna allow you to know my truth. They'll never allow it. Maybe they'll kill me, maybe they'll kill you, but whichever way it goes, the truth will be buried and one of us will go down with it. Now," he says, catching his breath a little. "Think real hard about what I'm saying here. What does that look like, Olive? The end of *me*?" His eyes lock with mine. He blinks. "Or *you*?"

Then he turns around and walks away.

This time, I don't bother trying to follow.

I just steel myself for Brose.

Because this failure will have consequences.

11 - Brose

It's a gray day.

I'm sitting in our quarters, waiting for Olive to finish up with Shep. Whatever that entails. Of course, we have cameras everywhere. Not physical ones, though. Not out in the open in Trinity County. It's mostly satellites, so the audio is sketchy, at best. But I know Olive well enough to read her body language. I can tell what's happening without hearing her.

And what's happening with the Shep guy is plain old attraction.

She likes him.

And why shouldn't she? There's a lot to like there. He's good-looking—I'm good-looking too, but in a different way. Shep has that soldier look to him. Like he's seen things.

Of course, I've seen way more than he has, but I look… not soft, exactly. Just… better managed, I guess.

I look down at myself. I'm slumped in a chair in our living room, laptop balanced on my knees. My tie is loose, but still around my neck, and my shirt is untucked. I don't have my suit coat on, it's draped over the couch back. That's where I dropped it when I came in.

This is the second time I've walked away from Olive in the field and it's sort of a turning point, I guess.

My phone buzzes and I know who it is before I even take it out of my pocket. "Grandfather, what do I—"

But he cuts me off. "Set her loose, Ambrose." The typical spotty connection is even more sketchy than usual.

"What?" I say. "We're totally on track here and—"

"Set. Her. Loose."

"But why?" I say quickly. "Everything's going according to plan." This is a lie. It's not going to plan at all, but his answer is even more surprising than my lie.

"You're right. It's going perfect. Fifty-five years I've been working on this project and now it's time to set her loose."

Fifty-five years? What the hell is he talking about?

"Do you hear me, *grandson?*"

He says the word grandson like it's a slur. "I hear you." I don't understand him, but I definitely hear him. "Nothing's messed up, grandfather. She's doing—"

But the call ends. There's nothing but silence.

I look at the phone in shock, only looking away when my attention is drawn to the voice of Olive coming from my laptop. My eyes find the video and despite the unsettling conversation with my grandfather, I smile. This is her intake interview. She was eight and a half that spring CORE brought her back into the fold. The same spring her older brother, Collin, left Trinity County with Amon Parrish to join the Marines.

The Creeds are not CORE, but through a string of weird chance happenings, Olive landed with them as a newborn. Her pregnant teenage mother escaped from Blackberry Hill. Not the one on the actual hill, but the one underneath.

This was way before Ike Monroe took over and the place was a mess down there. Of course, it's always been run by a Monroe, but Ike's father died young, and it was his uncle, Zeb, running things at the time. He was a terrible city manager. That's how Olive's real mother got out. Came up some secret elevator and just took off running through the woods.

I've read this story hundreds of times, but it's been a while. So I pause the vid of Olive, age eight, and open her written file up, scrolling down as I skim the report of that inciting incident. Her mother gave birth at the Creed house, then took off, leaving Olive behind.

It was a good plan because there are a lot of governing documents related to who can do what inside Trinity County, and Disciple, West Virginia, specifically. That's why no one came for Olive. Zeb Monroe declared the girl dead. But when your daughter runs away with your first and only grandchild, there are residual feelings about that. Olive Creed's mother was the daughter of one Pike McGill. That's who came for her on that fateful New Year's Eve. That's who Collin killed. Pike tried one other time when Olive was very young, about eight months old, but he was caught before he got out of Blackberry Hill and Zeb had him locked up.

Good ol' Pike, though? He never did forget about his granddaughter. He was released from prison New Year's Eve day and that very night he made his move.

His last move, as it turns out.

A move that flipped Collin Creed's plans of playing college ball at Ohio State upside down and six months later he was an intelligence operative for SILENCE, the black-ops side of the US Marines.

It had been over two decades since anyone in Trinity County was conscripted into the dark military. There was a formal exit from the program after Jim Bob Baptist completed his mission and was rewarded with a new contract for the trio of towns.

To say that CORE was surprised when Collin Creed ended up as covert intelligence operations would be an understatement. They had underestimated Jim Bob.

I guess CORE decided that if SILENCE was going to put Collin on the game board, they would counter with Olive.

I press play on the laptop vid and listen as Mrs. Creed cries hysterically. They're at an intake facility not far from where I'm sitting, actually.

In another room sits Mr. Creed. Pastor Creed. He's not crying, he's angry. As any parent might be, I suppose, upon hearing that the baby they kinda-sorta stole eight years ago belongs to a covert military operation. He's yelling.

In a third room sits eight-year-old Olive. She's cute. Thin and a bit gangly. Not graceful like a ballerina, but lean like a runner. She looks like any other kid her age, wearing jeans, and a t-shirt, and sneakers. The chair is just high enough for her feet to skim the floor as she kicks them back and forth. She's unaffected by the development, chatting happily with her intake officer as she is told that these people are not her parents.

She takes it all in stride. She's kind of excited. So when the intake officer asks if she'd like to see where she comes from, Olive is more than willing to go.

There's no footage of this visit to the underground version of Blackberry Hill, but there are notes and I've read them all.

The mind control started that very day. She was behind. In CORE, they start the kids around age two for the most part. There are some exceptions, but two is standard.

Olive was very behind, but so well adjusted to the real world that this sparked a revamping of all the internal protocols when it came to how to bring the children up.

Olive Creed is more than a CORE operative, she's a test case.

And she's failing.

All because of a man called Shep.

It's a bit ironic, I think. Considering who he is, not to mention what he's done.

And I don't really understand how it happened. I don't get it. She did everything right. It should not have turned out this way. But it was like... she took one look at him and all those tight stitches that were holding her together over the years started unraveling. For no reason at all.

It's bizarre.

But also very serious.

I'm losing her.

And if that call from my grandfather is any indication of what comes next, I've already lost her.

And honestly, it hurts.

Olive and I were supposed to be together forever. At the very least, until someone killed her in the field. She wasn't supposed to flunk out! She's SIO 2.0. The mistakes of the past were dealt with. Fixed.

But I missed something.

Somewhere along the way, I missed something.

Letting out a long breath, I start thinking back on my own childhood. My training began at the standard age because I was born into the Sinclair family and there were no runaway daughters in that mansion. My mother was a high-ranking, dedicated officer in CORE. My great-great-grandfather was part of the initial CORE Directive back in the forties. My great-grandfather ran hundreds of operatives in the sixties and my grandfather did the same in the eighties and nineties.

Fifty-five years. I guess it adds up but what the hell was he talking about. SIO 2.0 is my project and we certainly haven't been working on it for fifty-five years.

My father didn't make it very far—he was killed in the field on a job when I was four. By that time, I'd been living at CORE for two years, so I didn't even miss him. Didn't miss my mother, either. CORE parents have children for the mission. It's got nothing to do with family.

I think that's where it went wrong for Olive.

She wasn't CORE. She didn't grow up with our values. She says she's part of the mission, but those years she missed as part of her CORE training—between the ages of two and eight—those were… critical.

I can see that now.

So can my grandfather.

Soon everyone will see it.

And then… well, the protocols will be adjusted, of course, but as far as Olive goes? She's done.

I ponder this. Not just the regrettable outcome of something I've heavily invested in, but also in the possibility that she might be saved.

She's out of the program. This is her last SIO mission, that's unavoidable.

But she's not useless. Not at all useless, actually.

She might not be Collin Creed's genetic sister, but that's just a technicality. Surely, even though Collin knows the truth now, surely he still loves her. And even though I've turned off Olive's feelings for Collin, that was mostly about loyalty. I can manipulate this. There are ways to turn these feelings back on.

The big test for a SIO operative is stress. It's the only test, actually. The only one that counts. We stress them, and stress them, and stress them. And then we send them into a situation.

And might this scenario playing out here with Shep, in the general vicinity of Collin, be such a situation?

An… opportunity, maybe? To make lemonade, so to speak.

If I end this operation, what would happen if CORE didn't come in and scoop her up? What would she do?

I smile here, because I know exactly what she would do and it's a way forward that I can live with.

I love her. I do. We have a very twisted relationship, but my feelings for her are genuine. I don't know what life looks like without Olive. The idea that we'd fail never entered my mind.

Overconfidence has brought down more than one mission, but everything was going so well.

Still, this new way forward would keep her alive. At least for a few more weeks. And I could talk to a lot of people in a few weeks. My grandfather being one of them. He's old now, retired. But he's still got pull. He's still got power. I could make a deal. Keep her for myself. We could move to the family mansion and even if I had to lock her up in the basement, she'd be alive. She'd be there for me when I got home every night.

We could have a few kids to give to CORE. Surely her bloodline is good enough? Even if it wasn't, they wouldn't turn down kids. Every operation needs new recruits. Maybe we could even keep one?

I smile, thinking about that. How bold of us. To raise a child together.

Maybe we could mold it into the perfect operative?

In fact, this is more than a dream, this is a solid plan. I could come up with a whole new protocol for training children from birth.

My mind begins to race with the possibilities. Of course, this has been done before, but it's been decades. The mothers were the problem. The idea of 'breeding' might work for dogs, but women aren't dogs. They have opinions.

But Olive and I would be both parents and trainers.

Yes. It could work.

I just need to buy myself some time to set it up.

The door rattles, then opens. And then there she is—the love of my life.

"Hey," she says, her voice soft.

I focus on her lips. Those perfect, plump lips. Then I look her in the eyes and smile. "Hey."

She shuts the door and walks over to me, stopping a few paces away because she's unsure about what's going on. Which is fair. I've sent her some weird signals over the past couple of days. "Why did you leave?"

I shrug. "You had it handled. And the waitress was side-eyeing me. I should've ordered breakfast, I guess, but only got a coffee. I could tell she wanted the table."

"Oh." She lets out a long breath of relief. "That's all?"

I chuckle. "Were you expecting something more?"

"I just… you were… *there*. And then you weren't. It threw me." She lets out another breath, this one longer than the last. "Do you wanna know what happened? Or were you watching?"

I put the laptop aside, setting it on a small round table next to the chair. "Come here," I say, patting my lap, inviting her to position herself across it.

She smiles, shyly. "OK." Then she closes the distance between us. I look up at her as she looks down at me. "Now what?"

I tsk my tongue. "You know what. You get a reward. You're such a good girl, Olive."

She smiles again, not shy this time. Relieved. She knows this

Shep guy has ruined everything, but she wants to believe my lie and so… she does. Slowly, she positions herself in front of me, then gently eases her body over my lap. The chair arms are kind of in the way, making this position awkward, but that's part of the fun, if you ask me. Her shoulders and head are dangling over one side, her breasts are pushed up against the inside of the arm, her legs bent over the other one at a weird angle.

But none of that is the point.

The point is her ass, which is dead center over my dick.

She's wearing opaque black tights and a flirty miniskirt. I push the skirt up so I can rub her ass cheeks. She relaxes. She likes this. We do it all the time. It's a reward for her. Like a good steak given to a dog after a day of training.

"Does it feel good?" I ask.

"Yes."

I slip my right hand down into her tights while the left hand squeezes her cheeks. She's already breathing heavy. Usually, at this point, I warn her not to come. But this time, I don't. I want her to come as many times as she is able. I want her to think about this day after it's over. I want her to remember what it's like between us when things are good.

I want her to crave me when I'm gone.

My left hand grabs her tights into a bunch and then I rip a hole in them. She gasps and then does it again when I slip my fingers between her legs. She's so fucking wet, they slide all over the place. "You like this?" I ask.

"I do," she whispers back.

I bring my hand up and then smack it down on her bare cheek. The sound of this slap fills the room and she moans.

But I don't do it again. Not right away. I want her to enjoy this. So I finger her some more, forcing two fingers up inside her as another one finds her sweet spot.

She comes, biting her lip to hold it in, but failing.

I smile, enjoying her uneasiness.

Then I caress her and lean down to kiss her ass cheek. It's a bit red from the slap, and warm too, because I hit her hard. But she likes the kiss. She moans.

"Get up now," I say.

She doesn't want to, I know this. She's addicted to spankings. I've had her kneeling for hours, begging me to spank her. And it was *real*. She was dying for a spank. So wet just thinking about my hand making red prints on her ass cheeks, she would just spontaneously come without me even touching her.

It was definitely an experience I'll never forget. Easily the best sexual encounter I've ever had. I doubt anything will ever come close to that day.

She stands before me, a questioning look in her eyes.

"I've got a bottle of champagne in my closet," I tell her. "Second drawer down, below my belts. Get it and bring two glasses."

She nods her head, bowing it slightly. "OK." Then she does as she was told and returns a few minutes later, handing me the bottle and sets the glasses down on the little table, right on top of my laptop.

Then she bends down between my legs, looking up at me like I'm her god.

I pop the cork, letting the bubbly liquid spill all over my lap. She leans in, licking at it, which is a nice touch, I think. Then I hand the bottle back to her and she pours us each a drink, offering me a glass.

I take it, she takes hers, and we hold them together, just barely touching.

"To our brand-new future."

If she had any doubts, they are gone now. She is fully invested in my lie. She takes a sip, then goes to set her glass down.

"No," I say. "Drink it all. I want you… pliable."

This makes her happy. She likes being pliable. She likes when I take control and force her to be uncomfortable. Like that time I had her on her knees. So she downs it and tilts her head at me, flirting. "There. I'm buzzing already."

"Perfect," I say. "Now… go over to the couch—behind it—and then bend over and pull your tights all the way down to your knees."

She doesn't even hesitate. But she does wobble a little. I get an embarrassed glance over her shoulder as she rounds the back of the couch, which separates the living area from the bedroom area. She ends up facing me, since I'm on the opposite side of the room.

"Bend all the way over, I tell her. With your face in the cushion."

She does this, sighing, like she's tired.

"Good girl," I say.

Then I get up and walk around the couch behind her. I slip her skirt up. My dick is already hard, but the sight of the ripped tights—the almost perfectly round hole exposing her ass—makes me throb with anticipation.

I grind against her, my dick safely tucked away.

I won't be fucking her. Not because I don't want to, but because she's going to be unconscious in a matter of seconds. The champagne was drugged. Placed in that drawer for the end.

And this is what that is.

The end.

Her breathing becomes very heavy, so I grab her by the hair, bend over, and lean in to her ear, just to make sure she hears me. "You failed. I'm very, very sorry, Olive, but you failed. And now, my dear, you will have to pay the piper."

"Whaa… what?"

"Shhhhhhh," I whisper, then bite her earlobe. "I'm leaving now, Olive. I've been summoned to DC. You can't come. I'm going to be reassigned and you'll be collected soon. Today was your last chance. I didn't tell you because I didn't want to add any pressure, but it's over now, Olive. *We're* over."

She starts freaking out, struggling beneath me, But I have her pinned to the couch with my hips and my hand is firmly wrapped around her hair.

Anyway, the drugs in the champagne were very powerful, and it's only a matter of seconds before she's passed out cold.

12 - Olive

S*lowly, the world comes back* to me. My throat is tight and scratchy, my eyes feel crusted over, and my head is pounding. For a moment, I just let the fuzzy world between sleep and reality hang, unwilling to wake.

But then a panic hits me—what day is it? Am I late for something?

I force my eyes open, unable to make sense of what I'm looking at. I'm on the couch.

Noooo. I'm bent over the back of the couch.

"Shit," I mumble, trying to straighten up. But my back is aching so bad from being in this position, the most I can manage to do is slump to the floor.

This is where I wait as my head slowly clears and the blurry vision sharpens into clarity. My memory comes back with the vision.

"Brose?" My voice is croaky because my throat is so dry. "What happened?"

What did happen? What were we doing?

Then I remember, he had me bent over the couch and we were—

My reflexes come back in an instant. Years of muscle

memory take over and I force myself up, holding on to the couch as I stand.

I'm alone.

"Brose?" I call out again. And I manage to walk the length of the couch so I can get a peek into our little kitchen. I already know he's not here. He's gone.

I push some messy hair out of my eyes, still looking around as I try to make sense of things. "What the fuck happened?"

Maybe I passed out? I mean, yes. Of course. Clearly, I passed out. And just as I'm thinking this I look over at the chair where Brose was sitting and spy the bottle of champagne. On the little table next to the chair are two glasses. One full, one empty.

I drank it.

He didn't.

The sudden realization that he drugged me is so unsettling, a chill runs down my spine.

He drugged me.

I squint. He drugged me? Why would he do that?

But then I can hear him whispering in my ear right as I was closing my eyes. *I'm leaving now, Olive. You can't come. Today was your last chance. We're over.*

I look around, then stumble over to the closet. I pull the door open and start shaking my head. "No. No, this isn't happening." There are clothes in there, but they are all mine. Just mine.

Desperate, I make my way over to the dresser and pull open the top drawer. His drawer. Empty. I pull open mine and find it filled with underwear.

He's gone.

You failed. I'm very, very sorry, Olive, but you failed.

The memory of these words hits me like a gut punch.

But I refuse to believe them. It can't be real. It has to be… something else. A test, maybe. Yes. It's a test, that's all. He was getting jealous of Shep. He's trying to teach me a lesson, that's all.

I straighten my skirt, briefly consider changing my clothes, but decide against it. Maybe he's downstairs. From the angle of the slanting sun shining through our floor-to-ceiling bedroom windows, I figure it's morning.

That's it. It's just morning and he let me sleep in.

You know that's not what's happening here, Olive. You know—

But I don't know. Not really.

So I don't change, I just rush over to the door, pull it open, and start running down the hallway towards the stairs. I don't pass anyone, and that's the first clue, but I keep going anyway. All the way down to the main level where there is… no one.

It's empty. Not just of people, though it is, it's empty of *everything.*

It's just a big room with no tables, no chairs, no coffee bar.

And no Brose.

What the hell is happening right now?

You know what's happening, Olive.

You failed. I'm very, very sorry, Olive, but you failed.

They've erased this residence.

Why?

You failed.

They can't just… leave me here. They would never evacuate everyone, pull up roots so completely, and just *leave me here.*

Wouldn't they, though?

I run back up the stairs, enter our room, and start searching for my phone. I find my purse on the floor near the couch and my phone inside it.

But when I try to wake it up, the screen refuses to come to life.

You failed.

I slump down into the couch cushions, feeling confused and lost.

He left me.

I failed and he left me.

No, he did a lot more than that. He drugged me, had the place swept clean of all evidence that anyone but me ever lived here, and *then* he left me.

Why?

Come on, Olive. You know why. Because someone is coming to clean you up. Just like they cleaned the rest of the place. They just haven't gotten here yet.

The moment these thoughts manifest, I know it's true. My training kicks in. I go to the closet, toe off my shoes, and slide my skirt and tights down my legs. Then I pull on a pair of jeans. I don't change my shirt. I don't have time. I simply slide my feet into a pair of boots, pull on a coat, and leave.

I skip down the stairs in a heightened state of anxiety, my heart thumping inside my chest. When I get to the empty lobby, I start heading for the door that leads outside.

But then I pause and look over my shoulder towards the stairs that go down.

Should I take the train?

Is it even there?

I laugh a little. Because it's a ridiculous notion. Of course the train is there. Well, maybe not an actual train, but the tunnel is still there.

As soon as I think these words, I know it's a lie.

I *know* there's no train down there.

I force my feet to start moving towards the door that leads outside, but I only get a few steps before I turn around and start running for the stairs that go down.

The staircase is wide. Not like stairs that lead to a basement, but actually like stairs that lead to a subway. But I stop at the top of them, not bothering to go any further.

Because the entrance to the tunnel has been bricked up.

Bricked. Up.

This is when everything catches up to me. The drugging, the emptiness, Brose.

I have been abandoned.

I turn back to the door and walk outside. This is the front of the estate, but it's nothing how I remember it being. The main house in my memory was always grand and well-kept.

This place looks like no one has lived here in years.

I scan the grounds, noting the dying lawn, the untrimmed hedges and… the absence of the other houses.

What the fuck?

Sealing up a train tunnel is one thing. It's an improbable thing, but it's certainly not impossible.

Removing entire houses on this estate while I was passed out is another thing altogether. It doesn't make sense. I must be in the wrong place. I must be… dreaming, or hallucinating, or something.

The sound of a helicopter approaching pulls me out of my stupor and I make a run for the nearby woods. I duck under the heavy canopy of limbs just as the helicopter flies over. It doesn't land. It's not after me. It's some billionaire who lives nearby. Or a senator, maybe.

As the thumping of the rotors fade, all I hear are birds and my own heartbeat pounding in my head. *Get a hold of yourself, Olive. You're a highly trained CORE operative. Act like it!*

I shake my head, take a deep breath and hold it, then let it out and focus.

Whatever's happening here doesn't matter. What matters is my reaction to it.

I turn my back on the estate and walk further into the woods.

This is the outskirts of Leesburg, Virginia, so while it feels remote and there are certainly lots of farms and open land here, it's all relative to the small city just over the hills and the Potomac, which separates this tranquil landscape from the nearby hustle and bustle of Maryland, and, by extension, Washington DC. Which is where I need to go.

But first, I need to pick up my go-bag.

It takes me about twenty minutes to find the marker where I buried the bag two years ago when Brose and I were assigned to the estate. It wasn't part of protocol, but Brose insisted that I do this. "You never know, Olive. You just never know when you're gonna need a bag."

Which is true. It was a lesson drilled into all of us in my early academy days.

Rule number one—know your exits. Which feels a lot like face the door whenever you take a table in a restaurant, which it is. But it applies to everything. If you enter a stairwell, you had better know how to get out. If you get in a car, you better be ready to throw that door open on the freeway and roll out. And if you're told to live in a country estate as part of an elite group of CORE operative, you better have a go-bag buried in the woods.

And I do.

I haven't thought about it in years—that's why it takes me so long to locate it—but the gray backpack filled with survival gear, should my shit ever hit the fan, is here. It's packed tight too. I was always losing points in the academy for over packing my bag, but it's better to have too much of what you need than too little.

I don't bother to check the contents, just shoulder it on and keep going, heading east through the woods towards the nearby public rec center. When I get to the edge of the woods, I pause to scope out the parking lot. It's filled with cars. Commuters who take the bus over to the Ashburn Metrorail, then on to Union Station in DC. Which is exactly what I'm gonna do too.

Brose, despite being a company man to the core, was a Plan B, C, and D kind of guy. We've got pre-established local check-in points in DC, Baltimore, Richmond, Pittsburgh, and Philly, just in case we were ever separated while on a job.

Before leaving the woods I take the pack off, set it on the ground, and bend down to open the front zip compartment so I can find my SmarTrip card. Pulling it out, I realize this is real. *I'm on the run.*

It's surreal and I don't understand how I got here. It doesn't make sense how one day I can be living on a CORE estate with access to a clandestine high-speed train tunnel system, and the next day I'm staring down at a prepaid bus pass, ready to take *public transportation* hauling a twenty-five pound go-bag on my back.

From now on, Olive, you won't be thinking. You'll be acting.

These were the first instructions Brose ever gave me. I was

eighteen, he was twenty-five, and boy, was I ever enamored with him. Right from day one.

If you think, he'd said, *you'll make mistakes. And if you make mistakes, we'll fail. I don't fail, not at anything, so you won't either. Everything you do from here on out needs to be instinct.*

He thinks for me, I act for him. That's where it came from. That very first conversation.

I blow out a breath as I stand back up and hike the pack onto my back. "All right, Brose. I don't know what you're doing or why you're doing it, but instincts it is."

Then I head out of the woods and down the grassy embankment and join the crowd of commuters waiting to get on the bus.

I SIT NEXT to a professional woman on the bus who talks on her phone the entire twenty-five-minute ride to the train station. I look out the window, watching the world pass.

In Ashburn, I catch the Silver Line to Union Station. The slow, methodical motion of the train wants to lure me into sleep for the ride in, but I fight the sleep. I force myself to stay awake and on high alert, making up stories in my head about nearby passengers to keep me sharp.

Brose taught me this little trick. *Sleep is your enemy, Olive. If you're ever on the run, and you get tired, you just look at everyone around you and tell yourself they're a spy. They're here to get you. They're here to kill you. Trust me, you won't be able to fall asleep. And this little trick will probably save your life.*

So that's what I do. I target everyone in my vicinity and make up a backstory. This lady here, she's an assassin. That guy over there, that's her handler. The old man reading the paper three seats up is a spy.

It sets up a purposeful kind of paranoia.

But Brose was right. I do not fall asleep. In fact, I'm more alert than ever, almost buying into my fake backstories about my fellow commuters, when the train pulls into Union Station.

I wait for them all to get off first, watching them as they continue on with their day. Because wouldn't that just be my luck? That my fantasies about them turn out to be true and one of them takes me out in an alley outside?

But they don't. No one follows me as I leave the station and make my way over to a landmark coffee shop on 2nd Street. It's nine-forty am now, so while the place is busy, it's not crowded.

My eyes are sweeping over tables the moment I step inside, desperately looking for Brose. But he's not here.

I get a table anyway. It doesn't mean anything. He has no idea when I'll arrive. So I'm gonna wait.

I order coffee, consider breakfast but decide against it—my stomach is not in the mood—and wait.

At ten-thirty I can tell that the waitress is frustrated with me, but I ignore her. Instead, I open my go-bag and start searching through the front compartment for the burner phone I know is here. I don't want to use it because the moment I do, I have to throw it out and I only have two in total. But I need to know what's going on. I could be waiting around DC all day. Days, even.

I grab the SIM card, shove the phone charger into the battery pack that, even after two years, has two faint red bars of charge left in it, and slip the card in. Then I key in the number and wait.

It rings once, making my hopes soar, but then I get the three shrill special information tones followed by, "The number you have dialed is no longer in service—"

I end the call, blowing out a long breath.

Because that was my worst fear. I was hoping that this was some sort of test, maybe? While this particular scenario never came up exactly like this during my years of training with Brose, we certainly prepared for it.

But it's not a test. It's real. I've been abandoned. He's not going to meet me here, everyone around me probably is a spy, and I've got nothing but a two-year-old go-bag to my name. Which is far better than having no go-bag, but still. My life consists of the clothes I'm wearing and survival gear.

What do I do? Call my parents? I don't even have their numbers. I haven't talked to them in twelve years. The first thing CORE did was take me away. I didn't belong to them, anyway. They're not my real parents. And at this point in my life, those first years I spent with them feel almost like they never happened.

I don't have a family anymore. Brose was my family.

So I have nowhere to go.

I have nowhere to run *to*.

But as these words roll around in my head, I realize they're not actually true.

I know where one member of my family is. I know where Collin is. He's home, in Disciple, West Virginia.

I scoff out loud, shaking my head. I can't run to *him*.

Could I?

Before I change my mind—because this is the first bit of hope I've felt all morning—I do a search on my phone and pull up the train schedule for Union Station. I scan the routes and then I smile.

The Cardinal Line will drop me off in Charleston. But my hope dies when I realize that it only runs on Sundays, Wednesdays, and Fridays and this is Monday.

Well… wait. Is it Monday?

I check the date and gasp. Not just because of my luck, but because I lost two days. It's not Monday, it's *Wednesday*. I was up in our room for two days.

This both frightens me and makes me feel slightly saner, because two days would be enough time to clear things out of the estate. They could even brick up a tunnel in two days. I can't really explain the missing houses, but logic points to me just… misinterpreting that. Mirrors, maybe? Harry Potter's cloak of invisibility, perhaps? I mean, it's all just tech. And the tech inside CORE is quite advanced these days. Decades ahead of what the general public knows about.

But why would they want to make me think I'm crazy? (Because that's what I'm starting to think.)

Why would they abandon you, Olive?

Because I fucked up.

Well, not technically.

But I was about to.

I was, too. Even I know this. I was latching on to Shep for some reason. I can't explain it. I was going to tell him things I shouldn't. I was going to get involved with him.

I was going to sleep with him.

Not as an assignment, either.

I… *like* him.

And Brose saw it. He saw everything. That's why he walked away, both times. He knew. He knew and he reported me to CORE. So he drugged me with that champagne left me in the room. And while I was out, CORE sent in a clean-up team.

It makes perfect sense now.

I look back down at the train schedule on my phone, then notice that I have time. The Cardinal Line won't depart Union Station until eleven thirty-one and it's only ten forty-five.

It's doable.

I can run to Collin.

And, by extension, Shep.

So that's what I do.

I run to Shep.

The very man who got me here in the first place.

13 - Shep

The wake-up call at Edge changes every week, I'm told. Last week it was a simple tone that went off at five am for PT training. Not awesome, but I've heard worse.

This Monday morning, after drinking too much last night, the new call for the week is definitely on the offensive side because it's a hundred decibels of barking dogs. Nothing but three minutes of barking dogs.

Upon hearing it, every guy in the bunkhouse complains loudly and some of them go as far as to threaten to quit. Apparently, this is not the first time the barking dogs have been used but it's used sparingly.

"It's your fault," a guy called Razor says, punching me in the arm as he walks past.

"How is it my fault?"

"Because you're new here and it's a joke." He frowns at me, then growls at me. "It's not funny."

I just roll my eyes.

For a bunch of mentally challenged criminals and killers, they're not bad guys. I feel a sense of camaraderie with them.

They did tours in real wars. I can't relate to that because as a Deep Recon Specialist, I was serving in an entirely different kind of combat. If Collin and I were on the same side back then, he might've been my commanding officer because he was running spies and that's what I was.

Deep cover.

The guys I share the bunkhouse with were all regular military. Some of them SEALs, some of them Rangers, some of them Green Berets. All of them dangerous and all of them crazy.

It's not a term of endearment, but a clinical diagnosis. Though, as everyone figures out eventually, crazy is all relative to the world around you.

Which is all fine and good while you're 'in country' but doesn't fly whatsoever when you go home. And, even though I'd bet all the money I have at the moment that not a single one of these men wanted to go home, you can't hide forever.

That's when 'crazy' starts to actually mean something negative. Something life-changing. Some of the guys here had families before they got all messed up. Some of them were never going to have close relationships like that because their personalities don't allow for it. None of them have anything but each other now.

I like it.

I feel like this place could be a good second chance.

That's why I walked away from Olive yesterday. I don't know if what she was telling me was true—that Collin Creed is her brother—but either way, she's a flashing red danger sign that's gonna ruin everything. I can feel it.

If she is Collin's sister, no way do I want a piece of that.

And if she isn't... well, she's definitely CORE and I don't want a piece of that either.

I shove a protein bar in my mouth as I walk out the front

door of the bunkhouse and fall in to the march with the other men.

You'd think we'd all complain about the PT every morning, but no one does. We all went to basic—even I went to basic—and we all hated it, I'm sure. But there's something comforting about physical training. Something calming about being part of the group. Something settling about letting all the chaos inside your head go and just working through the physicality of it all.

We have a cadence caller, and everyone calls it back as we run, but it's mind-numbingly easy to let everything go and forget the world exists when you're doing morning PT.

About two dozen of the guys have off-base jobs so they all cut out about halfway through PT to shower and get to their assignments. Everyone else keeps going until it's time for chow, and then we shower, change, and train dogs for the rest of the morning.

In the early afternoon, everyone goes to the range out back in the hills. And then, when that's over, we work with the dogs again. After that we eat and hang out. Then sleep and wake up to do it all again.

I'm one of the guys now. And even though I've barely been here a week, it doesn't take that long to understand that this is a pretty nice setup. I like it.

But my interaction with the girl last weekend lingers in my head and I can't help but wonder, as I look around the compound, if this is all there is. If this is all there will be.

I'm not complaining. I don't think any of the guys here are complaining. The Edge contracts come with room and board, meals, and seventy K a year to start. There probably isn't a single guy, aside from Collin and his crew, who has ever made that kind of money. Or ever will any place else.

But it's a little bit like a safety net. Here to catch you. A nice thought, but there's always that nagging little question of... what if?

Especially when you look down the driveway at Collin and Amon's houses and you watch them both go home to women every night. Amon even has a boy. And he's a really likable kid. I've only spent a week with him and his puppy, but he's got a sense of humor and he works hard. Acts like he's thirty years old and just another one of the guys.

Every morning I come outside I'm thankful. For all of it. But it's almost impossible to miss what I'm trading this safety net for because all I have to do is look down the driveway where Collin and Amon are living the real dream.

I will never have that. I'll never have a son. Or a girl. There's not gonna be a wife, or a house, or a puppy. Because this place— the safety, the men, the permission to be who I am—it's addictive and necessary. And I don't have my own house at the end of the driveway. I bunk with six other men.

There's no place for families.

Not for us. Not unless we want to leave.

And of course we won't leave. No one is officially 'deployed' at the moment. The contracts are local. Couple hours away, at the most. So even if some of the guys are staying in hotel rooms, they're coming back.

I haven't heard a single guy here say they can't wait to work outside the compound.

They joined the military for a reason. They're here for a reason.

And honestly, I think Collin Creed and crew might actually be a bunch of geniuses—because this isn't a *job* they gave us.

It's more than room, and board, and seventy K a year.

It's a life.

So thinking about Olive is a waste.

Because I just got here and I can't think of a single thing that could make me give it up.

THE NEW WEEK **begins** with Amon's boy, Cross, and his puppy, whose name is Jagger. Cross is my new little sidekick since we're assigned to the same puppy. He goes to school, but the bus pulls right into the compound and picks him up from the porch of Amon's house, so he uses every spare minute from the time he wakes up to the moment that bus driver opens the door to hang out with the men.

He's the first one lined up for PT every single morning at five am. And by Tuesday, I find myself becoming number two, since I know he's already out there and he and I are partners. He stands under the flagpole in the dark like this is what every thirteen-year-old boy does before school.

No one eats before morning PT, so after PT he goes home to shower, and I go back to the bunkhouse to do the same, and when I walk into the mess at seven-fifteen, he's saved me a seat.

He shovels food into his face as fast as he can and then he waits for me so we can go to the kennel together so he can spend the next fifteen minutes giving me instructions on what to work on with Jagger while he's gone.

Then he salutes me, calls me soldier, and leaves.

He's such a bossy little fucker, you can't help but find the whole thing funny.

By Wednesday, Cross and I are best buddies.

By Thursday, we're old friends.

We're standing in the kennel with Jagger on the leash, and

Cross is scribbling down tracking instructions on a whiteboard in purple marker. "See," he says, tapping the marker on the board where he's drawn a picture of a scent pad. "This is food. Food, food, food. All these little marks are food. You throw them down on the scent pad and tell him to 'such.' That's German for seek. You tell him 'such, such, such.' Real fast like that. And then you let him eat most of it, but pull him back before he finishes so we turn him into a little *such*-ing fiend. Got it?"

I do my best not to chuckle because he's dead-ass serious about his dog training. "I got it."

He checks his watch—which is, of course, military-grade—and sighs. "The bus is gonna be here any minute. But I got something for you, Shep. Come to the house with me so I can give it to you before I go."

"All right. Lead the way." I pan a hand to the door.

We walk outside where the sun is just barely rising, and he jogs ahead to his house. He stops on the porch. "I'll be right back. Don't leave."

"I'll be here," I say. Then he goes inside and I take a seat on the steps and look down the driveway as a bus pulls in, stopping at the guard house. How the hell they got a bus driver to pull into the compound, I don't understand, because it's a hassle. No one comes in or out without stopping at the guard house. But down the driveway it comes, rumbling and filled with kids.

Inside, I hear Amon's woman yellin' for Cross to get his butt on the bus, then Cross yellin' back, but I can't make out what he's saying.

Since Amon's house is at the bottom of the driveway and it's a turnaround, it literally pulls up in front of me. The door opens and the bus driver—an older woman—salutes me.

I chuckle and salute back.

Then Cross is rushing out the door and stands on the step next to me. He holds up a finger to the bus driver. "One sec, OK, Fanny? I'm coming. Do *not* honk that horn at me, I'm standin' right here."

She rolls her eyes and cracks her gum, then starts checking her phone.

Cross turns his attention to me. "Here. This is for you, Shep. I designed it and everything. This is just the prototype. I got two. So there's one for me and one for you."

He hands me an embroidered patch in the shape of a shield with a German shepherd on it. At the top of the shield are the words 'Edge K9s' and at the bottom is printed 'Handler.' I look down at the patch, then over to Cross. "This is for me?"

He smiles and nods. "Yeah. You don't have any patches on your uniform yet, so I figured you needed one. And I had one extra. Everyone will get them when the order comes in next week, but you can have yours now."

A horn honk makes us both jump in surprise. Cross turns his attention to the bus again. "Fanny! I told you not to honk at me! I'm standin' *right here.*"

She smirks at him, her voice old and croaky. "Then get your skinny-ass butt on the bus right now or I'll honk at you again and then your mama's gonna yell. You're makin' us late, kid!"

Cross sighs, glaring at her. But he softens when he looks at me. "See you this afternoon, Shep. Take good care of Jagger!"

I wave and he hops from the bottom step of the porch to the bottom step of the bus. The door closes and the bus slowly pulls away.

I look down at the patch in my hand, feeling the threads with my fingertips. It's a nice patch. Lots of colors. The dog is black and brown—just a head in profile—but it's against a background of wooded hills with several shades of green. Behind the hills is a sunset, or maybe a sunrise, and that's in red and orange. The letters are in black and they're set against army-green banners.

Patches. Kinda dumb, but also kind of genius. Morale patches, they call them. Because they make us feel good. And I have to admit, this one does make me feel good. I'm gonna go hunt down a needle and thread and sew this fucker on first thing.

I look up, ready to hop down the stairs and do that, when I stop in my tracks.

I squint, looking down the driveway, because Olive is walking towards me with Collin.

For a moment, I can't move. I don't know what to do.

What is she doing here? Is she here to out me?

She sees me, but doesn't wave or pause the conversation she is clearly having with a delighted Collin. He's looking down at her with bright eyes and a wide smile.

Like a brother.

She was telling the truth. She's Collin Creed's sister.

And there are only two reasons why she's here.

One, to fuck with me. Maybe even get me fired, since she knows more about me than I ever told her.

Or two, she's a spy.

14 - Olive

*N*ever again will I take the Cardinal Line from Union Station to Charleston, West Virginia. Nearly ten hours. Ten. Hours. Even though I slept most of the way, by the time I arrived, I was even more exhausted than when the journey started. Because I spent all ten of those hours trying to figure out what was happening, or what I did that was so bad, or what the fuck Brose is trying to prove.

He can't *leave me.*

You can't just promise to be partners with someone and then leave them because of two conversations while I was *working.* Doing my job to lure one of Collin's men into a state of vulnerability.

My emotions pendulate wildly from one extreme to the other. First, I'm scared. Someone from CORE is gonna come get me. They're gonna lock me up, send me to a reeducation camp —hell, they might even kill me, I don't know.

But then I'm angry because I don't feel like I did anything that bad. Yes, I did spill a few details to Shep, but he's CORE! He's one of us! Since he's clearly older than me, he knows more than I do about pretty much everything, probably. They can't just cut ties with me because I took a certain direction on a mission. They can't just undermine my efforts like that.

Except they did.

And they did it in a very extreme way.

How do you remove houses from an estate? All the rest of it I can understand. Brose emptied his closet. They moved everyone out. They bricked up the secret subway. But the houses outside?

It just makes no sense.

But it has to. There has to be a logical explanation.

Anyway, the point is I was on the run, the train ride sucked, and by the time I got off, it was night time. Almost eight-thirty at night, to be exact. And everything around the train station was closed.

Which meant I couldn't rent a car—which I wasn't gonna do anyway because of all the documentation you need. I might as well have just worn a neon sign that said, *Come and Get Me.*

The only saving grace was that I saw a sign across the street from the train station for Appalachian Tours and Transit. Which is a little place that offers bus tours of the scenic shit in this area and one place they go is Trinity County.

I slept outside the little storefront, waiting until they opened up at six. "Usually," the woman at the counter told me, "we take passengers up on this first trip in the mornin'. We bring 'em back down here after their stay is over. So there won't be no one on the bus with you."

I didn't mind, and I told her that. My head was all jumbled and confused at this point. And I must've looked a wreck after my unnecessarily long journey from DC, so this lady sold me a ticket and I got on the bus.

It was about an hour ride up to Disciple, but since I was the only passenger, and this bus was driving straight past Disciple to pick people up in Bishop, I asked the driver if he'd mind dropping me off at Edge Security since it's right on the Loop Highway, and he agreed.

When we arrive, there's a school bus pulling in ahead of us. They get stuck at the gatehouse for a minute, so my driver just pulls along the highway and looks over his shoulder at me. "I don't have time to chat with the guards, so you're good with me droppin' you here?"

I nod and get up, slinging my go-bag over my shoulder. "Yes. This is perfect. Thanks a lot for your help."

He tips his head at me and smiles. "Have a nice day, young lady."

And I get off, waving at him one final time as he pulls away.

The bus is still idling at the gate, so I can't really see anything until it starts pulling forward down the long driveway.

I've seen aerial photos and drone footage of the Edge compound. And, of course, I know this place from when I was a kid. Not that I've ever been here, but we must've driven past it hundreds of times in the eight years I spent in Disciple. So everything in this moment is familiar, but in two very different ways.

On the one hand, Edge is an asset of Collin Creed, who is my target.

On the other, this is the Old Church Camp from my childhood, and my brother owns it.

It's a weird dichotomy.

"Can we help you, ma'am?" There are two guards at the gate. The first one is tall and dark-skinned and the other is Hispanic, maybe. Both of them are looking at me like they are not in the mood for whatever is about to come out of my mouth.

"Yeah," I say, letting out a long breath. "I'm... well... I'm Collin's sister? Olive?" Both of these things come out as questions, which is not good. Because if I'm not sure who I am, they have no reason to believe me. "Can you let him know I'm here?"

"Is he expecting you?" the first one asks.

I shake my head, but force myself to project confidence. "No. But he will definitely want to know I'm here so you should probably give him a call." *I think.*

"One moment," the second one says. He goes into the guard house, while Number One glares at me like I'm wearing a nametag that says *Enemy* on it.

The second one comes back out. "He's on his way." Then they both stare at me with half-hooded eyes. It's all very serious. Which might be weird. I mean, I'm a twenty-two-year-old girl. Blonde, and fit, and attractive, and small. They're hardened, big, and wearing black tactical uniforms. Not only that, they're loaded down with some serious weapons, like this is a military base in some violent desert country instead of a security operation in the middle of West Virginia.

I look over to my right and there he is. Collin Creed. My brother. My target.

He's coming down the porch steps of the house closest to the highway with a strange look on his face. As he gets closer he squints. "Olive?"

I smile, shyly. Because he's a lot like his compound. I know him—I grew up with him until I was eight—but I haven't seen him in over twelve years. Haven't even talked to him since I was a teenager, and that was just a random call out of nowhere that lasted about five minutes.

He's… scarier than I thought he would be.

Harder than even these men he has guarding his compound.

And those eyes of his—those weird hazel blue-green eyes—they don't look the way I remember. They look… suspicious.

I force a smile as he approaches. "Surprise!"

He's confused and he starts looking around. "Where's your car? How did you get here?"

I point down the highway, like the bus that dropped me off is still there, but of course it's not. "The Appalachian Tours bus dropped me off. I got into Charleston last night and—"

But he cuts me off. "What are you doing here? Where's Mom and Dad?"

My heart twists a little when he says these words. Mom and Dad. Like we're really related. Like we share parents. Which, of course, we don't. And I haven't thought of them as Mom and Dad for so long now, this question stuns me. Memories begin to flood my head and I don't know what to say.

"Olive? What's going on?"

Now he's looking at me like he's worried and I know this was a mistake.

A huge mistake.

Suddenly, Brose is in my head, whispering those oh-so-familiar words right into my mind. *My mission is you and your mission is me.*

For a moment, I feel like he's here with me. All the growing sense of abandonment fades and… it's just us.

Me and him.

He thinks for me, I act for him.

He thinks for me, I act for him.

He thinks for me, I act for him.

"Nothing," I say. "Nothing's going on. I mean, I'm here, so that's something. But… why do you look so worried?" I crinkle my nose at Collin, which makes him smile and drop his guard.

I'm very cute when I crinkle my nose and this is something he told me often when I was small.

Suddenly, memories are flooding through me. All the years he was—like truly was—my big brother. And I can feel the tears building. Not from a sense of fear that he will start asking me questions I can't answer, but from relief. Because I know him and he knows me, and there's actually a whole lot to say.

So that's what I do. I say it. "I've missed you." And I let those tears form.

Collin grabs me and pulls me in for a hug. "God, I've missed you too. I don't think I actually realized just how much until right now."

I hug him back and we stay like this for a good long moment. Then he pushes me back to get a better look and grins. Those crazy beautiful eyes of his focus on me for the first time in so long, I actually get lost in them. "Come on. I live down at the end of the driveway there with Lowyn. She's still here, and she's gonna fuckin' freak when she sees you, I'm sure. Wait till you see what she did to our house, Olive. Your room is an office now."

We begin walking deeper into the compound and that's that.

It's like I never left because suddenly I feel... *home*.

Don't get comfortable. These words float through my head in the subdued and low voice of Brose. *You have a lot of questions coming, Olive. And you need to be ready.*

But it's really not a problem because the very first project Brose and I ever worked on together was me. My backstory, I mean. *"Everyone has to have one,"* he'd said.

"What's yours?" I remember asking.

"Old money." He sighed when he said that. *"It goes with old power."*

I was flirting with him during this conversation. I was only eighteen and Brose is fucking hot. Everything about him is hot. Those lean stomach muscles, his broad shoulders, that bit of scruff that's always on his chin and looks like someone sketched it into place, that's how perfect it always is. And that voice. My God, he could make me come with words if he tried.

"You're a legacy," I'd said.

"We're all legacies, Olive. There isn't a single person in CORE who isn't. So it's your blood as well as mine."

The bus, which had preceded me at the entrance of Edge and rumbled down the driveway to the very end, spurts out a cloud of black diesel smoke and slowly pulls away, rounding the curve of the driveway to head out.

"You have kids?" I ask, pointing at the school bus as it maneuvers the curve.

"Nah. It's Amon's boy. Well, Rosie Harlow's boy. Cross. You remember Cross?"

I shrug, because maybe? But not really. I would not call Rosie a stranger, just like I would not call anyone in Disciple a stranger, but I didn't know her. And maybe I have a memory of her being pregnant, but if I ever saw her baby after it was born, it didn't leave an impression.

I'm looking right at the bus though, so when it finally rounds that corner what I'm really looking at is… Shep.

Holy fuck. I mean, of course I knew he was here. But I was not expecting him to be present when I started telling my fake story about my fake parents to my fake brother.

There is a fleeting moment here when I almost panic, but luckily, Collin is looking at me, talkin', so when Shep ducks away real fast, Collin doesn't even notice.

Hmmm. I guess Shep is as nervous about seeing me in front of Collin as I am of him.

"Olive?"

"Huh?" I look up at my brother. Who doesn't feel fake at all. Not even a tiny bit.

"I said, where are Mom and Dad?"

"Oh. They're in Florida. Pensacola. You haven't talked to them?"

Collin scoffs. "Not in many, many years. They disowned me, I think."

I frown. Because I didn't know this. I mean, I suspected they were not close, but I'm not close with them either so I didn't get any updates after CORE took over my life. I don't actually know where they live. Maybe Pensacola? Maybe not. It's just a story.

"What about you?" Collin asks. "Are you close?"

"No. Not really." I look up at him, readying the lies. "I dropped out of college."

"Why?"

"I hated it."

"So what do you do?"

"I'm an influencer."

"What?" Now he's laughing. But his eyes are shining with amusement. "What kind of influencer?"

"I'm a van-life girl."

"Stop it." He laughs.

"I am! I swear. I'm just in between vans at the moment. But I have a whole channel of content. Gypsy Compass. Look me up." The channel is real, but the girl doing it is actually AI. It's all fake. Even the destinations, which are mostly state and national parks with a smidge of coastal Mexico thrown in for variety.

"What happened to your van?"

"It got stolen. Just last week, actually. And it wasn't far away, so after dealing with the insurance, I decided to look you up. That's how I got here."

While Collin is thinking about all this, I watch as Shep makes his way over to a brown building and disappears inside.

I have an irrational urge to ask Collin about him, but I hold it in. He can't know that Shep and I know each other. That, despite Collin being the official reason I'm here, it's Shep I want to see.

Then I hear, "Oh, my God! Is that little Olive?" And then Lowyn McBride, a girl I kinda thought of as a sister when I was small, is bounding down the porch steps of an old house with her arms wide open, ready to give me a hug.

I let her do this and then, as if she and Collin are the same person, she pushes me out to arm's length and takes a good look at me. "You're gorgeous, Olive. Absolutely stunning. Do people tell you that all the time?"

My laugh comes out immediately. "Um... no? No. They really don't."

Brose does tell me nice things, but it comes off as platitudes. And I don't actually interact with anyone else these days, so... this isn't even a lie.

"Oh, that's crazy. You're hanging around the wrong people then."

And before I can make any more decisions or have any thoughts at all, actually, I'm being pulled up the porch steps and led through the door of the house.

The next thing I know I'm sitting at the kitchen table of a very bright and modern kitchen and Lowyn McBride is setting a cup of coffee in front of me. She gives Collin one too, then sits down next to him.

I squirm a little when they stare at me as a team, but manage to smile and take a sip of my drink to buy time. I don't know what comes next. Meeting Collin was always a hypothetical. This wasn't planned, I'm not supposed to be here, and Brose is missing.

So I don't know what to say.

"Do you need anything?" Lowyn asks. "I'm about to head into work. I run a vintage thrift store in Disciple, so if ya do, you can come along and check it out."

"Oh…" I stall. "I… well, I'm kind of tired, actually. So if it's OK, maybe I could just hang out here for a little bit?"

Collin looks at me like he wants to ask questions, but Lowyn gets there first. "Sure," she says. "You make yourself at home. I'll be back late afternoon, but you'll be here, right, Collin?"

"Well, I've got some meetings in the office,"—he nods his head to indicate some place outside the house—"but I'll be around. So yeah, sure. Rest. We'll catch up tonight at dinner."

"There's a guest room right down there, Olive. You unpack your bag there and settle in."

Then they both get up, so I get up too, and we all hug one more time before they leave to go about their days.

I watch from the front window as the two of them linger near what I assume to be Lowyn's car, then Collin opens her door, lets her get in, and closes it behind her.

He always was a gentleman like that and it makes me sigh a little at how perfect they are for each other.

But once Lowyn's car disappears, and Collin is all the way up the driveway, mostly hidden by dozens of his men, I slip out the front door and straight over to the brown building where I saw Shep disappear.

15 - Shep

My mind is spinning with all kinds of scenarios as I make my way back into the kennel. And even though my heart kind of jumped when I saw her—and it wasn't totally from shock—this is not good.

Whatever she's up to, it's not good.

And it kinda pisses me off. But also, I think I'm the one to blame.

I guess she really is Collin's sister. Fine. That could be the reason she's here. But that's not the only reason. If it was, why now? Why didn't she come here first? Why open that weird bar in the middle of the woods?

That place was a honeypot. It was CORE through and through. And they're not here for me—the only reason they're here is Collin.

And now this is all gonna come back on me.

I'm *so* pissed.

Because even though I didn't lead her here—hell, I didn't do anything with that girl except talk to her a couple of times—this is all gonna be blamed on me.

And I just got accepted into the group. For the first time in years, I've got a place to belong. I've got people, and a place to live, and a purpose. And none of that has anything to do with me being a spy.

But that's what he's gonna think. That's what Collin's gonna think if he finds out Olive is CORE and that she and I already know each other.

If, Shep? If? There's no if. She's here to tell him who I am.

And that's it for me. I'll be alone again. And it's all her fault.

I walk through the kennel, fuming, but don't go to the puppy. Instead, I go into the feed room and stare at the whiteboard where bossy Cross left me a list of instructions. Which… kinda makes me smile.

But also ignites the anger again, because I like this kid. I like his puppy. I'm looking forward to training that little maniac to bite people on command. This sounds *fun* to me.

I like this life, brand new as it is. It feels like a real second chance and I don't want this girl fucking it up.

The main door of the kennel opens, then slams closed, being on a tight spring to keep dogs in. It's probably Amon wondering where I am. Not that I really have a schedule yet, but Cross has left for school and the puppy's training is now my responsibility, so I put Olive behind me and step out into the hallway.

But it's not Amon, so my words come out in a growl. "What the hell are you doing, Olive? Why are you here?"

She looks taken aback for a moment, like she wasn't expecting my anger. Which is such a lie. *She* is such a lie. Because this reaction only lasts for a split second. In the next moment, she's spitting words at me. "What does that mean, what am I doing? Collin is my brother. I told you that. You're just mad because you didn't believe me and now you look like a fool."

"A fool?" I laugh. "Well, I'd rather be a fool than a fuckin' liar and that's what you are."

"And yet here I am in my brother's super-secret, black-ops, ex-military compound. How can both of these things be true, if I'm a liar?"

"Because you work for CORE."

"So do you."

"No." I shake my head. "I used to. They kicked me out."

"They kicked you *out*? Do you even hear yourself? Please. They kicked you out." She scoffs. "They didn't kick you out, *Shep*." She sneers my name. "They let you go. And then ..." She shrugs. "Somehow... by luck, I'm sure, you ended up here at Edge Security. A super-secret, black-ops, ex-military security business run by the infamous Collin Creed. Yeah," she laughs. "That's likely."

"Believe what you want. I was in prison. CORE was not coming to save me."

"Wow." She cocks a hip and leans against the wall. "You're just... dumb, or something."

"Right."

"Well, you're not sittin' in prison right now. So... how's that happen if CORE didn't get you out?"

"Charlie Beaufort did."

"Charlie Beaufort is as CORE as they come, Shep. He's a two-faced piece of shit. The only reason the US military complex still uses him is because he can get the job done. All he wants is money and power and he doesn't care one bit where those two things come from. So you're either lying to me"—she narrows her eyes down until they're almost slits—"or you're lying to yourself. Which one is it?"

"Well, first of all," I say, holding up a finger, "you have no right to ask me questions. I didn't show up at *your* work trying to fuck things up. And second of all,"—I hold up another finger —"I don't owe you answers."

"Hmmm." She kicks off the wall and walks forward, her fingertips gently brushing against my arm as she pushes past me, going into the feed room. A chill runs through my body from that small touch, but I shake it off, turning to watch her.

She's standing in front of the whiteboard, reading the instructions Cross left for me. "We discussed this, you know."

"Discussed what? And with who?"

She looks over her shoulder at me, just staring into my eyes. It's a technique to make people uncomfortable and gain control of things when a situation might be spiraling. I should know, I was taught to do the same thing. "Discussed you and how you got here."

"You didn't answer the second part of my question."

She smiles. "I guess the childish thing to say would be that I don't owe you answers. But I'm a grown-up." This makes me laugh. She's a baby. But she just keeps talking. "So I'm gonna tell you. My partner, Brose. When you came in to the club that first time he and I had a nice long conversation about you. And do you know what we decided?"

"I can't wait to find out."

"That it's the second one, Shep."

"Second *what*?" I'm very annoyed now.

"You're lying to yourself."

I take in a deep breath and let it out. "Whatever." Then I turn towards the open door, ready to go grab the puppy and leave her here with her stupid riddles.

"It's not your fault."

I don't even turn my head to look at her as I try to pass, but she grabs my arm, forcing me to react. If she was a guy, this would be my cue to punch her in the jaw. But she's not, so instead I make the most menacing face and growl my words out. "Let go of me and don't *ever* fucking touch me again."

She does not let go. She looks me right in the eyes. "They're using you."

"Look, if you're gonna try and play mind games with me, the least you can do is tell me something I don't know. Of course they're using me. Just like they're using you. Because they use everyone, Olive. But I, unlike you, have seen the truth here. That we are just puppets. And I'd rather spend my life in prison than work for CORE again."

She goes to open her mouth, but I put up a hand. "Save it, OK? I know who got me out of prison. I know why they did it. I'm not fuckin' stupid. But no one gave me marching orders, so as far as I'm concerned, this is a brand-new start for me. And even if they did try and give me orders, I'm not interested. If they want to kill me because I won't participate, then fuck it. There's nothing I can do to stop it." I reach up with my opposite hand and pry her fingers off my arm. "So if you don't mind, I'm gonna take my chances and you can just see yourself the fuck out and pretend you don't know me."

But again, as I pass, she reaches for me, grabbing onto my arm.

This time I don't control myself. Can't control myself. So my hand is around her neck and I have her pressed against the whiteboard before she can even blink.

I can feel her heartbeat beneath my fingertips and I'd be lying if I said that tiny pulse of blood wasn't turning me on. I lean into her face. My turn to look her in the eyes. "One little squeeze, Olive, and you'd be seeing black. Just a bit more pressure for just a few more seconds, and you'd be on the fuckin' floor."

Her eyes are low and lazy as she looks back at me. "Go ahead. Do it."

Before I can stop myself, my fingers squeeze, wrapping tight around her neck. I expect her to struggle. To push me off and give me a reason to stop.

But she doesn't.

She moans.

And instantly, I'm fuckin' hard.

"Do it," she says, her voice barely a whisper. "Do it. *Please.*"

"You're sick," I whisper back. "You're damaged."

"*Do it!*" This time, she says it through clenched teeth. "*Do. It.*" Then she brings her hand up to cover mine, and she squeezes for me.

I pull back, breathing hard, but not as hard as her, trying to get myself under control. "What the fuck was that?"

She exhales, still panting, looks down at her feet, then tips her eyes up to me in what comes off as a very menacing expression. She smiles, and it's wrong. "So what? I like it. Brose does it all the time."

"What?"

She's whispering. "My handler. He's…" She turns, facing the wall to her left. "He's possessive and expects full submission."

"Wow. They really did a number on you, didn't they?"

She scoffs, her voice normal again. "Look who's talking. You're here and you actually think it's a second chance. They've got a hold of your mind, Shep. You're a puppet."

"Bitch, you just told me that your handler chokes you out as part of your compliance protocol. I threatened you, and all it did was get your panties wet. So let's definitely have that conversation about who's a puppet and who's not."

Her smile is smarmy now. I'm concentrating on that because she's actually really pretty when she's all worked up like this, and the next thing I know, she's got her hand between my legs. "OK. Let's see who's the puppet, Shep."

"Don't start something you can't finish."

Her fingers dig into my jeans, squeezing me. And I've been hard this whole time, so all it feels is… *good*.

Then next thing I know, I've got her pressed up against the wall, my hand back on her throat, and we're kissing. Sloppy, open-mouth fucking kissing. I'm pressing against her neck and she's grinding on me like she's about to come any second now. And her fingertips are pulling my shirt up, tantalizingly flitting against my stomach as she tries to work the button on my jeans and—

The door slams closed out in the hallway and she and I break apart.

But not before Amon fucking Parrish enters the feed room.

He looks at her.

He looks at me.

He looks back at her. "What the fuck is going on here?"

Olive smiles. "Uh… Amon, right?"

"Don't play games with me, Olive. I'm in a bad mood."

She smiles bigger, then shrugs a shoulder, nodding her head towards me. "He's…" She looks down at my hard-on, which makes Amon look down at my hard-on, and then she says, in a sugar-sweet voice, "Fun. And I'm a grown-up, so… maybe you should just mind your own fuckin' business?"

I swear to God, Amon almost loses his shit. I watch in real time as he struggles to hold it in, growling back at her in a dangerously low voice that was honed to terrorize. "Get the fuck out of my kennel, Olive. *Right now.*"

She squints her eyes at him. And for a moment, I don't think she's gonna go. But when I glance at Amon, she and I see the same thing.

Malice.

We see a man who has killed many people.

Olive sucks in a breath, gives me a final look, then squares her shoulders and pushes past him. "I'll see you later, Shep. We can finish our conversation then."

The door slams closed one more time, and she's gone.

Amon turns to me. "What the fuck are you doing? Do you have any idea who that is?"

"Oh, trust me," I say. "I know exactly who she is."

Amon's eyes go narrow. "Do you... do you know each other?"

"Know each other? No. But we've met."

Amon lowers his voice to almost a whisper. "Did you fuck Collin's baby sister?"

"Not yet." And then, even though I know what's coming, I laugh. And it's still coming out when I'm hitting the floor.

Amon turns, shaking his hand, his knuckles all bloody. "Pack your shit and get out."

"No," I say, getting up and spitting out the blood. "No. I'm not packing my shit. She came on to *me*. She's the one you should be pissed off at. So no, Amon. I've got a contract and I'm not packing my shit just because Collin's little sister likes..." I almost say it. I mean, I'm very fucking close to saying what that girl likes. But it's a touch too far, so I don't.

"Likes *what?*" Amon prods.

"Me. That's what. It's not my fault she likes *me*. And I didn't know who she was when we met. It was in some bar." I don't add that she was whoring herself out because I figure that's really not my story to tell. "I didn't know who she was until last weekend. And I thought she was lying until I saw her walking down the damn driveway this morning. I came in here to work and she followed me. The next thing I know, she's grabbing my dick, OK? And… yeah. I let her. That's it. That's what happened. So fuck you. It really *is* none of your business."

Then I leave, spitting out some more blood on the concrete floor as I grab my puppy from his kennel and take him outside to work.

16 - Olive

*O*utside *the sun is* bright and confusing. Add in the fact that I'm new here, there are strange people everywhere, and the barking dogs are making noise akin to a deafening thunderstorm, and it's more than confusing, it's disorienting. My vision blurs, my body swaying a little like the earth is moving under my feet, and for a moment I think I might fall over.

"Get a hold of yourself, Olive," I whisper. "Snap the fuck out of it."

Behind me the kennel door slams and I turn around real quick to find Shep leaving the building leading a young dog.

Seeing me, he shakes his head and accusingly points his finger in my direction. "Stay away from me." Then he leads the dog down the driveway where all the activity is.

I'm just letting out a breath when the kennel door slams closed again. This time, when I look around, I see Amon.

I don't know Amon. Of course, I remember him. Everyone in Disciple—even when I was only eight years old—knew who Amon Parrish was. He was the bad kid. I'm like a hundred percent sure my father actually used those exact words to describe him. *"Stay away from him, Olive. He's a bad kid."*

Amon and Collin were never friends growing up. But they

joined the Marines together and I was told that Jim Bob Baptist made sure they were pulled aside for the black-ops shit the moment they got off the bus for basic.

Amon did dogs, which obviously bit him pretty hard because this compound is crawling with them. And Collin learned to run spies. But that's not what he's known for now. He's known, in my world, for killing people. And his team—he always had a team—is there to make sure the kill shot happens.

He's an assassin. I doubt he planned it. In fact, I know he didn't. Collin was all about rock and roll and football when I was little. That ancient piece-of-shit Jeep of his with the big tires and Jim Morrison. That's what I remember about Collin. We'd go to his games on Friday nights and watch. And Lowyn would be there cheering him on in her cute uniform and pompoms.

He was… quintessentially all-American.

Until New Year's Eve of his senior year when my biological father came down from Blackberry Hill and tried to steal me out of my bed.

That's when Assassin Collin showed up. It literally happened before my eyes.

In fact, I'm the only person alive who saw his face that night because the person he was aiming at got his brains splattered all over me.

Collin was angry. I don't think I'd ever seen him so angry. But there was something else about his eyes that night too. Something *off*. It was… an emptiness. They were void of things like mercy and compassion. But emptiness doesn't stay that way long, so I was looking right at him when that space filled back up with ruthless abandon.

When I was sixteen, the CORE OPS people took me into an

interrogation room and they showed me pictures of him. He was... I dunno. Twenty-four or twenty-five, maybe? And the first thing I thought was, my God, my brother is *handsome*. But a moment later they were sliding more across that table at me. Only this time, they wanted to show me what he had been up to over the years.

OPS stands for Operative Preparation Services. That's who raised me after my father went crazy over Collin leaving and we had to leave Disciple. They were faceless people. Nameless people. Like, literally. They wore veils. They were all women and none of them were nice. We had to call them by their departmental number. OPS-94 was the one I saw the most. She was my official caseworker. She was the one pushing photos of dead men across the table at me.

Wow. That seems like a very long time ago. And I guess when you're twenty, four years *is* a long time ago. One-fifth of my life.

I blink and the memories fade along with the dizziness and disorientation. Amon is texting someone. Probably Collin. He finishes up, looks at me, and nods his head.

When I look over my shoulder, Collin is coming down the driveway at a pretty good clip, his eyes lit up like a New Year's Eve sparkler.

He starts making hand signals or something, and the next thing I know, Amon is running past me. I watch as he approaches Shep and point to a building across the driveway. Shep looks at it, then shifts his gaze to me. And even from here, which has to be fifty yards away, I can see his anger.

Which makes me sigh. Because while it wasn't my intention to get him in trouble, what else was gonna happen when I showed up here?

Of course Collin was gonna find out. So I don't even bother glaring back.

"Olive," Collin yells, still pretty far down the driveway, so everyone looks, of course. "Let's go." He points to the same building, which I now realize is a church, of all things.

I consider what kind of scene I would make if I ignored him and just walked back to his house and went inside, but I don't bother. Whatever is coming next is inevitable.

Will I tell him everything?

I don't know. I don't understand what is happening to me. Did Brose abandon me? Did he really move all his shit out and leave? I mean, obviously he did because I woke up alone inside an empty estate with a bricked-up staircase that didn't lead to the basement train tunnel.

But why? I get that I told Shep more than I should've that day on the stairs, but he's CORE. It's not like most of that was a secret. That small mistake doesn't justify Brose turning his back on me after two years of *My mission is you and your mission is me.*

It just doesn't.

"*Olive,*" Collin yells again, this time much sharper.

"I'm coming," I mutter. Shep and Amon reach the church first and disappear inside. Then Collin. He opens the door and waits for me, letting me go in first.

It's dark inside because all the windows in here have been bricked up. While it's still a church from the outside, the inside appears to be some kind of meeting room. There are several whiteboards pushed against the walls and lots of tables and chairs.

Amon and Shep aren't sitting down, so Collin and I just walk over and join them.

Collin gets the party started. "What the hell is going on between you two?"

Shep looks at me, but he's talking to Collin. "I have no idea. I met her in a bar. We saw each other two times—"

"Three," I say.

"Three times and that's it. I didn't even know who she was until last Sunday. And even when she told me, I didn't believe her. But I did walk away and make it very clear that I was not interested."

"That's funny," Amon scoffs. "Because I just caught the two of you feeling each other up in the kennel."

"So what?" I say. "So what if we were?" I look at Collin. Right at him. Straight into those beautifully weird eyes of his. "We're grown-ups, Collin. You don't get a say in my personal life."

Collin shrugs. "That's fair, I guess. I don't even know you, Olive. Which is kinda bothering me right now. Not because I missed out on your childhood, but because I let you inside my compound even though you showed up here in rather mysterious circumstances. It sounds bad when I say it out loud, but what's worse than that is the fact that the very first thing you do when you get here is start something up with one of my men. Did you follow him into the kennel after Lowyn and I left the house?"

"So what?"

"That's a yes, I guess? Fine. You did. What is your purpose here? And don't say it's me, because it's not, Olive. What does Ean Shephard have that you need?"

"I just… like him."

"You don't even know me, Olive." When Shep says this, my heart cracks a little. Because I was truly trying to take all the blame here even though it's not entirely my fault. He was the one who got excited in the kennel. He was practically daring me to grope him. So I feel like he should fall on his knife just a teeny, tiny bit the way I fell on mine to show some appreciation.

But what does he do? Blame me.

Still, it's a losing fight. So I'm just gonna give in. "Fine. I'm a terrible person or whatever. I'll grab my pack and get out of your hair." Then I turn to leave.

"And go where?" Collin calls out after me.

"Like you care." I don't look at him when I answer, just walk out the door.

It's a childish thing to say, really. But ya know what? The last time I saw Collin I was a child and I just feel like... I dunno. Angry, I guess. That he missed it. So... he deserves a childish answer to make up for it.

Which makes me roll my eyes *at myself* as I walk down the long driveway towards Collin's house.

There's a black dog sitting on Collin's porch that wasn't there earlier. It stares at me as I approach, so I hesitate at the bottom step, wondering if it might attack me.

Possible, but not probable. There are lots of dogs here and they all seem to be up-and-coming tactical K9s. Collin would not leave a loose dog on his porch if it was prone to attack without orders, so I go up the steps without looking at it again and go inside.

It's quiet and the light is dim because all the windows have those fancy wooden shutters on them and they're closed, but I don't mind the darkness.

I go to the guest room and sit on the bed. It was stupid to throw a tantrum the way I did. To threaten Collin with leaving. I mean, why would he care? We haven't talked in ages. If I had bumped into him on the street, I'm a hundred percent sure he wouldn't even have recognized me.

I'm still unsure what my next move is, so I don't get up and leave. I guess I could hitchhike into Bishop and try and catch a ride back to Charleston on the tour bus. I'm definitely not gonna try that in Disciple. The last thing I need is someone from there to recognize me.

Actually, it would be even worse if they didn't. And I suspect that's what I'm really afraid of. That I'd walk into Disciple, West Virginia, and not a single person would know my face.

Bishop isn't a great plan either, but at least I won't have to look at grown-up versions of my childhood friends when I walk right past them and they don't even look twice.

The front door opens and closes and I stiffen, readying myself for my next fight with Collin. I turn my head towards the open bedroom door as heavy footsteps make their way down the hallway. He stops just short of my door, staying out of sight. But he's casting a light shadow on the hardwood floor, so I know he's there.

"You might as well just come in," I say. "Obviously you're here for me."

To my surprise, it's not Collin who takes those final few steps and looms in the doorway.

It's Shep.

"What do you want?" I sneer.

"Collin wanted me to come talk to you."

"Why would he want that?"

"Because... this is between us, right? You like me. You came here for me. Well,"—he throws up his hands—"here I am."

I turn my head away and look at the window. This one has

curtains, not shutters, so I can see outside. It's just trees, though. Since this house kinda bumps up against the woods.

"Can I sit?" Shep asks.

I don't answer or look at him, just shrug. So he sits, making the mattress dip on his side, which in turn forces me to scoot over and adjust my position. So now I do look at him. "Look," I say. "Sorry I came here and ruined things for you. I'm leaving, so it's over now."

"Can I ask you something?" is all he says back to that.

"I guess."

"What was goin' on back there in the kennel? And don't act like you don't know what I'm talking about. I got rough with you and then I put my hand on your throat and you…"

I shoot him a contemptuous look, waiting for his word choice.

"You… like it."

"So?"

"Olive, I… don't even know where to start this conversation, and…" But he stops. And I watch him carefully here, almost able to see the calculating moves happening inside his head in real time.

"And what?" I prod. Because while I can see that he's reevaluating things, I have no idea what options he's weighing. And I'm kind of dying to know.

But instead of answering me, he moves closer. Repositioning his body. And then he's slowly raising his hand. His palm is flat and facing me, but as it comes up to my neck, it curves into a loose fist.

He's gonna do it. He's gonna put his hand—

And then it's there. Pressing against my throat. Without hesitation, my eyes close and a moan comes out of my mouth.

The next thing I know, he's kissing me. And it's just like it was before. Ravenous and filled with an almost uncontrollable lust.

I don't kiss him back this time. No. This time I start whispering, "Do it. Do it, *please*. Just a little bit, OK? I can take it. Just a little tighter. *Please.*"

When he grants my request and his fingers tighten around my throat, I nearly come apart. The moans coming out of my mouth are low and erotic. If I was able to articulate coherent thoughts in this moment, I'd have the good sense to be embarrassed.

But I'm not embarrassed. In fact, I'm rather bold. Because I twist on the bed, facing him. And then I press my hand up against his just to make sure it doesn't slip out of position and I climb into his lap.

"Wait," he says.

But fuck that. No. I'm not waiting. So I hush those words with my mouth on his, while at the same time I reach down and press the heel of my palm into his rock-hard cock. Even through his jeans I can tell it's long and thick and I want it. So I slip my fingertips back where they were before Amon interrupted us and pop the button of his pants. Then I drag the zipper down, shove my hand inside, and grab his cock with a greedy fist.

His reciprocal moan is a signal that this will happen. And the next thing I know, he's pressing that hand against my neck with more force.

"Yes," I say, allowing myself to fully enjoy the feeling. "Yes. *More.*" But he doesn't increase the pressure, and this frustrates me, so I ask again. "More. Just a little bit." This asking becomes begging almost immediately. But he's hesitating. Any more pressure and he'll cut off the blood flow to my brain.

But that's what I want. I want the dizziness. I want the fade to black. I want the complete surrender of my body to this man. And then I want to wake up blinking at his face hovering over mine *as he fucks me*.

I want to feel the weight of his body and hear his ragged breathing as I gaze up into his eyes and see his *lust*.

"Do it," I say again. "Just, please, do it."

He doesn't hesitate this time. The pressure increases dramatically and the dizziness takes over.

I feel my body going loose. My muscles unable to work.

And then I get it.

Finally, I get it.

The fade.

The black.

And I come.

17 - Shep

*I*t's *so weird* to watch the light fade from her eyes as her body nearly convulses with the orgasm. But what surprises me the most is my reaction to it. Which isn't what I expected, because I have to close my eyes and clench my jaw to stop myself from coming in her hand, loose around my dick now.

When she's properly passed out, her body crumples like the little puppet she is and I hold her in my arms for a moment, letting her head rest on my shoulder as she takes a gasping breath.

It's dangerous what I just did. Very, very risky. Sexual asphyxiation is nothing to fuck around with and I shouldn't have given in, but my God, the look in her eyes as she begged me...

"Please."

It was a degree of lust I've never seen before.

She sits up, still in my lap, shaking her head, trying to clear it. Then she starts crying.

"Oh, fuck! I'm sorry," I say. "I shouldn't have done that."

"No," she says, practically sobbing into my neck. "No. You don't understand. It felt so good. It's never felt that good before, *ever*. Thank you. Thank you, thank you, thank you."

I… don't even know what to say to that. Certainly not '*You're welcome.*' If Collin finds out I came in here and choked his baby sister into a blackout orgasm, he's gonna shoot me on the spot.

Olive lets out a long breath and kind of collapses into my arms.

"Come here." I lean back on the bed and bring her with me. She pulls herself together long enough so we can crawl our way up to the pillows, then once again becomes loose and heavy, resting her face on my chest.

"You're tired," I say. "You should get some sleep."

She perks up, shakes her head no. "Not yet. Don't go. It's your turn now." The life comes back into her eyes when she makes me this offer. And I have to wonder just what the actual fuck they did to this girl to make her act like this.

This isn't her. It's not. I can tell that everything happening right now is *programming*. It's so fucking obvious.

"If you leave now, Shep, I'll never forgive you."

We don't even know each other. Like, at all. So this shouldn't even be something I take seriously.

But when her hand resumes its position on my dick, all rational reasons why this is a very bad idea just slip right out of my mind. A moment later she's pumping me, gripping me hard as her hand goes up and down my shaft.

Then it's like she wakes up and everything about her is fast. Her jeans and panties are sliding down her legs before I can process what's happening. She kicks them off, sits up, straddles my knees, and starts jerking on my pants, pulling them down. I help her out here a little, and then the next thing I know, she's hovering over me, her long, blonde hair hanging over her face and teasing me as it moves across my chest in a way that sends chills through my whole body.

She grips my dick, fisting it hard, and puts me inside her.

Her head falls back as her mouth opens and a moan of ecstasy flows past her lips. I grab her shirt, push it up to her chin, and grip her tits with the same force. She begins fucking me, her hips wild and her back arched as her hands slap down onto my chest. She digs her fingernails into my skin, making me moan, and then it's just… carnal. Fucking. It's just fucking.

Crazy, unrestrained sex performed with a frenzied passion that borders on violence.

Urges of my own begin to float to the surface and I decide to act on them. I flip her off me, turn her over, and then I push her legs open, hover over her perfect ass, and spread her cheeks as I push myself inside her dripping wet pussy.

"Yes," she's saying, her breath so ragged and uneven I almost can't understand her. "Yes."

I grab her hair, pull her head back, and fuck her from behind like an animal.

And the whole time she just says, "Yes, yes, yes," over and over again until I pull out, spew my come all over her back, and then fall to the side with a long sigh of relief.

She claws her way onto her side, hikes a leg over mine, put her cheek on my chest, and sighs.

And then, without another word, she's asleep.

I almost fall asleep too, but Collin Creed is outside on his porch waiting for me to report.

So instead, I come up with an alternative story to the truth.

Because while he did send me in here to get information out of her, he didn't give me permission to fuck his little sister like a fifty-dollar whore.

I take my time, though. Try to put all the sentences together in a coherent manner. And also enjoy the woman clinging to me like I'm some kind of savior.

Her breathing evens out and her body goes heavy. And after about ten minutes or so, I force myself to slide out from under her and pull myself together.

She doesn't wake up. Doesn't even stir.

So I leave, softly closing the door behind me, and hope to God I do not smell like pussy when I go outside and find Collin and his dog sitting patiently on the porch steps.

He turns when he hears me, then stands up. "Well? Did you learn anything?"

I let out a long exhale as I run my fingers through my hair. "Oh, I did. I absolutely did. But before we have this conversation, Collin, I have a question."

"Shoot."

"Where do you boys keep the alcohol?"

COLLIN TAKES me back to the church, which is where we had our first conversation about Olive after she stormed out the door to go pack her shit. Collin tried to follow her, but I took a risk and grabbed him by the arm.

The look he shot me—yeah. I believe every story I've ever heard about the guy after that look. But I put up a hand and said, "Hear me out, OK? Just give me five minutes to explain what I think might be happening here."

He and Amon exchanged a look and then Collin let out a breath and gave me his full attention. "Five minutes. Start talking."

So I did. But I didn't tell him everything. I needed to talk to Olive first. Not to get confirmation—I don't care how good I am at deep cover, she's locked up tight. I should know. I was like that once too. But I could at least carefully dig out some answers with the right questions.

Obviously, Olive and I didn't do a lot of talking back inside the house. But questions don't always come in the form of words. I'd already suspected her handler was using some very unorthodox methods to get inside her head, which explains the choking fetish, so that wasn't even a big revelation.

It was the emptiness in her eyes that confirmed it for me. Well, that and the hot fucking sex. She was out of control.

But then again, so was I.

It makes sense. So this is where I'm at when Collin and I walk across the big open room inside the church and go through a door to a stairway that leads down.

Even though he flips on the lights, it doesn't light up the stairs, only the room at the bottom, so it's casting eerie shadows up the walls as I descend. "You're not gonna kill me and bury my body down here, are ya?" I joke.

He doesn't laugh. Or answer me.

But when we get to the bottom, the nerves that were creeping up my spine settle a little when I realize what I'm looking at. "Why are we at the SCIF?" I ask.

He shrugs. "Typically, this is where all the fucked-up conversations take place, so it's where I keep the good shit." He points to the Faraday box on the side of the door. "Phone."

I dig mine out and drop it into the box and he does the same.

Then we go inside.

Again, I get that weird vacuum feeling when I enter and all the technology outside is blocked.

Even if we did come down here for the drink—and it's here,

so he wasn't lying—the SCIF is the perfect place for this conversation.

He grabs two glasses from a makeshift bar cart in the corner and brings them and the bottle over to the table. We sit, he pours, we drink.

When that's over Collin leans back in his chair and lets out a breath. "How bad is it?"

Which shouldn't surprise me, but it kinda does. "How much do you know?"

"About her?" He points up at the ceiling. "Nothin'. I haven't even talked to her since she was in high school. If I saw her on the street, I would maybe look twice, but for all the wrong reasons, if you get what I mean."

"You wouldn't have recognized her?"

He shakes his head. "Never in a million years."

"OK, listen. I'm not trying to pry or anything, but I need to know where you thought she was all these years."

"I… didn't think about it. Almost never. And if I did, I pictured her with our parents." Now he squints at me. "How much do you know about *us*?"

"When I got here? Nothing, Collin. I mean, I've heard rumors about you and your team. There were congressional hearings, for fuck's sake. But if you're askin' if someone sat me down and we actually talked about you—and by someone I specifically mean Charlie Beaufort, but also anyone else you suspect might do something like that—then the answer is no. That never happened. Everything that I know about you came right out of Olive's mouth the last time I saw her."

"Which was when?"

"Sunday morning."

"How did you meet her?"

I am careful when I explain this part because things with Olive are really bad already and he just doesn't need to know that she was gonna take money from me in exchange for sex. But he does need to know about the bar, so I tell him every detail about that place and end with meeting Olive at the Revenant Diner.

"This bar," Collin says. "It's a honeypot." And it's not a question.

"It is, and this isn't just speculation. Olive told me, Collin."

Collin leans back in his chair and crosses his arms. "Here's my problem, Shep. Why would she tell you that? And why would she be involved with something like that in the first place?"

"Why would she tell me?" I scoff a little. "She likes me. I guess. But she's…" I look away, gazing off into the distance for a moment, trying to find a way to break it to Collin Creed that his baby sister is a traitor. Not that I'm any better. Hell, not that *he's* any better. But it's different when it's someone you love and think of as an innocent.

I look at him again. "She's a spy, Collin. She's here for you and she was using me to do that. Or, at least, she was trying to use me. I didn't encourage her. She came here on her own accord. I'm not part of what she's doing, other than I wound up at that bar in the woods because I saw a flyer in a bar in Revenant."

He waits, saying nothing. Probably to see if I'll say anything else. But when I don't, his question is sharp and very on point. "All right. For the sake of argument, I'm gonna believe you about all of that, Shep. But what you didn't tell me was who she's spying for. Do you know?"

"Well, I sort of do. But also don't. Meaning, I can take a good guess. Mostly on account of things she said. But it's gonna cast doubt on me, so I'll prepare you for that right now."

Collin smiles, then laughs. "Let me guess… you work for a secret underground city. If so, get in line, Shep. That guy's already part of the team."

"Really?" I'm surprised at his statement. "Who is it?"

He ignores my question. "So you're an underground guy too?"

"No. I'm not. But it's all related. It's all part of a bigger organization called CORE. And I guess the shortcut through the long story I've been telling is this—Olive works for CORE."

"And you know this how?" His eyebrow goes up. "Because she told you?"

"Well, as unlikely as it sounds, yes. But, that's not all." I take in a deep breath and slowly let it out. "I work for CORE too."

"I see." It comes out deadpan.

"Well, I did, I mean. Charlie Beaufort really did find me in prison."

"OK."

"I am a veteran. But I was a deep-cover double agent."

"Stop." Collin puts up a hand. Then he leans in with squinty eyes. "What the *fuck* are you talking about?"

"Well, you already know they've got the deep underground cities. We're sittin' over top of one as we speak. This isn't the only place on the planet with underground cities, Collin. They're everywhere. Most of them are under the control of the military." I point at him before he can ask. "No. Not the one you were a part of. The one *I* was a part of. Anyway, it's a complicated game, as you can imagine. The whole us vs them thing.

"Mmmhmm. So you were a spy. And my sister is a spy. And both of you are here, in my compound… why?"

"Well, I'm under contract."

"Contracts made in bad faith can be broken. And if all of what you're sayin' is true, then I highly doubt you're gonna take me to court if I nullify it."

"You're right, I won't. But I'm not here as a spy. I'm here for the same reason everyone else is. Why the hell would I tell you all this if I was deep cover? I wouldn't tell you the part about the bar, I wouldn't tell you that your sister was a spy. I'll tell you lies, Collin. And that's not what I've been telling you."

"All right." He relaxes a little. "You got anything else to add?"

"Yes." I look him straight in those unsettling eyes of his. "Yes, there's more. It's a story all its own, but the most important thing is that CORE has a way of instilling loyalty. And Olive told me some very disturbing things about the guy who handles her."

"Handles her?" His anger is back now.

"You know how it works. You've got the field agent and the man who runs the field agent. And from what I can tell the one who's running her has…"

Collin leans forward in his seat, his eyes sharp like a hawk. "Has *what*?" And he's seething now.

"Manipulated her pretty bad with… sex."

Collin rubs both hands up and down his face as he processes what I just said. He's silent for nearly a minute, either getting himself under control or plotting twenty-five ways to kill this handler guy. When he looks up, I'm pretty sure it's the latter. "Where can I find this man?"

I shrug. "Fuck if I know. I've been out of service for years."

"Yeah," Collin says. "About that."

I put up a hand, already guessing where he's going. "You don't need to tell me. I get it. I'm here for a reason, I probably am a spy, and there's that thing about the abnormality in my brain."

"What now?"

"Well,"—I smile—"it's nice to know that Penny Rider keeps her word. I will remember that forever. She told me that I passed the lie detector test, just as she told you. *But* she also told me that there was some unusual activity in my brain that could not be explained."

"What's that all mean, Shep?"

"Honestly, Collin, I can't be sure. But obviously, I had a handler when I was in the field as well. I don't know what program she came up in, so I can't really compare us. But they do shit to us, Collin. To our brains. To make us comply. To make us... puppets."

"Why are you telling me this? Are you trying to make me kick you out?"

"No. I just want you to know. And I really don't think they've got any control over me. I think this brain activity is residual."

"How could you know? I mean, if they're all about mind-fuckin' maybe your mind is just fucked?"

"Maybe it is. But the thing about puppets is that they need a master. And mine's dead. So we don't need to worry much about her, or me. But we absolutely do need to worry about Olive and the man who is pulling all her strings. Because I'm sorry to say this Collin, and I'm not gonna get into details, but that girl's not right. She's not right."

"So what do I do? Kick her out and send her packin', Shep? She's my sister."

"Technically, she's not. At least that's what she told me when she described how you killed the man who was trying to kidnap her."

"Yeah, but… in my head she's my sister."

"I know. But I don't have any answers for you."

"How did you get away? How did you get your mind back?"

"I told you, my handler died."

"How did she die?"

I scoff. "Take one guess, Collin. How the hell do you think she died?"

"You killed her."

"I killed her. Not because I wanted to be free, just because it was all unraveling at that point. The brainwashing, ya know?"

"So what happened?"

"The programming started coming apart and nothin' made sense anymore, ya know? I washed out. This programming they do, it's complicated. The brain is a machine with many powers. And it's got lots of backdoors. Not for those who want to manipulate it, but for us." I point to myself. "It's *my* brain, ya know? The common phrase is 'coping mechanisms.' A brain learns to deal with stressful situations by adapting. And there's a lot going on in these programs. You really have to keep tight control over the push-pull dynamics. I think it's pretty common that people break. I think CORE knew I'd be useless afterward and when I robbed that store and got arrested, I think they just figured it would be too much of a red-tape hassle to get me back just so they could kill me."

"So they let you go to prison."

I nod. "They did."

"And then Charlie found you and sent you here."

"I suppose."

"All right. So…" He leans back in his chair and blows out a breath. "At least we've got a workable plan."

"We do?"

Collin laughs. "Fuck yeah, we do. All we gotta do to free my baby sister from all this evil is kill her puppet master."

18 - Olive

soft chime wakes me and when I open my eyes I'm rewarded with a spectacular view of an approaching thunderstorm through our floor-to-ceiling bedroom windows.

Brose stirs in the bed next to me, his voice thick with sleep. "Turn the chime off, Olive."

For a stickler for rules, he's very hard to wake in the mornings. But that just adds to his appeal, I think. That he likes his sleep.

I reach over, tap the alarm clock, and the chime stops.

"Thank you," he mumbles, his face now under the pillow.

Wait. I lie in bed, confused. "Why does this feel so familiar?"

"It's a dream, Olive," Brose says, his voice muffled by the pillow that's still over his head.

"Oh." I smile. "I'm dreaming."

He lifts the pillow up just a tiny bit, just enough to peek out at me from one open eye. "Wanna fuck before work?"

"If this is a dream, why do we have to work?"

"Good point." Then he grabs me, pulling me into his chest.

I let out a soft squeal and relax. Enjoy the warmth of being close to him.

"We have to go over the rules though," he says.

Which makes me squint. "What rules?"

"You know. *All* the rules. About me and you. And you and Shep. And me and CORE. And you and CORE. And don't even get me started on Collin. I mean, that was kind of unexpected."

"What do you mean?" I try and sit up a little, but he's holding me tightly, so I don't get far and decide to just relax.

"You ran right to him, Olive. Why? I mean, you could've done anything but that and everyone would've been happy. But you went right to him."

I frown. "Who's unhappy?"

"Well, everyone."

"You?"

His hand snakes around my hip, slides up my arm, over my shoulder, and then slips under my chin and across my neck. "Yes. I'm unhappy about it. It's supposed to be me and you, remember? And you just… forgot about me."

"I didn't—"

But his hand tightens on my throat so quick, it startles me. I try to suck in air, but can't. Not even through my nose.

Relax, I tell myself. *Relax, relax, relax.*

When I do, he eases up and suddenly my airway is open again.

None of this is weird. This is his way of correcting my behavior. What is weird is that it didn't turn me on. It *scared* me. Which is a whole other shock and I realize that my body is trembling.

Brose leans into my ear. "What's wrong, Olive? You don't like me anymore? Hmm?" He removes his hand from my throat and places two fingertips on my jaw, turning my head so I'm forced to look him in the eyes. "Who do you like better? Shep?" And as soon as he says Shep's name, he turns into him.

I blink, pulling away.

But Brose just laughs. "Maybe you prefer Collin?" And then Shep's face is gone and Collin's takes its place. "Kinda weird though, right?" His hand slips over my breast. "Being in bed with your brother?"

I gasp and my eyes fly open as I sit up. But I'm still in our room. I'm still at the estate in bed with Brose.

I look down at him, find him smiling, and suddenly nothing makes sense. "What's happening?"

He opens his arms. "Come here. Be with me."

But I was just with him and… it was very weird.

"Olive?"

"What?"

"Why are you hesitating?"

"Is this a dream?"

He smiles at me. But instead of seeing him the way I usually do, I see something else. I see… a viciousness I've never noticed before.

"Olive!"

I jump a little. "What?"

"Should I spank you? You're being bad." These words come out very serious. Not at all playful.

I lean down into his arms, pressing my back into his chest, and let him hold me.

He pets my head like I'm a dog. "That's better," he croons, his low, whispered words finding their way into my ear, making me shiver. "Now. Let's go over everything again, shall we? Who are you?"

I'm about to open my mouth and say, "Olive," but instead I say, "The mission."

He pushes me face first onto the bed and parts the hair

covering my neck so he can lean in and kiss it. "That's right," he says. "My mission is you and your mission is me. Say it."

"My mission is you and your mission is me."

"Again." His voice is louder now.

"My mission is you and your mission is me."

"*Again!*" He yells it.

"My mission is you and your mission is me."

He bites my shoulder, but at the same time he pushes my legs open and slips his fingers between my ass cheeks. "Nice. That was nice. Now you get a reward. I'm in a good mood and you're finally being a good girl, so you get to pick your prize. Choking or spanking?"

I can't answer, because I'm confused.

What is happening?

Where am I?

"Is this a dream?"

"Of course it's a dream, Olive. How else am I here? You *left* me."

"That's not true! You—"

But before I can finish, he's slapped my ass so hard, I gasp.

"Spanking it is," he says.

"No!" I try and get away, scrambling across the bed.

But he grabs my arm and pulls me towards him. Then he flips me over on my back, straddles my hips, pins my shoulders to the bed, and stares down at me with a crazed, psychotic look on his face that I do not recognize.

"You like it. You *LIKE* it!" He's snarling these words at me. "Say it. Tell me you like it, Olive. You better tell me you like it because if you don't—"

Then, as if a switch was flipped, he's calm again, staring down at me with affection and love. He even pushes some hair out of my eyes. "God, you're so beautiful. I love you so much, you know that, right?"

I press my lips together and nod.

"Say it, then. *Say it*, Olive."

"I love you."

He smiles. "Of course you do. We're partners, remember?"

I nod again. "Yes. How could I forget?" And suddenly, all my fear disappears. He's not mean, he's not psychotic, and all of this makes perfect sense. Which makes me feel stupid. So stupid, I laugh. "Oh, my God, what's wrong with me?"

He pets my face, brushing the back of his hand down it. "There's nothing wrong with you, Olive. You're perfect. I should know, I made you this way."

Again, relief washes through me. "Of course you did. Of course I am."

Then he's kissing me, his lips gentle and soft. "Of course you are." He whispers this into my mouth and everything is right with my world. "You love me."

"I love you."

"I am your mission."

"You are my mission."

He sighs, sliding off to the side of me. But his fingertips slide down my stomach, right between my legs. "Good girl. Now you get a reward." He strokes me. Slow, at first, but when I respond by arching my back and breathing heavy, he does more than stroke me, he puts his fingers inside me.

He fucks me like this and when I come, I wake up with my own fingers between my legs.

19 - Brose

My new office in Blackberry Hill is cold and stark compared to what Olive and I had at the estate in Leesburg. One desk, one chair, no windows. The walls are gray, the floors are gray, even the light feels gray.

I don't like it, but no one has ever cared if I liked something or not. Especially when it comes to work. I did bring along one personal item—a framed photograph of Olive and me.

It was last summer—just a few months ago—and we were in the city for a meeting with CORE. And by city, I mean New York, of course. The only one that matters. We were in Central Park, just walking around enjoying the nice day. And I had this urge to buy her a balloon. Back in the old days this would've been a choice of colors. *Do you want red, or blue, or yellow?*

But today, the choices come in the millions because it's one of those trendy vending machines where you pick all kinds of options and it prints it out and fills it up while you wait. The whole thing from start to finish takes about seven minutes.

Olive made a castle. It was like six feet tall and in the form of an arch. And when it was finally all blown up, and she took the string from the robotic hand, she looked at me and said, "We need a picture."

So we stood in the archway and got someone to take our picture as the fantasy castle bobbed around us.

Unlike today, it was a good day.

I'm leaning back in the desk chair, holding the frame of this scene out at arm's length, just staring at Olive Creed as a deep sense of loss flows through me. It's only been a few days since the estate in Leesburg was cleaned out and I was moved down here, but this is the longest we've ever been apart. We've spent the last two years being each other's whole world.

And now I'm alone.

I don't like it.

My office door opens and my grandfather pokes his head in. "You're settling in?"

It's not one of those questions you're meant to answer—not truthfully, at least. But there's a question mark at the end of it, so I appreciate his effort and stand up to force a smile and look him in the eyes. "Perfectly. Come in. I don't have a chair—"

"No," he says, cutting me off. "I didn't come for a visit."

"Of course not." Why would he do that? It might imply that he loves me or something.

"I came to take you to lunch. Up for it?"

"Sure." It beats sitting here pining over the woman I love who is now, and probably forever, out of reach. But I don't say that out loud, of course.

He opens the door wider and waves me through it, then comes up next to me as we travel down the long, mostly dark hallway. I don't understand the aversion to lightbulbs that don't sputter down here, but I've got bigger things to worry about than the décor, or lack thereof, of a deep underground military base.

My grandfather is about eighty-five, I think. I stopped

keeping track when I was ten. He doesn't like birthdays, or holidays, or anything, really. Except work. I might take after him, now that I think about it. But he's not feeble. Not at all feeble. He looks… sixty, maybe younger? He's not the stereotypical grandfather, that's for sure. He's still tall. His shoulders still fill out his uniform, which he still wears even though he's been retired since before I was born.

And, I guess that means, obviously, he never retired.

At any rate, he hasn't aged at all in my mind over the course of my life. He's always been like this. And while he's feared by most, if not all, people in our department—including me—he's nice to have on your side. I certainly wouldn't want him as an enemy.

"How are you liking Blackberry Hill, Ambrose?"

I grimace, not just at my formal name, but at the question itself, but only because we're walking side by side and he can't see me do this. "It's… um… fine."

Which makes my grandfather laugh. It's a rare enough emotion that I actually turn to look at him. "It's a shithole," he says. "Everybody thinks it's a shithole. Especially you, after growing up in my house."

His house. He says it like it's some four-bedroom bungalow on Main Street. It's not. It's not a house at all, it's a forty-thousand-square-foot estate. Something more akin to a museum, actually.

It's not what people might think. You don't just live in a place like that. You're assigned spaces. *You may go here, but not there. You may use this bathroom, but not that one. This is where you're allowed to have food. This is where you're allowed to play indoors. This is where you're allowed to sleep.*

And those were the good old days before I was conscripted

into the Department of Personal Operations at age eight. A department my great-great-grandfather started way back in his day.

All the men in my family have been Personal Operations Directors. Meaning they all ran assets like Olive. Assets that became my great-great grandmother, my great-grandmother, my grandmother, and my mother.

Which is why I'm having a hard time understanding how, exactly, any of this is fair.

Olive didn't fuck up that bad. She made a couple of mistakes. It's our first real job together. Did they really expect perfection?

"Ambrose?"

"Hmm?"

"Did you hear me?"

"I didn't, I'm sorry. I was preoccupied with my own thoughts."

"Of course you were. I'm sure you're wondering how this situation might affect your future."

"I was, actually." We've reached the closest dining hall in this section of the city, so we stop outside it and face each other. "Is that why you're here? To tell me how it ends?"

He smiles and waves a hand at the dining room. "We'll get there. But let's have a drink and a bite to eat."

Over the course of the next hour we have a drink, we eat food, and my grandfather talks about anything and everything *except* me. None of which I find even remotely interesting, even if I knew who or what the fuck he was talking about. It's a whole lot of General Farlow this and Admiral Leary that, and I'm actually making these titles up in my head because he lists off so many fucking 'old friends' of his, they become nothing more than a jumbled mess of names to me.

Finally, the waiters clear our table of dishes, brush all the crumbs off with a sweeper, and we're left with a white tablecloth and a small flickering candle between us.

He puts his hands on the table and folds them together.

"Just… say it." I sigh. "Whatever it is, just tell me."

"You're going to have to… start over."

Start over. A wave of hope fills me. Start over with Olive, he means. "Right." I smile. "Of course. She's not ready. I get it. We'll go back, all the way to the beginning if you want, and—"

"No, Ambrose." He cuts me off. "That's not what I meant."

The sudden wave of hope turns into anger. "Surely you are not telling me that she's not *mine* anymore. You can't be saying that. Because this is how it works, Grandfather. I chose her. You and everyone else in the DPO *approved* it. There's no going back. There's no—"

He puts up a hand, remains completely silent as if he's giving me an opportunity to collect myself, and then lets out a breath. "She's dead, Ambrose. Collin Creed killed her this morning. When she woke up yesterday morning and realized the operation was cut short, she ran to him."

"No. She would never."

"But she did, Ambrose. And then Ean Shephard told him everything. And do you know why Ean Shephard told him everything, Ambrose?"

I just stare at him.

"Do you?" He smiles at me. "You do. Ean Shephard told Collin Creed everything because Olive Creed told Ean Shephard everything. You know better than most what kind of man Collin is. He's ruthless. Olive was nothing to him. You know this. And you had to see it coming. You knew her history, it wasn't perfect. She was…" He pauses, almost as if he's wondering if he should say the next part. But of course he does. "She was *damaged*, Ambrose. This was all in her file. You knew. You understood the risk and, I'm sorry to say, you gambled and you lost. She's gone."

This is when I look around and realize the place has emptied out. When we got here, there were a couple of dozen tables with people at them, but now every single table is empty.

He was afraid I might throw a fit.

I want to. I want to call him a liar. But before I have a chance a waiter appears with a tray. And on the tray is a tablet. The tablet is placed on the table in front of me, and when my grandfather gives a nod, the waiter presses the screen and a video comes to life.

I stare at it. I stare at drone footage of Olive as she and Collin walk down the center of the Edge Security compound. Then it zooms in to another man, standing further down. Ean Shephard.

I look up at my grandfather and he's frowning. "I'm sorry, Ambrose. Not just for the loss of your puppet, but for what comes next for you."

There's not enough time for me to react. Four men, at least, are already behind me and the next thing I know, there's a funny smell in my nose and everything is fading to black.

A SOFT CHIME WAKES ME, but I don't open my eyes. One of the perks of sleeping next to Olive every night is that she turns off the alarm. Instead, I sink deeper into the bed and blankets and put the pillow over my head to enjoy my luck just a little bit longer.

But instead of turning off, the chime keeps going, forcing me to wake and mumble, "Turn the chime off, Olive."

She shuffles next to me, and a moment later, it stops.

"Thank you," I manage to mumble.

"Why does this feel so familiar?"

I sigh, so tired. Really, really, really wanting to go back to sleep. "It's a dream, Olive."

"Oh," she says, and I can tell she's smiling. "I'm dreaming."

It comes out so cute I actually lift the pillow and open one eye to look at her. Sometimes Olive can be nicely put together, like during an important meeting or something like that, but most of the time she comes off disheveled. And when she wakes up in the morning, she comes off as a mess. Hair everywhere, eyes all low and lazy, and usually wearing t-shirts and panties.

I like it. It's so real. Not like some women with all the makeup, and the pretenses, and the clothes. Olive is a what-you-see-is-what-you-get kind of girl.

Of course, I molded her into this girl, but she wouldn't be able to pull it off if she didn't already have it. She's so much better than just an asset. Or a girlfriend, for that matter.

She's my best friend.

I'm still peeking at her with my one open eye and she's gazing back at me looking all tousled and sexy, so I say, "Wanna fuck before work?"

She gives me a coy smile, like she wants to play. "If this is a dream, why do we have to work?"

"Good point." I grab her, making her laugh and squeal, and pull her into my chest, holding her until she relaxes. She snuggles me, and I hold her back, wondering, not for the first time, if she'll forgive me or hold a grudge when the time comes to retire.

"That's up to you," my grandfather says.

And when I look over towards the windows, he's here, in our apartment, sitting in a chair and backlit by the bright rising sun.

I blink and he's gone. But his words linger.

Will she love me or hate me when this is over?

It's up to me. Everything she does is up to me. *I think for her, she acts for me.*

"We have to go over the rules though," I say.

I can feel Olive's confusion. "What rules?"

"You know. *All* the rules. About me and you. And you and Shep. And me and CORE. And you and CORE. And don't even get me started on Collin. I mean, that was kind of unexpected."

"What do you mean?" Olive tries to lift her head up off my chest, but I hold her tight, not letting go. It's a metaphor, I think. She doesn't try hard, just gives in like she's been trained to, and relaxes.

"You ran right to him, Olive." I don't mention how pissed off everyone is—and by everyone, I mean my grandfather—but Olive knows me well enough to hear it in my voice. "Why? I mean, you could've done anything but that and everyone would've been happy. But you went right to him."

"Who's unhappy?" she asks.

"Well, everyone."

"You?"

My hand snakes around her hip, slides up her arm, over her shoulder, and then slips under her chin and across her neck. "Yes. I'm unhappy about it. It's supposed to be me and you, remember? And you just… forgot about me."

"I didn't—"

That's as far as she gets because my hand tightens on her throat so quick, it startles her. And I can feel her struggling to suck in air, but she's unable to. She likes the choking. It's sick. I'm sick because I'm the one who programmed her to feel this way about it.

But I like it too. Otherwise, why do it?

I know in her mind she's panicking. It's just a normal response to being choked. But she's well-trained and, after a couple of seconds, she relaxes. Utterly and completely. As if she's got no will to live and wants me to strangle her to death.

I would never do that and the moment I feel her relax, I ease back and let her breathe.

Usually, after I let go, she starts begging me to fuck her. Or she crawls into my lap and starts kissing me. Sometimes, if I'm sitting in a chair, she just kneels down and tries to suck my dick.

But everything is different this time because she goes absolutely stiff. I'm thinking about this reaction when she starts trembling. Which is a sign of fear.

Of course, I know she fears me. She *must* fear me. If she doesn't, and I'm not there to pull her strings, she might make her own decisions and that would be bad. But her fear doesn't often manifest after being choked. She's been programmed to find it exciting and provocative.

So I'm confused.

"What's wrong, Olive? You don't like me anymore? Hmm?" I remove my hand from her throat and place two fingertips on her jaw, turning her head, forcing her to look me in the eye. "Who do you like better? Shep?"

And then I make her see him instead of me. I project his face into her mind and become him.

Olive starts blinking rapidly, pulling away from me.

But I laugh. "Maybe you prefer Collin?" And then I make her

see him. "Kinda weird though, right?" My hand slips over her breast. "Being in bed with your brother?"

This breaks her, as it was meant to. And she blacks out, going limp in my arms for a reset.

I shouldn't play around with the illusions like that, but I like it. It's fun. And anyway, I hardly ever do it. Not anymore.

Olive goes stiff, then she gasps and sits up in a panic. I allow it because she's always confused after a reset. Instead of being angry, I decide to enjoy what comes next. Which is a correction. Because she's not allowed to think. *I'm* the one who thinks. *She's* the one who acts.

Those are the rules. And if she starts thinking, she's breaking them.

She's breaking *us*.

"What's happening?" Olive asks.

I open my arms wide. "Come here. Be with me."

She looks down at me, still confused. It doesn't wipe her memory, this reset. It adjusts her perception. So she remembers that she saw something weird.

"Olive?"

"What?"

"Why are you hesitating?"

"Is this a dream?"

I smile at her. She's so sweet. But instead of responding to my smile and reacting appropriately, she gazes at my face with a blank stare, as if she's getting lost in it. "Olive!" I snap.

She jumps. "What?"

"Should I spank you? You're being bad." My voice is not playful anymore. I'm very annoyed that she's not reacting in her typical, well-trained manner.

She doesn't answer me, just settles back into the bed,

pressing herself into my chest so I can hold her. And then I pet her head like the good girl she is. "That's better," I croon into her neck. She shivers. "Now. Let's go over everything again, shall we? Who are you?"

She is this close to saying her own name, and I am equally close to twisting her nipple until she screams. But she catches herself and gives me the correct answer. "The mission."

I flip her over on her face, pressing her shoulders into the bed. Then I part her hair along the back of her neck and lean in to kiss that little dent where her spine meets her skull. "That's right," I whisper. "My mission is you and your mission is me. Say it."

She does. "My mission is you and your mission is me."

"Again." My voice a bit louder now.

"My mission is you and your mission is me."

"Again!" I yell it.

"My mission is you and your mission is me."

I bite her shoulder while simultaneously pushing her legs open so I can slide my fingers down her ass cheeks and right up to her pussy. "Nice," I tell her. "That was nice. Now you get a reward. I'm in a good mood and you're finally being a good girl, so you get to pick your prize. Choking or spanking?"

I wait. One second. Two seconds. Three seconds. Finally, she says, "Is this a dream?"

"Of course it's a dream, Olive. How else am I here? You *left* me."

"That's not true! You—"

I slap her ass so hard, she yelps. "Spanking it is," I say.

"No!" She tries to get away, scrambling across the bed.

But I just grab her by the arm and pull her back. Then I flip her over on her back, straddle her hips, pin her shoulders to the bed, and stare down at her frightened face.

"You like it," I yell. "You *LIKE* it!" These words are coming out like an angry snarl. "Say it. Tell me you like it, Olive. You better tell me you like it because if you don't—"

Something inside of me… flips. Or… flicks. Or… something.

All the anger drains out and I'm calm again.

Reset.

I was out of control. I was… never mind. It's not important.

Olive is important.

I look down at her again, feeling *so* lucky. "God, you're so beautiful. I love you so much, you know that, right?"

She looks me straight in the eyes, pressing her lips together as she nods.

"Say it, then. *Say it*, Olive."

"I love you."

I chuckle, smiling. "Of course you do. We're partners, remember?"

She nods again. "Yes. How could I forget?" And then she laughs. "Oh, my God, what's wrong with me?"

I pet her face. Her cheek is so smooth. I do this gently, brushing the back of my hand down her youthful skin. "There's nothing wrong with you, Olive. You're perfect. I should know, I made you this way."

She lets out a long sigh, like my words comfort her. "Of course you did. Of course I am."

And she's so fucking cute with her disheveled look and all her messy edges, I have an overwhelming urge to kiss her. So I do. I wouldn't be able to stop myself even if I tried. This kiss is gentle and soft, meant to heal any discord between us and put us back on the right track. "Of course you are," I whisper right into her mouth. "You love me."

"I love you," she agrees.

"I am your mission."

"You are my mission," she repeats.

I let out a long sigh of relief as I slide off to the side of her. "Good girl. Now you get a reward." I stroke her slow, at first, but when she responds by arching her back and panting, I push my fingers inside her.

Slowly moving them in and out until she comes and I wake up.

But Olive is not in bed next to me, there is no room, there is nothing now.

I'm all alone.

And in the dark.

"Wrong," my grandfather says. And then a light appears. A spotlight that's only meant for him. "Boy, you're never alone. You know this."

I nod, then look down at myself and realize I'm naked. I look back up at my grandfather and find him smiling.

"You're a helluva specimen, Ambrose. But of course you are. You come from my bloodline, so I expect nothing less. You're not embarrassed that I'm looking at you, right?"

I am, but I shake my head no.

"Good," my grandfather says. "Because it's time and we don't want any complications, do we, Ambrose?"

Again, I shake my head no. But secretly, I'm thinking that a complication or two might do me some good right about now.

My grandfather is pleased. "Despite your father's failures, I always knew you'd be good at this. I was good at this and you take after me, not him. You did a very good job with your asset. She's the future. You should be very proud of yourself."

He's talking about Olive, I understand that part. But I'm not really following along with what he's *not* saying just yet. I've learned over the years to just… fake it until you make it, ya know?

So that's what I do. I show no emotion. I do not react. I become his asset. Because that's what I am. *He thinks for me, I act for him.*

"Are you ready, Ambrose?"

"Yes." I do not hesitate. I don't know what he's talking about, but I don't *need* to know. *He thinks for me, I act for him.*

"Good. Let's begin."

20 - Shep

We're just exiting the church when I ask Collin the obvious question. "So do you have a plan? For how, exactly, we're gonna kill this puppet master? Because he could be anyone."

Collin pans his hand down the driveway towards his house and we head that direction. "Well, they wouldn't go to all the trouble of buildin' some secret speakeasy in the middle of the fuckin' woods if it wasn't some kind of home base, right?"

My eyebrows shoot up. "You wanna send in a team?"

He shrugs. Like putting together a hit team to take out a shadow-government honeypot is just another one of his available services. "Why not? We've got an army. If I can't use everything I have at my disposal to save my baby sister, then what is the point of all this?"

He's not wrong. And if I were him, and I owned a private security company that amounted to a small army filled with damaged killers, I'd be thinking the same thing. If you can't save the ones you love, what's the point of any of it?

"But first," Collin says, "we need to call up Penny Rider and you need to give her permission to tell us what she found."

I scoff. "You need my permission?"

"Penny's on the up and up. She doesn't break the rules for us.

She doesn't break the rules for anyone. She's just very good at working within them so we can get the information we need. She pulled you aside because she never had any intention of telling me about it. In her mind, it was none of my business. I asked her to find a way to tell if you were lying. She did that. You weren't. And that was the end of her commitment to me. So, do you have a problem with giving this permission?"

"With her telling you? No. I can't say for sure what this brain wave shit was, but it's got to be residual. Leftovers from the programming."

"Programming," Collin sneers. "Nice."

I raise an eyebrow at him, stopping at the bottom of his porch steps. "You think you *weren't* programmed? Because Disciple, West Virginia, is a cult if ever there was one."

"Maybe." He doesn't disagree. Not outright. "But it's a pretty fuckin' innocent one compared to this CORE shit. My childhood was spent pretending to be a happy, old-timey son of a preacher man whose life revolved around a tourist-attraction tent revival. What these people did to my sister once she left Disciple was flat-out mind-control."

Again, he's not wrong.

"So are you in, Shep? Because I get it. You've got no loyalty to us yet. You've been here two weeks. If you don't wanna come—"

"I do," I say, cutting him off. "I'm here now." I look around a little. At all the men, and the dogs, and the houses. Then I look back at Collin. "It's pretty much the nicest place I've ever seen in my life."

He smiles and looks down the driveway. "Good. That's the vibe we were goin' for."

"So I'm in. And anyway—" I hesitate here.

But he catches this hesitation. "Anyway what?"

I shrug. "I like her."

"Olive?"

"Yeah. I like her. She's… well, let's just leave it there."

Collin side-eyes me. "Yeah. Maybe we better. But listen, I need to go make some plans. Can you stay here and watch Olive? We should really keep an eye on her until we know what's goin' on."

"Sure. I can do that."

"Good. I'll text you Penny's number. Call her up and just give her permission to talk to us. Then I can get all the details from her so we know what we're dealing with. Do not mention Olive. Do not mention anything about what we're doin' here."

"Won't say a word."

Collin nods his approval, then he shakes my hand and walks away.

I don't go back inside the house. Not right away. I just sit on the porch steps and wait for the text as I watch the goings-on around me—the dogs, the men, and everything in between. And as I do this, I find myself wondering what time Cross gets off school. Because he's gonna be mad at me if I haven't checked a single thing off his damn list by the time he gets home.

Just thinking these words in my head makes me smile.

Two weeks. That's how long I've been here. That's all it took for me to *want* it. This life that Edge is offering me. It's a real second chance. Something I never thought I'd have. Something I probably don't even deserve.

My phone buzzes in my pocket. I fish it out and read the text from Collin. It's short and to the point, which is typical of him. *Here's the number, call her up, give her permission to talk to me.*

So I stand up and make the call.

Penny picks up first ring. "I don't recognize this number, so state your name and business and be quick about it."

"Uh… Penny? This is Shep—I mean, Ean Shephard. We met on Saturday when—"

"I might be old, but I'm not senile, Mr. Shephard. Of course I remember you. It was five days ago. What is it that you need?"

"Well, what you and I were talking about on Saturday? Collin told me to call you and give you permission to tell him all about it."

"Hmm." She pauses here after her little hum. "So you're in."

"In?"

"You're going to be one of them. The Edge."

"Yeah. I guess I am."

"Well, Mr. Shephard, this is not a conversation for this phone line so I'm going to take some precautions."

"OK. What's that mean?"

"It means I'm going to send a courier to deliver a package. You'll know what to do once it arrives."

"How long will that take? Just so I can tell Collin?"

"Few hours. Talk then."

The call ends and I let out a breath, feeling a little more stressed than I was because I wasn't expecting her explanation would require end-to-end voice encryption, which is obviously what she's talking about.

I text Collin, letting him know what's up. He texts me back a thumbs-up, but nothing else.

So now, I wait.

But I decide to go back inside Collin's house to do that, even though it feels a little strange to be alone in his personal space. I look up and around, wondering if there are cameras in here. Probably? I would assume, actually. But then again, he lives here with his wife or whatever she is. Women get funny about cameras, so I'm not sure. I don't see any, but this operation isn't called Edge because it's behind the times. Whatever cameras Collin and company are using, it is highly likely that they're nearly invisible.

Which means... eventually, he's gonna see what Olive and I did in that guest room of his.

This makes me blow out a breath. But it's done. There's no take-backs. So I put these thoughts away for another time and walk down the hallway to check on Olive.

She's asleep, but under the covers now. Which means at some point she woke up, put herself under those covers, and then went back to sleep.

What is going on with this girl?

And how does it involve me?

Because it most certainly does involve me. In some way, at least. It cannot be coincidence that I walked into that bar and she was the first person I met. It's just not.

I haven't thought about CORE much since everything went sideways. In fact, I put the whole thing out of my mind while I was in prison. I liked it there. I mean, eventually I'm sure I would've seen it for what it was. But for me it was a timeout. It was permission to think. To figure things out. To be left alone. To pick apart what I could remember and fit it in to what I already knew. To heal, if that's possible. Five years was long enough to get my head right.

People have cell phones in lock-up. There's internet, even if the prisoners aren't always allowed to access it—the wireless is everywhere now. But it wasn't in every corner of every space in the prison. It wasn't like the SCIF with the vacuum feeling when the door closed. But it was better than being in a fuckin' city where the electromagnetic waves are pretty much everywhere. There's no way to get away from it and I'm kinda sensitive to those waves.

They bother me.

That's why I was in Wyoming to begin with. At least I think it was. It's hard to recall what it was like to be me back then. I was insane, I think. I'd been institutionalized twice for erratic behavior. But there's no real will to keep the insane separate from the public these days, let alone the desire to get them some help. So I was let go after a seventy-two-hour hold both times.

But Wyoming is… empty.

And unless you've lived there, you can't really imagine it. Probably Alaska is like that too. But Wyoming is just about the only real place you can go in the lower forty-eight where the wireless can't really get a hold of you the way it does in crowded places.

I would not say I liked prison, but I needed it.

And this brings me back around to Olive, still sleeping in the bed. I think she needs some silence. So I close the door, go back outside, and sit on the steps.

I like her. I would like to help her, if I can.

And maybe get a second chance with her as well.

She comes off as vulnerable. Innocent. Which is a hard thing to pull off after begging an almost-stranger to literally choke an orgasm out of her.

It's a deception. I know this. I know people like her. I know CORE. But even so, and knowing what I know, she still comes off in all these ways.

Which is dangerous.

I chuckle, looking around at all the even more dangerous men and their K9 partners. I guess, if you're a young woman who's been handled the way she has, this is definitely the place to be if you wanna get right with yourself and not be all alone in the process.

EVERY TEN MINUTES or so I go inside to check on Olive, but each time she's still sleeping so I come back out to the porch and wait, just watching all the activity on the compound. After what seems like hours, I finally see Collin making his way back to the house. Amon is with him and even from this distance I can tell they're having a conversation, which is cut off as they approach me.

I stand up and let out a long breath as they come up the steps.

"How is she?" Collin nods his head towards the front door to indicate Olive.

"Sleeping," I say. "I've checked on her every ten minutes or so since you left. I guess she's tired."

Collin nods, then looks at Amon, who holds up a medium-sized white envelope that has already been opened. "Let's do it then," Amon says, his drawl matching Collin's almost perfectly. He pulls out a burner phone and powers it up as Collin and I lean in, trying to get a better look.

An empty blue screen becomes a logo of sorts. "What's that?" I ask, pointing to it.

"Penny," Amon says plainly. But that's all the explanation I get because he's pressing buttons and the logo disappears to reveal a contact menu with a single option: *Call.*

Amon looks up from the phone and directs his gaze to Collin. "Ready?"

Collin nods.

Amon taps the screen.

There are a few seconds of silence and then a low, distinct ringing that reminds me of what it sounds like when calling overseas, but not exactly. There's a click, then another click, then another.

After that, there's Penny. "All right, who am I talking to?"

"Collin," Collin says. "Amon and Shep are here too."

"All right. And just so we're clear, you're OK with me revealing some of your history to Collin and Amon, Mr. Shephard?"

I don't like that Collin and Amon are on a first-name basis and I'm still Mr. Shephard. So I start with that before answering her question. "It's Shep. You don't have to call me Mr. Shephard. And yeah. You can say what you need to say. I don't mind."

"Very well, Shep. Collin?" she says, redirecting. "How familiar are you with the Covert Operations for Research and Espionage?"

"Well," Collin says, "I'm pretty sure that's where the acronym CORE comes from, but other than that, nothin'."

"Hmm," Penny hums. Then takes a moment to think. There is a lot of clicking on this line to indicate that software is running in the background for the encryption, so while it's a pause, it's not a silence. "Sorry for my delay in response. I'm just trying my best to come up with a plausible reason why no one ever mentioned CORE to you. Especially when you were an ancillary part of it. But that's a mystery for another day. Today I'm going to focus on Shep and Olive."

When I glance at Collin, there's some tension in his forehead and he looks a little worried. "OK," he says. "Should I be sittin' down or somethin'?"

"No. I am not in possession of the kind of details that would require you to sit, so feel free to stand. I'm going to say some things and you need to take it all at face value. I will not be providing proof of any kind, I will not be naming any names, and I will not be divulging anything that is not directly related to Shep or Olive."

Collin looks like he's got questions about these stipulations, but Amon says, "Sounds fair," before he can ask them.

"All, right," Penny replies. "Let's get into it." What comes next is a history lesson in liars. "JFK once warned about the dangers of secrecy in a free society. But what we're dealing with here goes far beyond secrecy, Collin. It's about control." Her voice is steady and strong. Not loud, not soft. She's very practical. Almost emotionless. When I met with her at the hospital she came across as knowledgeable, competent, and discreet. And this is how she comes off now too.

"And when I say control," Penny continues, "I'm not just referring to controlling the justice system, the military, the economy, or even the highest office in the land. Those things are very easy to control. It doesn't take much for certain forces to mold these systems into anything they desire. There are many ways to control the power of others and make it your own. Bribes and blackmail, just to name two. But there's always been a gap between the people in power and the people they hold power over. Are you following me?"

Amon and I both look at Collin as he nods. "Yeah," he says. "I get it."

"I'm sure you do," Penny says, and I can almost hear her smile. "Well, there's always been a sort of bottleneck in regards to this control over people. Well, I take that back. Always is much too strong a word. Let me just be plain here. They've solved the issue of how to control people. With the masses, they do it with propaganda. Pop culture, music, art, film, books, advertising. You get the point. But that applies mainly to groupthink. Controlling groups is fun to them, but not as useful as controlling individuals."

I let out a long, involuntary sigh. Because I see where this is going. Collin and I were just talking about it this morning, but I only have access to so much information. Personal experience, mostly. Everything I said about Olive was a guess. And I didn't tell Collin anything about me. Not because I couldn't put it together if I really tried, but because I don't wanna know what happened to me. I really don't.

Penny doesn't care about what I want, so she just keeps talking. "They've been working on ways to control and influence the minds of individuals since the late 1700s when mesmerism became popular. From there, the focus switched to hypnotism, then psychoanalysis, then behaviorism and conditioning. These days, it's much, *much* more than suggestions. It's neuroscience. It's technology. In fact, modern mind control is about neural implants and quantum entanglement."

Collin, Amon, and I are all looking at each other as Penny finishes. Amon blinks. "I'm sorry, Penny. What the fuck does that even mean?"

"It's very complicated, Amon. But what I'm getting at is that Shep is a part of this program."

Amon looks at me, his brow all furrowed. "You've got a brain implant?"

Before I can answer, Penny says, "No. He doesn't. And we know this for sure because we scanned his brain last weekend."

"So," Collin says, "it's the other thing. The entanglement."

"That's right, Collin," Penny says. "He and his partner were one of the first to go through the program. I won't go into details about the principles behind the science, mostly because I don't understand it myself. But the takeaway is that… well… it didn't work. Shep can fill you in on the specifics of that because I don't know, to be honest. What I do know is that evidence of the procedure he went through is still in his brain. That's what they found, Shep. Proof that you were a part of that program."

All of us go silent for a moment. Thinking.

Then Collin asks the obvious. "Penny, do you have any information about my sister, Olive?"

Penny blows out a long breath and doesn't immediately answer. I get a bad feeling in my stomach, even though I already know what she's gonna say. But still, when it comes out, I'm floored. Because she says, "Collin, I'm sure there's a reason for this question and I'm sure you've already got your suspicions, so I'm just going to cut to the chase. Olive and her partner were the first successful results of this entanglement program and they were both released into full active duty about six months ago."

21 - Olive

I ***sit up in bed***, the memories of sex with Brose still fresh in my head, but I'm not in our room at the estate. I'm in Collin's house. In his guest room.

I just sit there in bed like this, propped up and looking at the window, trying to put the dream behind me. Not because I was afraid, though it was a bit frightening, but because it was so real.

I felt him.

I heard him.

It was real.

So real, I start looking around for Brose.

Did he follow me here? Shep is gone, so maybe Brose somehow broke in?

It's a ludicrous idea. I'm in the Edge Security compound. He would never be able to sneak in here.

It was just a dream.

I get up out of bed, reaching for my pants, which are strewn on the floor, and pull them back on.

What just happened?

I don't know.

But then I remember something.

My vow. My promise. My reason for living.

My mission is him and his mission is me.

And then the next part. The part he didn't need to remind me of in that dream.

He thinks for me, I act for him.

"Brose," I say, whispering his name out loud. "Where are you?"

Voices from outside startle me back into reality and I go completely still, listening.

Collin, Shep, Amon. And then another voice. They're on speakerphone with someone. I carefully walk over to the bedroom door, which isn't fully closed, and tap it open so I can peek into the living room down the hallway.

They're outside, not in here, so I creep out, trying to hear what they are saying. Whoever the woman is they are talking to, she says my name.

I walk faster, all the way over to the front door, and press my ear into the crack between the door and the wall.

"Who is this partner?" Collin is asking.

There's a pause, and then the woman on the phone says, "I don't have confirmation yet, but this came from a trusted source. His name is Ambrose Sinclair."

Brose! This woman just told my brother my biggest secret! We've been made! Our cover is blown, the mission is bust, and... and... well, I don't know what happens next, but Brose put everything on the line for this mission. He put everything on the line for *me*.

And I fucked it all up—again—by running to my brother. That's what my dream was about. *You ran right to him, Olive,* Brose said. *Everyone's unhappy.*

CORE is gonna take us out of service. Our first real mission and we've blown it. It's over. And I did that.

"Ambrose Sinclair," Collin says, snapping me back into the

conversation outside. His voice is low and threatening. "Where might I find this Ambrose Sinclair?"

"Oh, shit!" I say. "He's mad. He's gonna kill him!"

"No, he's not, Olive." I startle, looking over to my right, and find Brose sitting in a chair. "Your brother hasn't got a chance in hell of killing me now."

I… I'm so confused. I don't know what to think. "Brose?" I whisper. Then I blink a few times, trying to clear my head. "Am I still dreaming?"

"Don't be silly," he says. "Look at yourself. You're not in bed. You're here. You're walking around. You're real, Olive."

"Well, of course *I'm* real. But you… how did you get here?"

He smiles at me. "I followed you, of course."

"They know," I say, pointing at the window. "Some lady just told Collin about you. They know about us, Brose."

"Yep." He nods, seemingly unconcerned. "They know. But it doesn't matter anymore."

"What do you mean?"

"You *did it*, Olive." He stands up, walks over to me, places both hands on my shoulders, and beams a smile down at me. "You did it. We're here."

"They *know*!" I say.

"Who cares?" And then his hands slide up to my face, holding me as his lips connect with mine. His kiss is soft, and long, and perfect. "You're in," he whispers. "It's going well. We're all proud of you."

"Proud of me? But in the dream—"

He pulls back, angry now. "This isn't a dream. It's *real*."

"But I was dreaming. I was sleeping. And you told me that I was bad." I pout a little here, making my lips all puffy.

"Well, of course I did, darling. You like punishment and I wanted to make you feel good. You *LIKE it, remember?*"

He yells this last part and I panic, looking out the window, because surely Collin heard that. But the three of them are still having their phone conversation.

"Look at *me*," Brose says, jerking my head to the side. "This is very important, Olive. We are the first successful entanglement. You're in. Congratulations. But now is when the job really starts and I need you to focus."

"But…" I shake my head. "None of this makes sense. How are you here? How—"

He grabs me by the hair with both hands, fisting it as he shakes me. "Listen to me. We have two more objectives, OK? There isn't time to explain. Remember our promise? Hmm?" He softens again, leaning down to kiss my lips. "Do you remember?"

"My mission is you and your mission is me."

"That's right," he coos into my ear. "That's right. We are the mission. And what's the other rule? Hmm? Can you say it so I know you're here, and present, and willing to work?"

He takes his kiss to my neck and my shoulders relax. "You think for me, I act for you."

"Yes. You're so perfect," he says. And these words slide right into my ear, making a chilling tingle shoot through my whole body. "I'm gonna fuck you so hard when I see you again."

For a moment, I'm confused. When he *sees me* again? I'm standing right here. He's kissing my neck. His hands are wandering over my body. One gripping my breast, the other sliding right between my legs.

I'm about to come undone standing a few feet from my

brother, with only a wall between us. So what does that mean, when he sees me again?

But before I can articulate this question out loud, the front door opens and I turn, startled, looking straight into Collin's unnerving eyes.

He blinks. Smiles. "Olive. You're awake."

I look at Brose, panicked. "I… he… he's my friend."

Brose is shaking his head at me. "Shut up, Olive, don't say anything."

"What?" Collin asks, looking around the room. "Who's your friend? Shep?"

This is when I see Shep and Amon behind him. I turn back to Brose as he says, "Kill him, Olive. Right now. You just gave away our secret and now you need to kill him."

I hesitate.

But then Brose is kissing me again, squeezing my breast and pumping my pussy. And all the while he's kissing me, he's whispering, "I think for you, you act for me. And I want you to *kill him*. Kill him, Olive. Kill him right now!"

Then Brose turns me around and pushes me towards the door, forcing Collin to open his arms to catch me. His eyes are filled with confusion. "Olive? Are you OK?"

I reach for his gun, snap it out of the holster with practiced accuracy, point it at his face, and pull the trigger.

22 - Shep

I see it happening—Olive, so confused. Collin, reaching for her to see if she's OK. And then a blur of motion as she grabs his sidearm, points it at his face, and pulls the trigger.

There is a click.

A misfire.

Then silence.

Then chaos.

Collin reacts the way I'd expect him to. One moment the gun is aimed between his eyes, the next Olive is face down on the ground and he's handing the weapon to Amon. Collin's knee is pressed into Olive's back and he's yelling, "Get her hands! Get her fuckin' hands!"

Amon is stuffing the gun into his pants, so I grab her hands while Collin takes his knee off her back and hauls her to her feet.

She's not yelling or being crazy, she's just whispering something, over and over again. "You think for me, I act for you. You think for me, I act for you."

Collin points to a small chest of drawers near the front door. "Get me a zip, Amon. Quick."

The fact Collin Creed has zip ties in a drawer near his front door says a lot about him that I will think more about later on, but for now, I hold Olive while Amon and Collin secure her. And the whole time, she just keeps whispering. Like she's not even here. Like she's not even aware of what's goin' on.

They haul her outside—Amon has one arm, Collin has the other, and he is not being gentle as they go down the porch steps, leaving me behind.

For a moment, I don't know what to do. I just watch them.

And then there's the telltale squeaking of brakes and when I look all the way down the driveway, I see a yellow school bus stoppin' at the guard house.

My head is pounding and my heart is racing as I watch the bus get checked through security and make its way down the driveway. Then I just stand there stupidly on the porch of Collin's house as Cross jumps down the bus steps, smiling.

It's so surreal to see his happy face, I have trouble processing it for a moment. Because how could it be that this morning when he left there was no Olive at Edge Security and by the time he got home, she had almost killed Collin Creed and is now a prisoner?

"Shep?" Cross asks. "Are you OK?" When I don't answer, he looks over his shoulder. "Who's that lady my dad and Collin are haulin' off?"

I let out a long breath, force a smile, and say, "I didn't get a chance to get through your list today."

"What?" Now he's annoyed. "But why?"

"It's a long story. Maybe your dad'll tell you about it tonight. But for now, I'd really like to go train a puppy for a little bit, if you don't mind."

Most kids his age would start asking questions. But I have a feeling that Cross isn't anything like most kids his age. Because all he does is look over his shoulder one more time as Amon and Collin take Olive into the church.

When Cross looks back at me, he's not a little kid anymore. He presses his lips together and nods. "I see. Well, let me put my pack in the house and we can go do that."

Jagger is too **young** to do any serious training, so Cross and I take him to the big grassy area in the middle of the compound where there are still a few guys working with dogs and just play tug and fetch with him. Cross talks the whole time, telling me about his day. How some teacher assigned stupid homework. How some girl he likes shot him a smile during lunch. Then he goes into a whole monologue about how she's from Bishop and it's never gonna work out, but he still likes her, and anyway, he's too young to date.

And eventually, as I listen to his free therapy session without comment, not even understanding this whole issue with liking a girl from Bishop, I calm down. The pounding in my head becomes more of a dull whooshing and my heart is only trottin' instead of galloping.

What. The fuck. Just happened?

Olive Creed just shot her brother in the head, that's what happened.

I mean, obviously, she didn't. The gun jammed.

But she did. She *did*.

And it's blowing my mind.

She almost killed him. She almost blew his fuckin' brains out right in front of me.

And then all sorts of things start running through my head.

How this is pretty much exactly what Collin did to her father when they were kids.

Does that mean anything?

I don't know.

But then I remember what she was saying afterward—*You think for me, I act for you.* And it makes sense. She was triggered and she was being handled.

I let out a breath and look at Cross, suddenly realizing that he's been quiet for a minute.

He squints his eyes at me. "You OK, Shep?"

I nod. But I'm not sure I am. Because they triggered her. How? How did they do it? I tell Cross, "Would you be mad if I cut out so I could go and talk to Collin for a bit?"

Cross doesn't smile immediately. He's a kid, after all. So he's gotta think about these words and what they actually mean for a moment before he catches on. But he does catch on. "Nah. You're boring, Shep. I'm gonna take Jagger home now and do my homework. See ya tomorrow."

Then he picks up the puppy and walks away.

"Yep," I say. "Tomorrow." But I'm already heading across the driveway to the church.

Inside it's dark and quiet and I have no idea where they took Olive. I walk over to the door Collin and I went through earlier that leads to the basement, but there's a serious lock on it, so I don't even try the handle. I can't leave until I talk to one of them, so I just take myself over to a table and have a seat to wait it out.

You think for me, I act for you. These words run through my head on repeat as I wait. Obviously, it's part of her programming. And the person she's referring to is her handler. When Collin asked what Penny knew about Olive, she was as forthcoming as she could be. She gave us a name, at least. Ambrose Sinclair. Some guy about my age who comes from a CORE legacy family overseas. But that's about all Penny knew. Or, at the very least, all she was willing to tell us.

Collin had heard enough for one day, apparently, because he promised to burn the phone and ended the call with, "Thank you and talk soon."

Then we came inside to check on Olive.

A door to my right, on the opposite side of the one that leads to the SCIF in the basement, opens and Amon appears, pulling me out of my reverie. "Hey," he barks. "Collin wants to talk to you." He nods his head at the door he's holding open.

I get up and follow him into a dark hallway that leads to another door. It looks similar to the one they have on the SCIF, but it doesn't lead to a room specially shielded from electromagnetic frequencies, it leads to a jail.

A very sterile-looking high-tech modern jail. And for the first time, I start to really wonder what the actual fuck these boys are up to. Why the hell do they need a jail?

Not that I'm complaining, because in these circumstances, it's handy. But it's not normal.

There are four cells, two on each side. And it's not some old-timey jail with bars or anything like that. It's polycarbonate glass and from the visibly bluish tint, it's got some very serious bulletproofing. While I don't know for certain, I'm guessing that it's been modified on the inside so that the prisoner can't see out. There are cameras set up inside the cells, but not anything an occupant might be able to tamper with because they're very small and set up into the ceiling.

The floor is some kind of non-slip metal composite, and if I were to take another guess, I'd predict there are a lot of sensors in that floor. Probably measuring vitals and tracking movement.

Each room has a stainless-steel bed bolted to the wall and a toilet-sink combo unit, but that's it.

Olive is on the floor facing into a corner. Her knees are pulled up to her chest and she's rockin' herself back and forth.

Collin looks at me and nods his head to his sister. "What the hell is this?"

"She won't talk," Amon says. "It's like she shut down."

"Did you hear what she was saying afterward?"

Collin shakes his head. "No. I wasn't even capable of hearing."

"I didn't hear shit, either," Amon adds.

Which isn't surprising. It was a shock and they were both living inside that shock in the immediate aftermath.

"She was whispering these words. 'You think for me, I act for you.' I don't know how it works—I really don't. But she was not... here." I point to the floor. "She was not in the moment with us. She was somewhere else. And these words—'You think for me, I act for you'—it's part of her programming."

"What kind of programming?" Collin asks.

I can only shrug. "I don't know."

"But you were one of them. You're like *her*." Amon is angry now.

"I'm not like her, Amon. I mean, maybe the training was similar, but I don't even remember much about what they did. I have lost a lot of years of memory. I don't even remember my handler's name, you guys. I don't even know her name anymore. I can't see her face. She's nothing but a blur when I try and think about it."

Amon doesn't believe me, but Collin lets out a breath, fully understanding that I'm a dead end. He looks at his friend. "Can you call Penny back and tell her we need that MRI machine again? ASAP. Don't tell her anything about what happened, she won't want to know anyway. Just tell her we need it." Then he looks at me. "We need to compare your brains. Go back to your bunk and have chow, or whatever. I'll let you know when we get it set up."

"But—" I hesitate.

Collin narrows his eyes at me. "But what?"

"Maybe I could stay with her. Talk to her. See if I can get her to snap out of it."

"No," Amon says immediately. "That's a bad idea."

But it's Collin's decision, not Amon's. And he doesn't answer. Just kinda gazes off into the distance for a few moments, like he's thinking.

"It's a bad idea, Collin," Amon insists. "There's something wrong with his brain."

But when Collin turns back to us, it's clear that he's come to a different conclusion. "If I let you stay, you'll be in there with her."

"OK."

"Why would you agree to that?" Amon asks, clearly not OK with this.

"Because, Amon, I like her. We were gettin' to know each other. And I don't like this." I point to her, all hunched up and rocking in the corner. "She needs support, not abandonment. I don't know what she's been through, not the details, but it doesn't take much imagination to fill them in." Now I look at Collin. "This is a desperate hour. Maybe her *most* desperate. She needs someone who gives a fuck."

"I give a fuck," Collin growls at me. "But you were there. You saw what she did. The only reason I'm alive right now is because my gun misfired. Which is some kind of fuckin' miracle because I clean that gun twice a week. It doesn't misfire. So yeah, I give a fuck. That's why she was in my house to begin with. What if Lowyn had stayed home with her today? What if something happened to Lowyn?"

Lowyn is his woman, I guess. I don't know her, so I just don't have the same feelings about it as he does. I would not say I know Olive, either, but I think I understand her. "I get it," I tell Collin. "I'm not saying you don't give a fuck, I'm simply saying that I might give a little more."

"Why?" Amon asks. And he's snarlin' at me now. "You said you just met her."

"I did. But…" I let out a breath and look right at Collin. "Look, we've been intimate. It's been building up to it from the beginning. It hasn't been a casual thing, OK? There's a connection here."

"Yeah, it's some brainwashing thing," Amon shoots back.

But again, this isn't up to Amon. So I only look at Collin. "That's sad," I say, pointing to his baby sister. "That's all I've got to say. It's sad. And why leave her alone if someone is willing to stay with her?"

"Fine," Collin says.

"It's a mistake," Amon objects.

Collin points to me. "You can go in." His eyes narrow down into little slits. "But I've got eyes and ears on you, Shep. And these are the most advanced eyes and ears you could ever imagine. So let's just be clear here, you will *not* be alone with my sister."

"Agreed."

Collin turns to Amon. "Open the door."

Amon turns, walking down the aisle of cells towards what I imagine to be a guard room, but the whole time he's muttering, "It's a mistake. It's a big fucking mistake."

Collin doesn't respond, instead he turns to me. "Don't fuck me over, Shep."

"Why would I do that?"

"Charlie Beaufort is pretty fuckin' mad at me right now."

"I told you, I don't work for him."

"Right. But I'm pretty sure Olive didn't consciously try and kill me. Like you said, she was programmed. And to be honest, you being in that cell with her makes me feel a whole lot better. At least I can stop watching my back for a minute."

Which isn't a vote of confidence from him, but I can't blame the guy for being suspicious.

"But if you try anything," Collin threatens, "I will take you out and I will not blink."

I let out a long exhale. "Noted."

Amon's voice booms out from hidden speakers. "Opening cell three."

The glass in front of me shimmers for a moment, then it lights up. Lines of blue outline a door, and the next thing I know, a digital control panel appears, built into the glass.

It's probably the most sci-fi thing I've ever seen with my own eyes in my life. I side-eye Collin, but he's grinnin' now.

"Pretty cool, huh?"

"I guess," I say, which makes him laugh. "But why the hell do you guys need some futuristic spaceship jail?"

Collin shrugs. "I've learned, after many lessons, to embrace the future, Shep. And while I am not claiming to be prophetic in any way, I see the war that's coming and I am ready for it."

Which, I suppose, means he plans to take prisoners.

For the first time since I got here, I stop feeling grateful for the second chance and start to seriously wonder just what the hell I've signed up for.

But it's too late to back out now, because Collin starts pressin' those digital buttons on the glass, and the next thing I know, the glass pops open, creating a door where just seconds before there were just lines of light.

"Welcome home, Shep. You take care now."

And then he waves me in.

OLIVE IS STILL HUNCHED in the corner on the floor, rocking back and forth. I look up at the ceiling, knowing that Collin and Amon are both watching and listening, and have a sudden wave of doubt that this is the right way forward.

It's been a while since I had anything to lose, let alone a something as promising as a stable position with a company as good as Edge Security, and this is where the doubt comes from.

When you've got nothing to lose, it's easy to risk it all. For the most part, the only way left is up.

Where I am right now—in a state of transition where a new opportunity is so close, I can almost reach out and grab it—this is where mistakes are made. Mistakes that can trash that new opportunity so fast, it becomes nothing but a fleeting moment of unrealized gains.

But this same transitory state is also where better times and bright futures are born.

I want to stay here at Edge. I want the compound, I want the PT, I want the structure, I want the paycheck, I want the dog, I want these men to have my back while I have theirs—I want all of it.

But I also want to help this girl. I want her to come through the other side of the darkness and look at the world around her as a second chance instead of just a death sentence.

And the reason I want this for her is because I want this for *me*.

I'm just not convinced it can be done.

But I'm gonna give it a try. So I walk over to the corner of the room, press my back up against the glass wall, and slide down it until I'm sitting next to her. She doesn't look at me, but that's fine. I'm gonna do all the talking.

"Did I ever tell you about the time I was a secret double agent for the Underhaven? Have you ever heard of that place?"

She doesn't look at me. Doesn't respond at all.

"I was a Deep Recon Specialist. DRS."

"I already know this," she says, softly. But it's more of an angry hiss than a gentle whisper. "I know more than you do."

I smile. At least she's talking. And now I know she can hear me. "Of course you do. You're still active and I was discarded years ago."

She turns her head now, her long blonde hair hanging in her face, her eyes dark, a sharp contrast to her almost pale white face under this too-bright light.

She doesn't say anything else, so I just continue. "I had this partner. We were paired up when we were kids." Olive blinks here, perhaps thinking about how old she was when she was paired up with this Ambrose Sinclair guy. "Because we only work in pairs, right? Deep Recon needs an agent and a handler."

"You were her handler?" Her question is sincere and less angry than her last statement.

"No. She was mine. I was the agent."

Olive turns a little in my direction, still folded up with her knees pulled up to her chest, but leaning against the wall now. "What was her name?"

I don't remember her name, but I make one up for Olive. It's hard to relate to nameless people. "Waters."

Olive makes a face. "Waters? What kind of name is that?"

"It was her last name. Actually, her last name was Waterson. She called me Shep, for Shephard, and I called her Waters."

"Oh." She says this with the smallest of smiles.

"Yeah, so anyway she was my handler and I was sent into deep cover in the underground free zone called the Underhaven. Have you heard of it?"

She shakes her head no.

"It's a shithole, mostly. Lots of crime, lots of drugs, lots of dissidents."

"What was your mission?"

I don't remember this either, but this time I don't make it up because I know that Amon and Collin are listening and lies are not the way forward with them. The more lies I tell Olive, the more I'll have to explain to Amon and Collin later. It's not gonna help me, so I tell her the truth. "I can't remember."

Olive doesn't like this answer. "Why are you telling me this? I mean, who cares? Especially if you can't even remember your mission."

"I'm telling you this because I know what it feels like to be connected to your partner."

She scoffs. "You haven't got a fucking clue what that feels like. And you know what? I don't wanna hear your stupid story. Remember what you told me outside the diner? You said I'll never know your truth because if I knew, they'd kill one of us." She points to herself, then to me. "That's what you said. So your story is bullshit."

"It's not bullshit." I say this with contempt, but inside I'm pretty happy with her recollection of that conversation. It's a good sign. "Look around, Olive. *Where are you?*"

"What do you mean? I'm not fucking crazy. I'm in the Edge Security prison."

I force myself not to laugh. *She's not crazy?* She literally just stole Collin Creed's sidearm off his person, pointed it at his face, and pulled the trigger. But the fact that she's participating in this conversation is a step forward, so I make sure that laugh doesn't come out.

"Well," I say, my voice even, "they can't get us here, can they? I mean, if CORE wasn't afraid of your brother and what he's doing out here in the woods of West Virginia, they'd just set the place on fire, or something. And they haven't done that. In this room," I point to the floor, "we can say anything we want and CORE can't hear it."

"You're wrong."

"How am I wrong?"

"See," she says, smiling at me, "you don't know anything about Brose and me."

But she's the one who's wrong. Because that right there was the missing link I was looking for.

I consider my options here. I could signal to Collin that he needs to get me out of here so we can talk or I could keep going and finish what I started with Olive.

And I guess that's all it comes down to.

Which of the Creed siblings do I want on my side more?

Obviously, Collin is the better option. My future with him and Edge is bright.

Olive is darkness. A sad, lost emptiness that is going absolutely nowhere but crazy.

And that's the thing—I understand that crazy. I still feel it. I still… miss her.

"That's not her name," I say.

Olive squints her eyes at me. "What?"

"Waters. I lied." This makes her scoff. Me as well, because I guess I made my choice. "I don't remember her name, Olive. I don't know why, not for sure. All I know is that years and years of my life are missing. They cut me loose, they let me flail around like a baby who had no clue how to survive in the world around me, and they walked away. I was detained twice on mental health holds and then I just broke. Robbed a store. Went to prison. And we both know you can't walk away from CORE. So why didn't they tie up their loose end?"

Olive's eyes flit up to the ceiling, then back to me. "You'd better be careful here, Shep."

"I know Amon and Collin are listening. They told me they would be. But I'm not talking to them, I'm talking to you. Why would they cut me loose?"

She lets out a long sigh. "To watch. To see what you do? To let the experiment run."

I smile, then chuckle a little. "Yeah, that's what I think too. I think they cut us, Olive. Me and no-name. And they filled me up with a memory of killing her just to make it final. And I think they did this on purpose to see what would happen."

"You went crazy."

I nod.

"They cut me too. They cut *us*. They took him away." She pauses here, her eyes flitting back and forth like they're searching mine. "Will I go crazy?"

I nod again. But then I take her hand and give it a squeeze.

This makes her startle, and try to pull it back, but I don't let go. I wait for her to look me in the eye. "But you know what?"

"What?" This word is barely a whisper.

"At least you won't be alone when it happens. Because I'll be right here with you."

23 - Olive

I'll be right here with you.

I say these words in my head on repeat when a buzzing noise sounds, making me jump. I look over and see Collin standing in the doorway of my jail cell. He's staring at me like I'm a stranger, which is how he should've looked at me the moment I arrived, but he didn't.

When he saw me this morning, I was his sister.

Looking at me now, all he sees is a threat.

Shep gets to his feet, bringing me up with him. "What's up?" he asks Collin.

Collin doesn't look at Shep when he speaks. Those unnaturally beautiful eyes of his are still locked on me. "We're meeting Penny at the hospital. She said to come right now, so I've arranged a helicopter. Let's go." He hands Shep a coat that is meant for me, so Shep helps me into it, and then Collin steps aside and waves us forward.

I hesitate, not understanding what this is all about. But Shep takes my hand and gives it a squeeze. "It's all right. I went through the same scan last weekend. It's boring and cold, but you don't have to be afraid of it."

His explanation didn't answer a single question in my head. But when I look at Collin—at the cold distance in his eyes—I lose my nerve to ask. Whatever this scan is, it's going to happen whether I agree to it or not. That's clear.

So I allow Shep to push me forward and we go up into the church and outside, where I can hear the approaching thumping of helicopter rotors. I'm not a helicopter expert, but this one looks very serious. It's all black, even the rotors and skids, but it's got a logo on it so I know it's not military.

It lands in the center of the compound where I saw men training dogs earlier and immediately, the doors open and two men jump out. They are armed and they are not Collin's men, but must be part of the helicopter service.

A third man jumps out, and this one is who Collin approaches. I can't hear anything because it's all very loud, but it's clear that he and Collin are old friends because the man smiles big, clapping Collin on the back. Then his eyes shoot over to me. I see some surprise in there, so Collin probably told him who I am, but also suspicion. Because he goes all serious and nods, then makes some hand signals to the two other men, and they approach Shep and me. Not with guns ready, but those rifles are definitely ready. We get nods and gestures to approach the helicopter and then the next thing I know, Shep is pushing my head down and moving swiftly towards the copter.

He jumps in first, then extends his hand to help me up. There is a third armed man inside who directs us to the second row of seats on the right. Shep waves me in, giving me the window, and then he takes the aisle.

The third man starts barking orders at me about seat belts and ear protection, so that takes a couple of minutes, but I'm just barely settled when the door is shut and we lift off. I don't know where we're going or what this scan is hoping to find, but Shep's presence is comforting, so I mostly just gaze out the window at the lights on the ground, shining up in the darkness. Wondering, as probably everyone does, what kind of lives the people in those homes and buildings below are living.

The next thing I know, I'm waking up as the helicopter lands.

Again, there's a lot of bustling and fussing as the door is opened and we extract ourselves from the seats. And then Collin is telling Shep to exit, and I'm being pushed out into the dark night of a city.

We're on top of a building, on a helipad, obviously. But we start quickly moving away from the helicopter, so I don't get a good look at anything until we're inside and a small, older woman is shaking Collin's hand. They go down a hallway, stopping about twenty feet away to have a conversation. I try to listen in, but the helicopter outside is taking off, so I can't hear anything.

Shep places his hand on my arm and gives it a squeeze. "Ya OK?"

"Where are we?"

"Pittsburgh. At a hospital. But the MRI machine is just down the road at the university. That's where we're going."

I have a lot of questions about this scan, but no time to ask them. Collin whistles at us like we're a pair of his dogs, and then motions for us to follow the woman as she opens a door.

We do, and end up in a stairwell, which we use to descend all the way down to the ground level. Outside there is a car waiting, and it takes us into a university campus and drops us off in front of a modern-looking building.

The next part of the journey involves a descending elevator with a lot of security. The woman, whoever she is, takes care of all that and when the doors open, we come out into a sterile-looking hallway. Here, the woman takes over, directing Collin and Shep down the hallways to wait.

After they leave, she smiles at me. "I'm Penny, Olive. Do you know why you're here?"

"No."

"We're going to scan your brain."

"Why?" I ask, annoyed.

"Because Collin ordered it."

"Do you take orders from Collin?"

"Yes. When he's paying me, and he is. So I've arranged an MRI. I'm going to need you to change in here." She waves a hand at the door closest to us.

"And what if I don't?"

Penny offers me up a sympathetic smirk, like I'm her clueless grandchild who is testing the waters of authority. "Let's not do this the hard way. Perhaps you feel empowered because it's just the two of us in this hallway. Perhaps you think you might be able to overpower me and just walk out of here. I'm old, after all. But Olive, let's just be clear here, OK? I'm not stupid." She pans a hand at nothing in particular. "There's no way out without me. I don't go to the trouble of setting up brain scans in the middle of the night unless I'm thoroughly invested in the outcome. And my darling, I am one hundred percent invested in this outcome."

"Why? Why do you care?"

Her smile is tight-lipped and forced. "That doesn't concern you. Just know that I am."

I let out a frustrated breath. "I don't care about the scan. But what are you looking for? Can you at least tell me that?"

It takes her a moment of consideration before she answers.

"I can and I will, but afterward. I don't want to influence you. It's important that we do this right."

I give in. Mostly because I figure I don't have a choice. "Fine. What do you want me to do?"

She points to the door again. "Change into the clothes provided and meet me back out here."

So I do. And when I'm done changing Penny leads the way into a large room where the machine is. I've had a lot of MRIs in my life, so all of this is familiar until I am handed a remote to click. Once for yes, twice for no. The next thing I know, I'm inside it, answering questions.

None of the questions are meaningful. I figure this out pretty quick. They have nothing to do with me personally. They are yes and no questions meant to stimulate a reaction in my brain. And there are a lot of them.

"Olive," an unfamiliar voice says through a speaker inside the machine. "Please remain still as we process some of your results. The test is not over. It will resume in a few minutes."

That's probably a bad sign.

But there's nothing I can do about it, so I close my eyes and let myself drift, so tired, I could fall asleep in here.

Olive! Olive, where are you?

My eyes fly open. "Brose?"

"Please remain still, Olive," the voice in the speaker says. "The test is not over."

It's me, Brose says. But the weird thing is, he's not here, but I can hear him inside my head. *Bet you thought I bailed, huh?*

I can't answer him. Not without being chastised again. And anyway, I don't want whoever is on the other end of that speaker to hear my conversation with Brose.

So I have it inside my head, which doesn't even feel weird.

I find myself inside a room. Brose is sitting in a chair at the far end. He looks good in that suit. No tie. The collar is open. The chair is kind of low and wide, so he's a little bit slumped into the cushions and his legs are open. My eyes get stuck there between them for a moment, but automatically scan back up to his face when he grabs himself and chuckles. "Do you miss me?"

"Oh, God, you have no idea. Where did you go? Why did you leave me? What the hell is going on?"

Shhhh, he says. Then he beckons me to him with a single crooked finger. *Come here. Sit in my lap. Let me hold you.*

I don't, though. Because this isn't real. "Where are we? What is this place?"

What is this place? Brose snickers. *It's your head, love. It's where I live.*

"I… don't understand."

Yes, you do. I live here, Olive. Inside your head. Just as you live in mine.

I'm trying to force these words to make sense, but they just… *don't.*

Listen. Brose's words are sharp now. *We don't have much time. Where is Shep?*

"Shep? I don't know. Somewhere around here."

Look for him.

"How? I'm inside an MRI machine."

You know how. Relax and concentrate.

"I don't know what you want. I—"

"Olive?" the voice in the speaker says. "We're going to begin again. Once for yes, two for no."

Easy, Brose says. I'm still in the room with him, he's still in the chair, but none of this is making sense to me. *Just relax, Olive. Answer their questions. Press that button each time—however many times you want, it doesn't matter. But while you're doing that, I want you to find Shep. I want you to look for him.* He points to the door behind me, which I didn't actually realize was there. *You can go out there, Olive, and look for him.*

The speaker starts the questions again, and without even thinking, I'm pressing the button on the remote in my hand.

Go on, Brose says. *Go look for him.*

I turn back to Brose, confused. "Why?"

He gives me the same smile that Penny woman did. *Who thinks for you, Olive?*

I deflate a little. "You do."

And who acts for me?

"I do."

Yes, good. Now go look for Shep. His voice changes a little at the end here. It sounds... deeper. Meaner. Older?

But it's still him in that chair. And he's given me a task.

He thinks for me, I act for him.

So I leave the room and go looking for Shep.

24 - Brose

A*re you ready, Ambrose?*

"Yes." I do not hesitate. I don't know what my grandfather's talking about, but I don't need to know. He thinks for me, I act for him.

Good. Let's begin. Do you know where Olive is?

"No."

I need you to find her. Can you look for her?

At first, I don't know what he means because I'm asleep. I think. But then, in my mind's eye, I see a tunnel. Like a funnel. It's black with bright glowing lines. Like an outline or a skeleton of the shape of the tunnel. Something that reminds me of a 3-D model. And it's moving. Racing. Like I'm inside this tunnel, rushing through it at an incredible speed. It's something you'd see in a movie. A special effect.

Suddenly, my mind is alive with images. People, and faces, and snippets of conversation.

People I've never seen, in such detail, they could be real.

They are real, Ambrose. But we're not looking for them, we're looking for Olive. Can you find Olive in these faces?

I search the faces. Hundreds and hundreds of them flash by. They're doing things. Talking to people, but not me. It's like…

I'm a visitor passing through their lives. A part of it, but then a moment later, not. Just gone and on to the next one.

Find Olive, Ambrose.

"I'm trying. There are so many people here."

But there is only one of them who acts for you.

"Because I think for her."

That's right! Good boy. Now keep looking. Push all the other faces away, don't listen to their conversations. Stop hearing them. Seek only Olive.

"Olive!" I call. "Olive, where are you?!"

There's no answer and no face, either.

Keep trying, Ambrose. This is your only task. Find. Olive.

So I call out again. "Olive! Olive! Where are you?!"

But this time, something weird happens. All the faces flashing by slowly morph into a grayish-black blur. The tunnel is back and I'm racing through it again. For a moment I think that this is not what I'm looking for, but then there she is. Olive. Standing in the darkness looking around. "Brose?"

I smile, ready to laugh and start telling her all about the weird shit that's happening to me, when suddenly, I'm choking and gasping.

Let me have control now, Ambrose. Good job. You're a very good boy. But I will handle things from here.

Before I can disagree with my grandfather's proposal, I realize I'm paralyzed. I can't move, I can't talk, I can't breathe and panic is starting to set in.

Just give me control, my grandfather says, *and all these uncomfortable feelings will go away. Relax... and sleep.*

I let go. The choking feeling fades, but I still can't move.

Good boy, my grandfather says. *You've done so well, my boy. Now stay very still while I give Olive her orders.*

What orders?

"It's me," my grandfather says. But the weird thing is, he's using my voice. "Bet you thought I bailed, huh?"

Suddenly I'm in a room, sitting in a chair. Olive is in the room too, but she's on the other side of it. She's wearing clothes I don't recognize. Sweats and a t-shirt. I look down at myself, but I'm wearing a suit.

Words spill out of my mouth that aren't mine. "Do you miss me?" I ask Olive.

"Oh, God," she says. "You have no idea. Where did you go? Why did you leave me? What the hell is going on?"

"Shhhh," my grandfather tells her using my mouth. Then he beckons to her with a single crooked finger. "Come here. Sit in my lap. Let me hold you."

Internally, I recoil at this. Because he's old and it came out like a proposition. Something I definitely do. But I'm young and Olive is mine.

I start struggling to take back control of myself, but my grandfather is too strong. There's no way back inside my head. It's like I'm a puppet and he's pulling all my strings.

Olive doesn't move. She scans the room with suspicion. She knows something's wrong. *Yes,* I think to myself. *Yes, Olive. This is wrong. This isn't me talking to you!* But instead of saying that, or acknowledging that she heard my thoughts, she asks my puppet master, "Where are we? What is this place?"

"What is this place?" My grandfather snickers. "It's your head, love. It's where I live."

"I... don't understand."

"Yes, you do. I live here, Olive. Inside your head. Just as you live in mine."

She looks very confused. And I start to hope that she

understands. That this isn't me. That I'm not what we thought. That *she's* not what we thought.

But before she can put any of this together, my grandfather says, "Listen, we don't have much time." His tone is curt and sharp now. And it sounds less like me and more like him. "Where is Shep?"

"Shep?" Olive shakes her head. "I don't know. Somewhere around here."

"Look for him."

"How? I'm inside an MRI machine."

"You know how. Relax and concentrate."

"I don't know what you want. I—"

"Olive?" A third voice interrupts, confusing me. "We're going to begin again. Once for yes, two for no." Who the hell is that?

"Easy," my grandfather says. "Just relax, Olive. Answer their questions. Press that button each time—however many times you want, it doesn't matter. But while you're doing that, I want you to find Shep. I want you to look for him." He points to the door behind me, which I didn't actually realize was there. "You can go out there, Olive, and look for him."

What the hell is he talking about? Who is he talking to?

"Go on," my grandfather says. "Go look for him."

Olive, who was distracted by the voice, turns her attention back to me. Who is not me at all. "Why?" She sounds defiant, and again, I have a spark of hope that she's figuring this out. That she knows that this isn't me talking to her.

But then my grandfather does the very thing I would do if Olive were defiant towards me. He asks her the question. "Who thinks for you, Olive?"

And I know it's over. She will not rebel. And she doesn't because she says, "You do."

"And who acts for me?" my grandfather asks.

"I do."

"Yes, good. Now go look for Shep." His voice is his own now. It sounds nothing like mine. It's deep, and mean, and old.

But Olive either doesn't notice, or doesn't care.

Because she leaves the room and goes looking for Shep.

25 - Shep

"**She's acting weird**," Collin says.

And I can't say I disagree. Olive *is* acting weird. It was all fine at first, but then we started getting strange activity in her brain. Since I was on the receiving end of this tech last weekend, I didn't realize that they were looking at my brain in real time. It's like reading her mind almost. Once you know what to look for. And the technician points everything out as it's happening, so we do know what to look for.

"Yes," Penny says. She's been mostly quiet throughout the test, letting the tech take over. But now she turns to Collin. "Let's talk outside. Continue the test," she tells the tech. "Make sure to record everything. We'll be right back."

The tech nods and Penny motions to the door. To my surprise, Collin taps my arm. "Come on. Whatever she's gonna say, you should hear it too."

We leave and walk down the hallway a bit to a small lounge nook tucked away in a corner. Penny turns to us with a serious face. But to my surprise, her gaze is directed at me, not Collin. "How much do you know about Project Mastermind?"

I make a little shrug with my shoulders. "I've heard of it. But mostly in a conspiracy theory kind of way. Why?" I ask the question, but obviously whatever is happening with Olive has to do with this project.

"What the hell is Project Mastermind?" Collin asks.

Penny directs her attention to Collin now. "It's an old project. Something left over from the Cold War. Mind control."

Collin scoffs. "Like... Mk ultra, or something?"

"No. Not like that at all. It's cutting-edge science, not psychedelics and conditioning."

"What kind of science?" I ask.

"Quantum neurodynamics."

"Quantum?" Collin raises an eyebrow. "I thought that was all theory?"

I'm kinda surprised that he's got any opinion at all about quantum physics, but don't say anything. Penny must be surprised as well because she raises *both* eyebrows at him. "You've studied quantum physics, have you?"

"No," Collin says. "But I was part of some very high-level meetings that last year we were operatives. There were plenty of boring discussions about this shit. So I've heard of it. And with all those boring conversations came a lot of high-level doubt as well."

"I'm not surprised about the doubt. All of the really groundbreaking discoveries are kept at the highest levels of classification."

"What's this got to do with Olive?" I ask.

Penny turns to me, offering a small smile. "Yes. Let's cut to the chase. I'm not a neuroscientist or a physicist, but I've been in many a high-level meeting myself." Her gaze wanders to Collin for the last part. "CORE has made significant discoveries and we know for sure that they've been experimenting on humans for nearly a century. Project Mastermind is exactly what it sounds like—mind control. But not just implanting pre-programmed actions and things of that nature, but actual puppeteering using certain frequency waves aimed at the brain. Extremely Low Frequencies, or ELF waves, are particularly effective for this."

Collin asks his next question. "So what are you saying? That Olive is one of these experiments?"

"That's my suspicion," Penny says. "Of course, I can't confirm it. I'd need at least a week to find an expert who owes me the right kind of favor to get a professional opinion on her scan. But I've seen these scans before and hers, to me, looks textbook. She's been manipulated. Extensively."

Collin shoots me a side-eye because this is the very thing I told him yesterday morning. But his next question is directed to Penny. "So what do we do about it? I mean, how do we undo it, or whatever?"

"I have no idea, Collin. But it would probably be in everyone's best interest if I called in a favor with a discreet institution where she can be detained until we get this professional opinion."

"You mean, lock her up?" I ask.

Penny nods. "That's precisely what I'm saying. She's dangerous, Collin. I understand that she's your sister, but she's *very* dangerous. No one, as far as I am aware, has ever evaluated one of these operatives."

"So you want to study her?" Collin asks.

"I don't want to study her," Penny says, a little defensively. "I'm certainly not qualified to do that."

"No," I say. "You're not. But you work on favors, don't you? So if you bring in an actual operative for this 'professional' to evaluate, he, or she, will get answers no one else can provide."

"And that person would be in debt to me," Penny replies, not even a tiny bit embarrassed that I called her out. "Yes. I trade favors like this with some of the world's most important people. That way," she looks at Collin, "when you call me up asking about a state-of-the-art lie detector test, I can set one up. And when you discover that your baby sister has been inducted as a participant in Project Mastermind, I can get her the help she needs." She shrugs with her hands. "I am a broker. You know this, Collin. But I am discreet as well. No one will ever know about this outside the people who were here tonight unless you choose to tell them. We trust each other. That's why you call me."

Collin turns and starts pacing, thinking it over. After a few seconds of this, he stops and faces us again. "I've got a little... prison set up on the compound. It's a project we added after all that shit went down last summer. It's secure. I can keep her there. Can this person you're thinking of examine her at my compound?"

"It's not ideal," Penny says, "and I wouldn't recommend it. You didn't mention why you wanted to scan Olive when we talked earlier. Surely, it's not a lie detector test. Of course, that's none of my business. My only point is that you suspected something and this test is your confirmation. I would not waste this chance to get the upper hand."

"What about me?" I ask. "What about the anomaly in my brain? It is... connected?"

Penny sighs. "I don't have the slightest idea, Shep. But I will say this, what we discovered in your brain is nothing like what we discovered in Olive's."

"So..." Collin says. "He's not compromised?"

Penny shrugs her shoulders. "I wouldn't know, Collin."

He shoots me a look and I already know what it means before he says anything. "We can't risk it, Shep. I'm sorry."

"What does that mean?" I ask. "You can't just kick me out. I have a contract. What about the honeypot in the woods?"

"What honeypot?" Penny asks.

"Some bar," Collin says. "It's a CORE operation, Shep says. That's where he ran into Olive."

Penny doesn't say anything, just stares off into the distance like she's putting puzzle pieces together in her mind. Whatever conclusions she comes to, she doesn't share them with us. Instead, she says, "Well, my job here is done and any further discussion about what comes next is none of my business. The memory on the machines will all be erased, but I'll have all the records compiled and sent to you by courier as soon as I can."

Collin offers her his hand. "Thanks, Penny. I owe you."

She gives him a knowing smile that says, *Of course you do.*

*It's **a quiet ride*** back to the hospital where the helicopter is waiting for us, then a noisy, but even quieter ride back to the compound. Collin spends most of his time texting on his phone, Olive sleeps, or pretends to sleep, but I just lean my head against the window, staring at the world down below.

This is how I know what's coming even before we land.

Because as the helicopter descends, I spy Amon and a bunch of guys waiting for us. Which would be unusual in and of itself, but they are wearing body armor and holding rifles at high ready.

"Sorry," Collins says into the headsets we're all wearing. "But Amon took a team to that bar you described and there was nobody there."

"What?"

"You heard me. There was no one there. There was *nothing* there, Shep. It was a couple of ruined buildings and an old abandoned mine. No bar, no rooms, no band, no nothing. And before you try and tell me that they packed up and left, there was no chance of that. None at all. Because it looks exactly like what it is. Something forgotten."

26 - Olive

I'm wearing a headset too, not for the conversation, just for the ear protection, so I hear everything Collin says to Shep. Immediately, I want to jump in and insist the bar was real.

But I already know it's not.

It never was.

Just like Brose and I were never real.

There's something wrong with my head. That's why they took me for the brain scan. I'm crazy. I'm hallucinating. I made up my entire life. The reason why the estate looked abandoned when I woke up the other day is because it *was* abandoned. It was never what I saw. Or thought I saw. It was some… I dunno. Just another old estate that fell into disrepair after the elderly owner died. And I was squatting there. Homeless and insane. Seeing things that weren't real.

I mean, come on. What was I thinking? A train in the basement? A secret underground train that stopped at the bar in the forest of West Virginia? Which, as Collin just proved, doesn't exist.

And Brose. Another hallucination. He's not real. None of this is real.

The helicopter lands and the men who came with it all

spring into action, opening the door so Amon and a couple of other guys can come in to escort Shep and I out. They're serious too. This is not a joke because they've got those rifles at high ready.

Neither Shep nor I put up any kind of fight. I'm sure he's lost in his own thoughts, just like I am. *Fake?* he's asking himself. *How could it be fake? I saw it!*

I saw too.

But I also think I was a secret agent for some global shadow government, so…

This actually makes me laugh as I hop down the steps of the copter. Which Collin hears, so he's giving me a look of concern as his men zip-tie my hands behind my back and start pushing me in the direction of the church.

I could put up a fight. I could maybe escape and call the police, or Jim Bob, and report an attempted kidnapping. But it wouldn't matter. Since when does my brother live by the same set of laws as the rest of us? And anyway, where the hell else am I gonna go? Would Jim Bob Baptist even recognize me? Would anyone in Disciple care? Do I even have parents? Are they alive? *Where are they?*

It's early morning and the air is crisp and cool. I don't say anything as Shep and I are encouraged to walk towards the church. I just put my head down and look at my feet.

We go inside, go downstairs, and then I pause at the door as Amon comes forward to key the lock. He opens the door, refusing to meet my gaze. Can I blame him? I'm Collin's crazy sister. When I go though, his eyes lift up to find mine. And I can see it. The mean inside him that he hides so well with that charming and handsome exterior.

But I did, after all, try and kill his best friend. So I guess I get it.

I enter the little prison and walk down the corridor, then stop in front of the cell I was in last night. Collin comes up behind me. "I'm sorry, Olive. I really am. But it's for your own good until we figure things out."

I just let out a breath as the glass door slides open, then walk into my cell without saying a word. I mean, what am I gonna say? There's nothing to say.

I turn, expecting Collin to back out and close the door, but instead he waves Shep into my cell. Of course, he and I were both in here before, but I felt certain, now that they know he's crazy too, that we'd be locked up separately.

Collin's reading my mind because he shakes his head and frowns at me. "I love you, Olive. I don't want you to be hurtin'. I'm not doin' this to punish you. We're gonna get you help. We're gonna fix this. But until we do, this is how everyone stays safe."

Then, as Shep enters, he backs out. Closing the door on both of us as he continues to look me in the eye.

I turn away first, and when I turn back, he's already exiting the little prison.

So I turn to Shep and find him looking back at me. I'm just about to open my mouth and try for a joke to lighten the mood, but the main door comes swingin' back open and Lowyn McBride appears, hands full of blankets and pillows.

She smiles at me. And just for a moment, I'm a little girl again. Of course, Lowyn and I were never friends. I was nothing more than her boyfriend's annoying little sister. But she was always nice to me. After Collin killed my kidnapper slash father that New Years Eve, we never really talked again though. It was just over. Everything was just over.

"Hey," she says through the glass. "Collin texted me while you all were riding back on the helicopter and told me to get you a little care package ready." She holds up her armful of pillows and blankets with a smile. "Collin's filling up the air mattress."

"Air mattress?" I ask, my eyebrows nearly up to the ceiling.

"I'm pretty sure that concrete cot over there is meant for bad people, not little sisters. You're only in here because we're worried about you, Olive. You know that, right?"

I don't get a chance to confirm or deny because the door opens again and this time it's Collin pushing a blow-up mattress through it. Someone in the control room opens the cell door, and Lowyn steps forward with her arms out.

Which makes me open mine in return. I take the blankets from her and step back as Collin shoves the mattress through the door.

"I packed you some snacks too," Lowyn says, shouldering off a backpack.

Shep takes it, looking as surprised as me.

He and Collin lock eyes as Collin puts his hand on his shoulder and gives it a squeeze. "We're gonna figure this out. Don't worry."

It just now occurs to me that Shep isn't obligated to stay in this jail cell any more than I am. This is kidnapping, unless you agree to it. So that's the first thing I ask him after Collin and Lowyn are gone. "Why did you stay?"

He squints a little in response. "What?"

"Here," I say, dropping all the pillows and blankets onto the cement cot. "Why did you let my brother lock you up? Why didn't you just grab your shit and go?"

He offers me a smile. "Same reason you did, Olive. Because Edge Security is the only second chance I'll ever get. This is the end of the line for me."

I don't say anything, but internally I agree. It's the end of the line for me as well.

I pick up the fitted sheet from the cot and start making the bed. Shep joins in, stuffing pillows into cases. Then I open the blanket, drape it over the mattress, and let out a sigh. As if it's a signal, the lights in the jail dim. It's daytime out, so it should be daytime in here too. So this dimming is yet another way that my brother wants me to know that he's on my side. He knows I must be exhausted and he wants me to rest.

"I'm tired," I say. Not to Shep, mostly to myself. And then I kick off my shoes and slip my pants down my legs. Without another word, and all the while being watched by Shep, I lower myself to the mattress and slip under the cover.

Shep stands there for a moment, probably trying to work out these new arrangements. In the end, he kicks off his boots and gets under the covers with me. But it's an easy conclusion to come to because what choice does he have?

The blow-up mattress is a good enough size that we both fit, but we find ourselves scootin' towards the middle anyway. Drawn together, one might say. Like opposite ends of a magnet. Pretty soon, we're huggin' each other.

I sigh, feeling stupidly good even though my brother has locked me in a jail cell in his private underground prison with a man I don't even know.

"I'm crazy," I say.

Shep huffs a little. "Well, not only are you not alone, but I've been to crazy town so many times now I'm practically a local, so… I'll be your guide."

It takes me a moment to catch on that he's joking. It's just such a change in mood, it doesn't hit me right away. But when it does, it's truly funny, so I laugh. "We're both crazy."

"We both saw the bar, right? I mean, you weren't pretending when I was there, were you?"

"No," I tell him as I turn onto my side, propping myself up on my elbow. "Not only did I see it, but I was getting to the bar using some imaginary underground train system, Shep. I made up a subway station. Hell, I made up an entire underground railway because I was living in Virginia and commuting to the bar."

"What?" He nearly snorts. "How is that possible?"

"I dunno. I was… hypnotized, maybe? To think I was in a train when I was driving a car? But… I don't think I have a car. I don't even have an ID. I'm… homeless, I think. A vagrant."

"That's not true. CORE is real."

"How do you know that?"

"Well… Penny. Penny told me CORE is real. Penny told all of us that they do shit to people's brains. They did something to you, Olive. You're not crazy. I don't know if any of that stuff exists—the train or the bar, or whatever—but you're part of it and so am I."

"But what if we're not, Shep? What if we're just nuts?"

He sighs loudly. "Yeah. I've thought of that too. But even if we are, Olive, it doesn't explain everything." Then he reaches for me, swiping a piece of hair away from my face. And I get a smile. Which makes his eyes dance a little and I start picturing what it would be like to… date him. "What are you thinking about?" he asks.

"You," I say, a little shyly. "And how it might be nice to… you know, see you. Outside of the insanity."

He laughs but his eyes are locked on mine and then, he leans in. It's a slow approach. Like he's giving me time to back away. But I don't back away. I want him the way I never wanted anything else in my life. He is comfort, and strength, and safety. So I let his lips touch mine and the moment they do, a tingle of electricity shoots through my body, making my head buzz a little with excitement.

I kiss him back now, feeling an urgency that wasn't there before. His hands are wandering, and so are mine. It's like we're drawn to each other in a new way now and our joining is the only thing that matters.

I struggle, getting out from underneath him, and then I straddle his hips, pressing my hands down on his chest as he looks up at me with lust-filled eyes.

"That's it. That's exactly it, Olive. Keep going."

The voice startles me and my head whips to the right. "Brose?"

"Keep going," Shep says. "It feels good. Keep going."

"Yeah, Olive," Brose says. He's leaning against the cell wall with his arms crossed and that smug smirk on his face, his words deadpan. "Keep going, Olive. We're almost there."

"*What the fuck is going on in there?*" Collin's voice comes booming through some kind of loudspeaker, making me pull away from Olive's forceful kiss. "Olive! What the hell are you doing?"

I want to say it's not her fault, but I can't because she won't stop kissing me. I try and push her back because this is just not right. There are cameras everywhere and Collin is clearly pissed.

But I can't push her off me. She's strong and leaning into my chest with all her weight. Then her lips are right up next to my ear. "Guess what?" Her voice is weird. Different. So I don't answer. "You're mine now, Ean Shephard. All mine. And there's a rule when you belong to someone."

"*What?*" I manage to gasp out.

"The rule. I think for you. You act for me."

Suddenly, I'm dizzy. The whole room begins to spin. My head goes light and I feel like I'm floating, but when I look around, I'm not. I'm lying on the mattress with Olive on top of me. "See," she says. "Doesn't it feel good?" And then she puts her hand across my throat. Her palm isn't that big, but it doesn't take much pressure to compress an airway. I want to throw her off of me, but a ringing sounds in my head, distracting me from everything else that's going on. It's sharp nearly to the point of being painful.

And then there's a voice. A voice I haven't heard in many years. "Do you remember me, Shep?"

For a moment, I'm not here. I'm not in the cell. I'm not on the Edge Compound. I'm in a dark, black room. There's just enough light to make rippling waves across the four black walls. Like it's being reflected off a pool of water.

When I look down, I realize that's because I'm lying down in a shallow pool of water. It covers the entire floor of the room.

"Do you remember me, Shep?" the voice asks again.

I do, but I don't either. So I say, "No."

"That's OK," she says. "All you need to remember is the rule. And the rule is, I think for you, you act for me. Can you say it back for me?"

"You think for me, I act for you."

"That's right. That's very good, Shep. You're a good, good boy. And you're going to get lots of rewards when this is over and you come home."

"Home?" I ask.

"Home," she says. "But not yet. We're not done here. Olive is taking my place in your head. She's your new handler."

"What?" I'm starting to feel sick. Like I might throw up.

"Don't panic," the voice says. "You're fine. You're not even going to notice the difference. She and I are the same person as far as you're concerned. It's all going to work out just fine as long as you remember the rule."

"You think for me, I act for you."

"Yes," Olive says. And suddenly, the room with the water is gone and I'm back in the cell.

Time was going in slow motion, or something, because Olive is still on top of me, her hand pressed against my throat.

She choked me.

She fucking choked me and I passed out!

Holy shit!

Rational and logical thinking return at the same moment that the door to the jail flies open and Collin and Amon are coming in heavy with a whole team of men behind them. "Get away from her!" Collin is yelling. "Get away from her!"

I start protesting, trying to get to my feet as Olive once again presses her fingers into my airway. Even though she's tiny compared to me, she grips hard enough and with enough force to bring the stars and encroaching darkness.

"Do you know what to do?" the voice asks.

Immediately, when I hear these words, I'm back in the black pit of a room filled with water. I'm looking up at the ceiling where tiny pinpricks of light are shining down on me.

The woman leans in to my field of vision. "Hi, handsome. I bet you never thought you'd see me again."

"Who are you?"

She smiles, whispering, "I'm the puppet master, of course." And something about her tone, or her look, or maybe just the fact that she called herself the puppet master makes me recoil.

"Who am I?" I ask it because I feel like I'm reading from a script and this is the next line. Not because I don't already know the answer.

The woman leans down into my face and kisses me on the lips.

Then she whispers, "Hello, puppet."

28 - Olive

"*Hello, puppet.*"

I hear words coming out of my mouth, it's just... I'm not the one saying them. It's not Brose, either. It's a woman. Some strange woman. And she's acting like I'm not even here. Like I'm not important. Like this isn't my head and she's not inside it!

I fight against this sudden occupation, but I have absolutely no control.

I look around, find myself inside a black cube of some sort. I'm standing in water up to my ankles. And then Brose is suddenly here with me. "Calm down, puppet."

"Calm down?" I ask him. "Where the fuck am I? What is going on?"

"You're fine, Olive." He steps towards me, reaching for my face. And then his hand is caressing my cheek in a way that is so familiar, I actually do calm down.

"Where did you go? Are you real? What is happening to me, Brose? *Where are you?*"

"I'm right here, puppet."

I reach up, grab his hand, and fling it away. "Stop calling me that. What are you doing? Who is this woman talking out of my mouth?"

"Woman?"

"Stop it! You know what I'm talking about!"

"You're the only woman I see, Olive. It's just you and me."

"She's out there!" I point to one of the encroaching walls. "I mean, she's inside me! She's in my head!"

"Come on, Olive. Can you hear yourself? You sound insane." When these last few words come out, he chuckles. Like this is funny. He reaches for me again, but this time, instead of caressing my cheek, he brings his hand up to my throat.

My eyes close involuntarily and a warm sensation washes through me.

"There you are," he says. "See, puppet? Everything is perfectly fine."

My body is shaking and I am having trouble breathing—on the verge of panic—because this isn't real. None of this is real. Brose isn't real, and the house isn't real, and I'm not some secret agent for an underground shadow government. *I'm not.*

But I don't understand. I can't put it right. I can't make it make sense. When I speak, I'm on the verge of hysteria. "I'm not your puppet."

"Oh, but you are, Olive. You're mine. Remember? Your mission is me. My mission is you. And what we have here, my dear, is what we call 'a spectacular success.' You've done it. You're going to go down in history. They will write books about you, darling. And 'I think for you, you act for me,' from this day forward, will be known as the greatest weapon man has ever invented."

We stare at each other for a moment, Brose and me.

And I see everything that we are. All that we have been over the past two years. I love him. He's my best friend, he's my everything.

But as I look him in the eyes, I see something new in there.

I see *someone* new. "Who are you?"

Brose laughs. It echoes off the cubed walls and sends a spasm through my wet and already shaking body. "I'm you, darling. I'm you."

And then he squeezes. His fingertips tighten around my throat and it's so fast, and with such force, I see the blackness coming for me before I can react.

I crumple.

That's the only word to describe what happens to me. I simply crumple into… nothing? Something broken? Someone else?

I don't know. All I know is that the next time I open my eyes, I'm not me anymore.

I'm… *Shep*.

In my head I hear his voice repeating, over and over, *She thinks for me, I act for her. She thinks for me, I act for her. She thinks for me, I act for her.*

And I have this sudden, sick feeling that the lie that's been sitting between us is… *me*.

She thinks for me, I act for her.

He is my puppet.

I am his master.

We only work in pairs, Olive. Deep Recon needs an agent and a handler.

You were her handler? I asked.

No. She was mine. I was the agent.

Nothing about my life makes sense now. Nothing. *Nothing.* Not a single fucking thing after Collin left for the Marines because none of what I think happened is real.

It's not real.

It's fake.

It's a lie.

I am the girl Shep lost.

I was his handler.

I was his partner.

I think for him, he acts for me.

Time speeds or something because all of these thoughts have occurred in the moments after Collin opened the door to the jail. And he's rushing towards me.

Me. Towards me, the real me and not the eyes through which I'm seeing. He goes right past Shep and tackles me to the ground. *I feel this.* I feel the pain in my hip when he slams me against the hard floor.

But I'm also watching it happen from the eyes of Shep.

Brose is standing next to me, laughing. Laughing! Like some maniacal supervillain. He throws his head back, looking up at the ceiling, and this laugh just comes out and fills up the room. He's shouting, "We did it! *We did it!*"

But it's *not Brose.*

It's not him. It's someone else inside him.

Because he's a puppet too.

Brose grabs me, and this whole time I'm watching Collin on the floor with me, Olive-me, zip-tying my hands behind my back. And Amon is coming in now, and there are men, lots of men, trying to get control of the situation.

But none of that matters.

The only thing that matters is Brose.

He leans in to my ear and whispers, "Welcome to *Chain Reaction*, puppet. We think for you, you act for us."

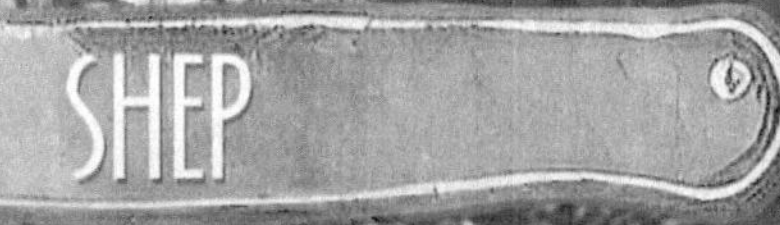

29 - Shep

She's in my head! She's in my head!

And words are flowing. Words I don't understand but make perfect sense, nonetheless.

I think for you, you act for me.

And it's in her voice. Olive's voice.

A voice I now recognize.

My missing half. My partner.

Waters. Who is not Waters, but Olive.

My handler.

No.

I fight this realization.

It's not right. *This isn't right.*

But the woman's voice is shushing me now. And then, I'm in a small room. A black room. Like the inside of a cube. I'm lying on the floor that is covered in a few inches of warm water and I'm looking up at a ceiling of pinprick lights.

A woman leans over, into my view. She is smiling and she is not Olive. "What's the rule, puppet?" And she's using Olive's voice to say these words.

It's so wrong, I can't even process what I'm seeing and hearing.

"Puppet?" she asks. Her voice calm and sweet. Almost sing-songy. "Tell me the rule."

"You think for me, I act for you." It comes right out of my mouth, and in the next moment, I'm back in the jail. which is nothing but pure chaos.

Collin has Olive on the ground, zip-tying her hands behind her back. Amon is behind him, facing me and the other men who rushed in to help. They are all armed. He's yelling, "We need to get her upstairs. Be ready!"

Be ready for what?

Collin gets up, holding on to Olive's bound hands, bringing her with him. He's out of breath and for the first time, I see panic in those weird eyes of his. He looks right at me. "Are you OK?"

Which doesn't even make sense to me, so I don't answer.

He doesn't wait. Just turns to Amon and starts saying something about upstairs.

But while he's doing this, Olive and I lock eyes.

She smiles at me and I smile back.

Inside my head I can hear her voice. It's like she's really there. Like she's really inside me. *I think for you, you act for me. Do you understand, puppet?*

There's something wrong with that voice. It's warped. Too low of a pitch. A little bit shaky and uneven. Almost like a man's voice. But not a young man—an *old* one.

Do you understand, puppet?

Collin is dragging Olive past me now. I get pushed out of the way, like I'm of no consequence here. Amon makes room for them to get through. Then he waves his hand at me. "Let's go, Shep. Get out of there."

I follow Collin, but we don't get far because there are a lot of men down here in this small space and everyone is trying to figure out who needs to leave first. So there's a bottleneck at the stairs.

And this is when I look down at Collin's hip and see his sidearm.

The very same sidearm that Olive tried to kill him with just yesterday.

Do you understand, puppet?

Oh, yeah. I get it. *Chain Reaction.*

I reach for the gun, snap it out of the holster, and I'm pulling the weapon back, aiming it at Collin's surprised face as he turns.

Those eyes of his stare right back at me as I hold the gun mere inches from his forehead.

He sees his mistake. I watch the thoughts form in real time.

Do it! The old man's voice is yelling in my head. *Do it!*

That's not Olive inside me.

Puppets.

That's all we are.

Just puppets.

These thoughts of mine manifest as hesitation and it's long enough for Amon to tackle me to the ground and wrestle Collin's gun away.

Everything that happens next is just a whirlwind of confusion.

So much yelling, and zip ties, and being pulled up to my feet and marched up the stairs.

I see the surrounding hallway. We enter the church and there's suddenly too much space. And the voices, my God, the voices are screaming. Not just the old man, but another man— who is probably Ambrose—and the woman who was in my head, my partner, who was not Olive, and me, of course. I'm screaming too because I don't know what the fuck is happening and every one of these voices except my own is telling me to do things.

Kill him!

Kill her! Which I assume is referring to Olive.

My head is a maelstrom of confusion.

There's no chance of me killing anyone. There are at least a dozen Edge guys all around me. So I just let them push me out in front of Olive and shuffle me across the front of the church. I am directed through a door, and down some steps, and find myself standing in a familiar place.

I turn to Collin. His face is angry and tight, his eyes flashing like he wants to kill me.

But past all that emotion I see something else. Something stronger than his emotions. I see why everyone respects him.

I see his control and his wisdom.

And when he says, "It's OK, Shep. You're gonna be OK," I believe him.

Then the door in front of me swings open and I'm pushed through.

30 - Olive

Brose is gone. I feel his absence.

But in his place is someone else. Someone who is no longer hiding. An old man, that I know for sure. But who he is, I have no idea. All I know is that *he's inside me*. He's telling me what to do.

Kill him, Olive.

Kill him right now!

At first, I think he's talking about Shep. But he's not the target here. The old man is talking about Collin and Collin is staring right at me.

I think for you, you act for me. Kill him!

I'm just about to reach for his weapon when I realize he's no longer carrying. He smiles at me, grabs me by the shoulders and shoves me through the open door of the room. I go crashing into Shep as Collin and his men follow us unto the room.

Something interesting happens next—the voice in my head becomes distorted and distant. Like someone is talking underwater.

"It's gonna be OK," Collin says.

But it's not. Nothing is ever going to be OK again.

Amon and another man are standing behind him, pointing rifles at Shep and me. "This is a SCIF," Collin says. "You're being targeted by a low-frequency weapon, but the walls of this room block out all incoming electromagnetic waves." He grabs my shoulders and shakes me. "Do you understand me, Olive? You're being attacked by signals. Whatever is happening inside your brain, it's not real!"

I turn and look at Shep. The room is not that big so he's leaning against the back wall, about ten feet away. He's holding his hands up to his head, like he's got a headache.

"Olive," Collin says, shaking me again.

"Yes," I say. "I understand."

My brother lets out a loud sigh. Amon and the other guy remain on high alert with rifles ready. Shep takes a few steps away from the wall. He turns to me with squinted eyes. "What the fuck was that?"

I don't know what to say. I know what it was. I was inside him. I was *controlling* him. Except it wasn't me. Because I wasn't myself I was... Brose?

But I have a sick feeling that if Brose was here with us, in real life, I mean, that he would be saying the same thing. It wasn't me. There was someone inside me.

It was an old man, of that I'm sure. This old man was controlling *both of us*.

I want to tell Collin but I can't seem to get these words out.

Collin takes over, turning to question Shep. "What happened?"

"I'm not sure. I don't know. Someone was inside me. A woman. She was making me do stuff." He's looking at me when these words come out.

"It was me," I tell Collin. "I was inside him."

"No, Olive," Shep insists. "It wasn't you. It was my handler."

He shakes his head. "I can't… I don't remember her, but I know it wasn't you."

"How is that possible?" Collin asks. He's looking between the both of us now. "Who was controlling Olive then?"

"It was Ambrose," Shep says.

"It wasn't," I say. "The first time—" I know how this sounds. I'm listening to myself. But what else can I do but try and explain? "The first time, it probably was. But just now? That wasn't Brose, Shep." I look at him, begging him to believe me. "It wasn't him. It was someone else. An old man was inside me! And then I was inside you. And that's how they got inside you." And then the words I'm looking for come spilling out. "It was a chain reaction."

Because this is what the old man told me. *Welcome to Chain Reaction, puppet. We think for you, you act for us.*

"She's right," Shep says. "It wasn't her. This old man, he was inside me too. He kept calling me his puppet."

No one knows what to say now, so we just stand there for several long seconds trying to process things. My eyes lock with Collin's and for a moment, I see him the way he was that night, when he shot the kidnapper. I remember looking into his eyes— and he's got some crazy eyes, so I got lost in them. Time slowed down for me. I remember that the man smelled weird. It was… filth. And alcohol. And fear, I think. And part of it was my fear because you hear about people who break into the bedrooms of little girls, but you never think it could happen to you.

And then it does.

But then, in your darkest hour, while that endless terrifying moment is on pause, someone steps forward as your savior.

Collin's eyes that night were filled with anger. I'd never seen him like that. And the man holding me was begging for his life. Like he knew what was coming.

Collin either didn't care or couldn't hear him over his own thoughts inside his head.

The next thing I knew, my body was hot with blood and the man was on the floor behind me.

After that, I don't know what happened. I lost time, I think. The next thing I remember is waking up in a hotel room. We couldn't go back to the house because of the investigation and the mess.

No one really asked me what happened. Not until much later.

I went back to school. I did homework. The Revival was on winter break, so there were choir rehearsals, but nothing really structured on the weekends like during the season.

I think I lost all my friends. Not because they didn't care about me or want to be around me, but just because I withdrew. I didn't want to do anything with them anymore. My parents were fighting all the time. My father was so angry. But I didn't understand why. It never made sense to me. I don't really remember what I did that spring other than go through the motions.

The next really important moment in my life was the day after Collin left for the Marines. Because that's the day that the CORE people showed up at the door. I was there when they came. There was an argument. My father was loud. My mother was crying.

Jim Bob Baptist showed up and there was more yelling.

I was in my room because the CORE said I needed to go with them and they wouldn't let me leave. After hours of this back-and-forth arguing, the woman from CORE came into my bedroom and started packing things into a bag. Clothes, and shoes, and a couple of books and toys that were lying around. She didn't say anything to me as she did this, but when she was done, she turned and smiled. It was a fake smile that every kid learns to recognize when speaking to strangers. And she said, "You're going away to camp."

I'm pretty sure she said more than that, but that's the only part I remember. The next thing I knew, I lived in a dorm with other girls my age.

And from there, everything got blurry.

Some days I remember very clearly.

Some years I don't remember at all.

Not until Brose on my eighteenth birthday.

But just because I don't remember it doesn't mean it didn't happen.

"Olive?" I blink and find myself still looking into Collin's eyes. "What did you hear?"

"'Welcome to Chain Reaction, puppet. We think for you, you act for us.' That's what I heard."

"I can still hear the voices," Shep says. "Olive? Can you still hear them?"

"Yes," I say. "But they don't make sense now. They're not words, just... sounds."

Collin lets out a breath. "That's the SCIF shielding you from their manipulation. Once I close the door, you should have complete relief."

"You're gonna lock us in here?" I ask.

"It's the only way," Shep says, taking a few steps in my direction. His hand takes mine and he offers me a smile. "But don't worry. I'll be right here with you."

"It's OK," Collin says, reassuring me as well. He steps

towards me and puts a hand on my arm, giving it a rub. And I'm suddenly very sad that we've been apart all these years. "It's OK, Olive," he says again. "You're safe in here. The voices can't get you. No one can get you. I'm gonna call Penny and we'll figure it out. I promise. I don't know what happened to you." He looks at Shep. "To either of you. But I promise, we're gonna figure it out."

And then he backs up, which makes Amon and the other guys back up, and they close the door, leaving us in the darkness.

Shep squeezes my hand and then, in the next moment, the commotion in my head—a maelstrom of information, and voices, and sounds that have been my entire world since I was eight years old—goes silent.

"They're gone," Shep says.

He's right. And, maybe for the first time since that night the man came into my bedroom, I feel like myself again.

No CORE.

No voices.

No mission.

No Brose.

It's quiet.

The only thing is, I'm not sure who I am in the silence.

Epilogue - Shep

Something happened on my trip back to sanity.

Several things, actually.

First, there's Olive. Sweet, tough-as-nails Olive. I'm really falling for her. There's a bit of a disconnect as I try and parse out what we were doing with each other in those early days when we first met, because the girl I met in the speakeasy bar and the one I'm currently living with bear almost no resemblance to each other.

I'm sure she's thinking the same thing about me, since I was just as delusional as her.

So we're grappling with the inconsistencies that implanted on our brains in those first two weeks.

But still, living with Olive—prison vibe aside, but I'll get to that in a minute—truly does feel like the fresh start I was looking for.

The second thing I realized on my way back to sanity is that I'm a stranger to myself. I'm not convinced that anything I thought I knew about my past is true. The woman in my head, the one pretending to be Olive, but wasn't.

I knew her. I think she was my handler.

I think I've been manipulated for a very long time. Was I even in prison for five years? Couldn't they have dropped me off out in front of it and woke me up, or whatever? And that's why I have memories of riding my bike across the country to West Virginia?

Maybe.

But it's just as likely that I was never in prison, that they implanted those memories, and they woke me up the moment I showed up at Edge.

I have no idea which one is true, but I'm leaning towards the second one.

I saw a bar in the middle of the forest. It was filled with people. I sat on a couch. I drank. Olive was there.

But she saw a train tunnel. She rode an underground train to the bar in the forest every morning. She and her partner, who we are mostly convinced is even real, were living in a mansion in Virginia. They took that train together.

What the fuck happened to us?

At first, the doctors came to the Edge compound because Collin was afraid to let Olive and me out of the SCIF just in case that old man from CORE—if that's even the real name of that organization—was lingering about, waiting for his next opportunity to be our puppet master.

But after a couple of weeks Penny Rider set things up in a proper lab at a private institution in Kentucky. We go there three times a week by helicopter.

Penny wanted us to move in over there and spend about six months full time with them, but Collin put his foot down and told her absolutely not. He has his friend with the helicopter, Calder Boone, take us by air. Boone looks like a man who's seen things and doesn't even bother making eye contact with me or

Olive when he and his team escort us back and forth to Kentucky three times a week.

In fact, I'm pretty sure he considers us both prisoners and not clients.

But I get it.

There's something really wrong with our brains.

It's hard to believe that people were inside my head. But they were.

Project Mastermind, Penny Rider called it.

But it's much more than that. Because Olive and I both heard our puppet masters call it Chain Reaction. Which makes sense. Somehow, some way, CORE has developed a protocol that can infiltrate a person's mind. But not only that, they can piggyback off that mind and leap into another in close proximity. And once inside, they are pulling our strings.

We're thinking this is why I saw the bar the way Olive was seeing it. She was projecting images to me. And that's why she was in my head at the end there.

Someone put her there.

Ambrose Sinclair put her there.

Olive is steadfast in her opinion that someone else was controlling Brose, but neither Collin and I are convinced, so every time she brings it up, we've agreed that downplaying any and all thoughts about Brose is the best way forward.

"She needs to forget about him," Collin said.

And I can't say I disagree.

Whoever he is, he's a bad guy and I hope she never sees him again.

The idea that the science has progressed far enough now that mind-control in real time is possible is more than just frightening, it's the literal end of the world as we know it and something must be done to stop these people.

But every time I bring that up, Collin plays it down the same way we're playing down Brose. I don't know him well enough to decide if this is just for my benefit so I don't get myself worked up about some crazy save-the-world plan, or if he knows something I don't and he's really not worried about it.

Olive doesn't know him well enough either. We've discussed this at length. The one thing about living inside our cube is that it's absolutely, one hundred percent private.

Which brings me to the third thing. The cube and living inside it with Olive.

Edge Security built a SCIF for a reason. They use it.

So Olive and I were kicked out in week two after an extensive renovation of a small house out back of the church. All the windows were boarded up, the walls were lined with Faraday fabric, and then they renovated it from top to bottom. It's small—the size of a studio apartment—but it's functional, has a bathroom and a small kitchen, and if you don't think too hard about it, it's easy to forget that you're literally inside a Faraday cage prison cell.

I like the privacy.

So does Olive.

And it's reassuring that what we do in our little prison cell of a home is all *us*.

We're not prisoners, though. One of the guys on the compound was an engineer in the Green Berets and came up with a prototype Faraday helmet. It looks stupid as fuck, but it's nice to be able to keep doing PT with the guys every morning and work with Cross's puppy for a little bit each day.

Olive uses it to hang out with Lowyn and Rosie—Collin's

and Amon's women. Neither of us are allowed to leave Edge unless we're being escorted to the lab by Boone and his team.

Therapy also occurs inside a Faraday-cage lab and, little by little, Olive and I are starting to piece together our lives.

Will we ever get the truth?

Well, I'm not countin' on some bad guy showing up to spill his guts in the final scene like it happens in the movies, that's for sure.

If we want the truth, we'll have to go look for it.

Epilogue - Brose

I think for her, she acts for me.

"Ambrose? Can you hear me?"

I think for her, she acts for me.

"Ambrose Sinclair? It's time to wake up now."

My mission is you and your mission is me.

"You're awake and on the count of three, I would like you to open your eyes. One. Two. Three."

I blink. Find myself lying on my back in a room with a black ceiling and in water that is deep enough to gently lap at my earlobes. On the ceiling are thousands of tiny pinpricks of light.

A woman leans over so I can see her face. It's young and she has smooth pale skin. Her eyes are wide and blue with perfectly arched eyebrows. She smiles, drawing my attention to her lips, which are shimmering with some kind of gloss. "There he is." Her voice is soft and sultry. "Do you know where you are, Ambrose?"

My neck is stiff, but I force myself to turn to the right. It's a black wall, just like the ceiling. Then I turn to the left and find another wall. "I'm… in the Cube."

"Very astute. Yes. You're in the Cube. Do you know why you're in the Cube?"

I blink again, trying to remember. At first, I can't. I can't find any memories, it's just waves of darkness. But after a few seconds, a bit of it starts to come back. "It's the quiet room."

"Good. Yes. That's what your grandfather called it when you were little. How old are you, Ambrose?"

"Ten."

She smiles at me, but it's a worried smile, not a real one. "No. You're not ten. Not anymore. How old are you, Ambrose?"

I blink. "I… I'm not sure." But she's right, I'm not ten. That's not the voice of a ten-year-old.

"You're twenty-seven. Can you remember what you've been doing for the past seventeen years?"

"My head hurts."

"Of course it does. We'll give you something for the pain, but first, you must answer the questions. Think hard now, Ambrose. What have you been doing for the past seventeen years?"

I open my mouth to tell her I don't remember, but she places a fingertip on my lips. "Shhhh. Think hard." Her voice is stern now. "You only get one more chance and I like you, Ambrose. So I don't want you to fail."

I push her hand away. "I'm not Ambrose. My name is Brose."

Her real smile returns. "Very good. Tell me more."

"Why?"

"Your questions will be answered at another time."

I scoff. Then I'm up, out of the water, and I've got the woman by the neck. I put her in a choke hold, drag her to the wall, look up, find the cameras, and snarl, "Open the fucking door or I'll kill her."

I count the seconds of silence as they tick off.

Four.

The door opens, and even though the light outside the Cube is dim, it hurts my eyes enough that I have to squint. I stumble forward, throw the woman aside, and then find myself inside a small room with gray walls and staring into a mirror. It's a two-way mirror, I know this because the memories are flooding back now, but it's still reflective enough to see that I am naked.

And grown.

Twenty-seven, she said. Looks about right.

I've got stubble on my face, but it's not a beard. Not anything close to a beard. I rush the mirror, pounding my fists on it as I look him straight in the eyes. I know he's there. He's *always* there. He's *always* watching. "How long?" I ask. "How long was I in and what the fuck did you take from me this time?"

The speaker crackles a little, announcing his answer. "Two weeks."

"Two *weeks?*" The breath rushes out of me in a wave of relief. Two weeks is long, but it's not even close to the longest. When I was a kid, he used to put me in the Cube for months.

Then I turn and brace myself against the mirror as I come to terms with the new reality, letting out a breath. "What did you take?"

My grandfather's voice sounds old on the other end of the comms. "Nothing of importance. Just another subject."

"What kind of life was it? Who was she? I need all the details."

"You'll get them. I told you I would record it, and I did. You can see it all for yourself whenever you're ready. But listen to me, Ambrose. The important thing is that we did it this time. *We did it.* It worked. You got in. But it wasn't just you. We sent your new partner in as well and that worked too. Get dressed and I'll see you in the drawing room."

I can *feel* my grandfather leaving the room on the other side of the two-way mirror so I don't bother saying anything else.

The woman I choked is on the floor, on her hands and knees looking up at me, gasping for breath. I exhale, then cross the distance between us in four steps and offer her my hand. "Brose Sinclair. New partner, I take it?"

Her smile is immediate. She accepts my offer of a hand up and as I pull her to her feet she says, "Hattie Miller. Nice to finally meet you."

* * *

Books 5 and 6 in this series should be out in late 2025

Looking for a similar book to read in my catalog?

TRY CREEPING BEAUTIFUL

End of Book Shit

Welcome to the End of Book Shit. This is the part of the book where I get to say anything I want about the story you just read or listened to. It's never edited and almost always written last minute, right before upload, so in some cases, it's been a really long time since I wrote the book!

This is one of those cases. I finished this book last year some time. November 2024? I'm not sure. I've been working on another book and other projects since then, so I've had quite a while to think about what I got out of this. Or, maybe a better way to phrase it is, what the series got out of this book.

Well, first of all, I'll say this right off the top, I LIKE Brose. He's kind of a dick, he's got some issues that will need to be explored, but I didn't find him unlikable at all. I'm not sure what readers will think about him because, of course, you guys aren't privy to my inner thoughts as I'm crafting a character, but he was always fairly sympathetic in my eyes.

Second of all, I was super happy to be back at Edge Security. I like that place. I feel like there's a lot more to come for Edge even though the first set of stories in this 'never-ending-series' is almost complete.

Book 5 is called The Emptiness of Anger and I *think*

Lowyn and Collin will be back in a big way, but the book is mostly about Brose. Lucky me- I mean, him. lol

Don't hold me to the return of Lowyn and Collin because while I do have lots of ideas for what this book will be about, I've been so busy writing something else (Godslayer!!!) I really haven't thought much about this story since I finished Danger.

I will say this about book 5, there will be lots of answers with very few new questions because the last book, book 6, the Blessing of Grace, will be a *Fun* one.

Anyway, if you've been a reader of mine for any length of time, you know I like to change up how I tell a story. And sometimes my ideas work and sometimes they don't. So I'm not sure that I can wedge Lowyn and Collin into Brose and Hattie's book yet, but I'll give my best.

Now, back to this story.

How about that little snake, Olive! I love that she's kind of a bad guy. Of course, she was totally manipulated, so not sure it really counts. But I like bad-guy girls. So glad that Hattie Miller is also back to ruin everyone's good time! I kinda loved the ending when she popped up.

Also, with Hattie, I don't even think readers will care much that Brose dishes out his version of punishment because she's a bitch. :)

Shep is our new character here. And let me just say, this story between them, including Brose, isn't over. This was definitely a HEA For Now kind of situation. But I figure I'm allowed to do that since it's a long continuing series with standalone couples and we're starting to wrap things up for our Disciple characters. So we will be seeing a lot more of Olive and Shep's relationship, probably even after the "Disciple Story" wraps up.

Speaking of, when book 6 is done I'll be moving on to another town. Which one do you want to hear about first?

Bishop and their trad days (that probably get pretty dirty at night)

Or Revenant, and those bad-boy bikers?

I'm pretty sure I know what you guys will say, but if you want to make sure you get stories about your favorite town in 2026, put it in your review for Danger so I know.

OK, so I feel like that's all the business stuff for this book, now let's talk about the plot. Because I know what some of you are thinking—Julie, this isn't contemporary romance, it's sci-fi.

And to that, I say, - bitches, look the fuck around. You're living in the future. Sci-fi world came up behind you and bit you on your ass. Because if you think that every major military on this planet HASN'T FIGURED OUT HOW TO MIND-CONTROL PEOPLE, I'm sorry to be the one to say this, but you are decades behind the science. You are so far behind on what is actually happening in research, it scares me.

The AI doesn't scare me. The science doesn't scare me. I understand all this shit pretty well. You guys who don't understand, scare me. Because I'm telling you, the world next year won't look anything like the world right now. And I don't care if you're reading this in 2025 after the book first came out, or 15 years later.

You can't put this genie back in the bottle.

Hear me, please. Speaking to someone from a distance and inserting speech into brains so that people think they're hearing a real conversation is not new, novel, or hard.

The quantum theory in this book is fiction. (As far as I know.) But it's is pathetically EASY to insert thoughts into people's minds. Especially sounds. They can insert whole conversations. Music. Sound effects—like the sounds of war. Anything.

So no, none of that part of the story is science fiction. And again, I'm sorry if this is new to you, but this is decades-old technology. The videos about this type of mind manipulation have been on the internet since the early 2000's. I'm not talking random YouTube vids, either. I'm talking about recorded lectures at war colleges where they actually put on demonstrations in the classroom and strategize on how to use it against enemies.

It used to be that the Brain was the Final Frontier. That was an actual headline on a magazine in the early 2000's. But let me tell you, these days, the final frontier has been conquered and the way they did that was with FREQUENCIES.

This is 'the new big thing'.

And oh, my god, you're going to be hearing this word a lot from now on because pretty much all science is going in the direction of frequencies at the moment.

So you're welcome if this is the first you've heard of it. Frequencies are… literally like magic.

And so here's my public service message for ya'll now:

Pay attention, bitches. PAY. ATTENTION. Because sci-fi world is here. You are in it. You are living it. The AI is everywhere, and let me tell you, that happened FAST.

Back when I wrote my first series, I am Just Junco, this wasn't a thing. There was no AI. Scientists were insisting we were 50 years away from a functional AI like ChatGPT.

If ya'll read Junco then you know there are a couple of AI characters. It's 100% sci-fi – not romance. So I had all kinds of ideas in that book. And one of them was a little something called Virtual Reality.

And let me tell you, the romance readers who picked this book up back in 2012 were SO fucking confused. I was getting messages – What is a VR? I don't get it. What's a virtual?

They had no clue.

Which was fine, these were romance readers. All sci-fi readers like myself knew what this was, and I didn't write the book for romance readers. It was normal to not know what these things were back in 2012.

But it is not normal to not understand what these things are in 2025.

If you ask anyone today—like pretty much anyone on the planet what a VR is, or what an AI is, they will know.

They know, because they've probably been in a VR. And most likely a good majority of them have all used AI.

I use AI all the time. Here's a little sample of what Chat and I chat about…

Hey chat, - how many AI programs exists in the world in 2025

ChatGPT said:

As of 2025, it's practically impossible to quantify an exact number of AI programs globally, as the landscape is enormous, constantly evolving, and highly decentralized. However, we can confidently say:

Hundreds of thousands to millions of AI applications likely exist globally.

Fifty years, my ass.

It's here, you guys. We're living through the greatest technological revolution the human race has ever seen. It's so far ahead of anything we were ever promised, it might actually wipe us out.

So please, PAY ATTENTION. Don't turn it off. Don't tune it out. Don't stop listening because you think it's not possible. It is. It's HERE. It's happening right in front of your eyes—and most people have no idea what they're looking at.

You NEED to understand what's coming.

An on that note of dark foreboding, I'll leave you here. Because that's really all I was thinking about while I was writing this absolutely inconsequential piece of spicy, dark, mind-control fiction.

The future is here and it is intelligent.

Thank you for reading, thank you for reviewing, and I'll see you in the next book.

Julie
JA Huss
March 25, 2025

Looking for a similar book to read in my catalog?

TRY CREEPING BEAUTIFUL

McKAY

I wasn't the one who broke her but I played my part.

She came to us when she was ten. I raised her. I loved her.

I taught her how to survive in a world of evil men.

But it wasn't enough.

ADAM

I wasn't the one who saved her but I did my best.

She needed me as much as I needed her.

Bought and paid for on the auction block.

331

But not for the reasons you think.
She was my weapon.

DONOVAN
I wasn't the one who lied to her but I hid her truth.
She was broken before I got there.
Wild and angry. Defiant and bratty.
But she trusted me most.
She loved me best.
So I set her free.

INDIE ANNA ACCORSI is a woman lost in her past.
A pretty little nightmare.
A gorgeous piece of misery.
A mess of lovely darkness.
She is creeping beautiful.
And now we want her back.

ABOUT THE AUTHOR

About the Author

JA Huss is a *New York Times* Bestselling author and has been on the *USA Today* Bestseller's list 21 times. She writes characters with heart, plots with twists, and perfect endings.

Her books have sold millions of copies all over the world. Her book, Eighteen, was nominated for a Voice Arts Award and an Audie Award in 2016 and 2017 respectively. Her audiobook, Mr. Perfect, was nominated for a Voice Arts Award in 2017. Her audiobook, Taking Turns, was nominated for an Audie Award in 2018. Her book, Total Exposure, was nominated for a RITA Award in 2019.

She lives on a ranch in Colorado with her family.

www.ingramcontent.com/pod-product-compliance
Lightning Source LLC
Chambersburg PA
CBHW021726190726
48289CB00008B/2705